EXTINCTION POINT: KINGS

Also by PAUL ANTONY JONES

Published by 47North

THE EXTINCTION POINT SERIES
Extinction Point
Extinction Point: Exodus
Extinction Point: Revelations
Extinction Point: Genesis

Toward Yesterday

Published by Good Dog Publishing

Ancient Enemies (Dachau Sunset - short story)

EXTINCTION POINT KINGS

PAUL ANTONY JONES

Cover design by Lance MacCarty
(www. LanceMacCarty.com)

Published by Good Dog Publishing

For Wolf, the inspiration behind Thor

And for Bear

SVALBARD ISLANDS

CHAPTER 1

Emily Baxter, her head bent to avoid a flurry of snow carried in the teeth of an icy wind, stepped through the open hatch of the Caretaker machine and out into what could only be described as desolation. A thin layer of snow had already begun to settle over the ramp leading to the ground, deep enough to leave footprints behind as she made her way ever-so-carefully down to the frost-hardened tundra. If it had not been for the heavy fur-lined parka, she would already be on the way to freezing to death. Rhiannon, dressed in a similar coat, followed behind Emily, one hand resting on her friend's right shoulder, as Emily guided her down the ramp.

Thor, on the other hand, seemed quite at ease. The big malamute trotted alongside Emily as though it was a summer day and they were out for a leisurely stroll in the park, instead of standing on permafrost while a razor-sharp subzero wind sliced at the exposed skin of their faces.

"Careful," Emily warned, "it's slippery."

"Oh. My. *God*," said Rhiannon, with an exaggerated shiver, "Are we back in Alaska?" Her eyes stared sightlessly ahead of her, unblinking."

Emily smiled grimly. She knew full well that Rhiannon understood *exactly* where they were. "Welcome to sunny Svalbard Island," Emily said, "where even the polar bears wear thermal underwear. Assuming there are any polar bears left, of course."

Rhiannon's giggle was short-lived. "Do you see him?" she asked, her tone turning serious, her head pivoting left then right as though she weren't blind.

Emily raised her hand above her eyes to shade the glare bouncing off the sheets of white stretching away in all directions. She scanned the landscape. A mountain range, craggy and gray, lay directly to the east of them. To the west, the frigid waters of the Greenland Sea, and about a kilometer or so from where they stood was what looked like a small town.

"I don't see—" Emily paused as movement to the south caught her eyes. The glare bouncing off the snow was a little disorienting but..."There's something. It could be them."

A group of four vehicles, snowcats similar to the one she and Rhiannon had used to drive across Alaska to the Stockton Islands, pulled sharply to a stop, a flurry of snow bursting from beneath their tracks. There was a momentary pause, then the door of one of the snowcats flew open, and several figures covered in white from head to toe jumped out and sprinted for cover. Soldiers, from the way they unerringly took up their positions, Emily guessed. She could not remember if Mac and his team had packed snow camouflage when they had set out on the submarine *HMS Vengeance* to find the seed bank here on Svalbard, but she was sure they would not be reacting this way if they saw her. *Well*, she thought, *pretty sure*. Then again, the *Machine* probably looked a little off-putting. Still, chances were these soldiers watching her from behind rocks and snowbanks were new survivors rather than Mac and his crew, which meant they might very well shoot first and ask questions later. Like dead last; *literally.*

Emily was about to back into the Caretaker vehicle when another figure, dressed in similar white camouflage, jumped from the lead snowcat, paused for a moment then ran forward, hands raised above his head. He was yelling something at another one of the men dressed all in white, but the wind and distance smothered his words. Still, there was no mistaking the stocky build and shock of red hair; it had to be her husband, Mac.

"I see him," Emily replied to Rhiannon's question, unable to keep a smile from her face, "And apparently, he's made some new acquaintances."

Emily felt Rhiannon's hand squeeze her shoulder tightly.

"Not sure if they're friendly or not, so maybe you should just stay...well, okay."

Mac had started walking toward where Emily waited on the ramp of the *Machine*, his hands still high up in the air as if he were surrendering to her. Even over the wind and the crash of waves hitting the shore, Emily could hear the tall man in white yelling, at Mac she presumed, in heavily accented English to stop. Mac ignored him and just kept walking toward her. *If they shoot him he doesn't stand a chance*, Emily thought anxiously. And if they did shoot him she would make them pay in ways they could not dream of.

The *Machine* was more than capable of destroying everything and everyone on this island if she instructed Rhiannon to make it happen. Adam, Emily and Mac's son and the first child born since the red rain had erased life on Earth as humanity had known it, had instructed the vehicle they had ridden in to bring them here to the island to find Mac. Just how Adam had known exactly where his father was, was not something Emily understood fully. But then there was still so much she didn't understand about Adam. *Actually, scratch that*, Emily thought, she knew next to nothing about the changes their son had gone through after the Caretakers had kidnapped him, if she was honest. Still, one thing was absolutely certain, Adam's abduction had set in motion a chain of events that had almost cost Emily her life, thanks to the machinations of Dr. Sylvia Valentine, that power-hungry bitch. But Adam had told her that their ride, the *Machine* as she and Rhiannon had named it, was more an animal than a mechanical device as humans thought of them. It had an intelligence that allowed it to make complicated decisions on its own, if it had to. So, if the *Machine* thought any of its riders were under threat, there was no telling how it would react.

Mac stopped about ten meters from the bottom of the ramp, his hands were still raised but he slowly dropped them to his sides as his eyes moved first to Emily, then Rhiannon, then the hulking alien craft standing over them. No one said a word for a few long moments.

Finally, Mac spoke, the tone of his voice half-hopeful, half-doubtful, "Emily?"

Before Emily could answer, Thor leaped from the ramp and bounded through the snow. Mac staggered backward as the malamute jumped up and placed his two front paws against Mac's chest.

If that dog's tail moves any faster he's going to take off, Emily thought, unable to suppress her smile of joy.

"Surprise!" said Rhiannon, and that was enough to demolish the thin wall of tension that Mac's uncertainty had erected.

"Stay here," Emily said to Rhiannon, sliding the girl's hand from her shoulder. She slipped and slid down the ramp in three long steps, stumbling through the almost knee-deep snow to her husband. Pulling Thor away, she threw her arms around Mac's neck, hugging him so tight she thought she might snap him in two. Mac slipped his arms around her waist and pulled her just as tightly to him. They embraced like that for almost thirty seconds, entwined in each other's arms while the freezing wind pulled snow-devils from the ground that whisked past them like spirit ballet dancers. Finally, Emily stepped back. She kissed her husband gently on his chapped lips. "We have to get out of here, right now," she said.

"Can't," said Mac, looking back over his shoulder, "The Norwegians have my men." He nodded in the direction of the four snowcats.

"The whole crew?" asked Emily.

"No, just the landing crew. The rest are back in the Vengeance. It's moored offshore a couple of clicks from here."

"I can order the *Machine* to destroy them," Emily said, matter-of-factly.

Mac looked askance, his eyes moving to the *Machine*. "Yeah, uh, about that, what the—"

"I'll explain everything when I can," Emily said, interrupting him. "Right now, I need to know what you want me to do about the men...the Norwegians that were holding you captive."

Mac thought about it, his eyes betraying the uncertainty he felt, flicking back and forth between Emily and the Caretaker machine. "As averse as I am to the use of force, under the circumstances, I think a show of power might help make them understand they really shouldn't bugger around with you."

Emily nodded. "Give me a second." She turned and walked back up the ramp to where Rhiannon waited.

"Try not to hurt anyone," Mac called after her.

"Well? What's going on?" Rhiannon asked, attuned to the crunch of Emily's boots on the snow-covered ramp.

"Mac's here but we have a little...problem that you're going to have to help us deal with."

"What *kind* of problem?"

"Nothing we can't handle. There are survivors here, Norwegians, Mac says. They've taken his crew captive. We need to show these people we're not messing around. Okay?"

Rhiannon sighed, "Okay. What do you need me to do?"

"Just follow us with the *Machine*. If things get out of hand..." Emily allowed her words to fall off. She knew Rhiannon would not hesitate to defend her and Mac, or his men, if she had to.

Rhiannon extended her left arm. Emily placed it on her own shoulder. "Thor, come," she yelled, then led the girl and dog back inside the *Machine*. A minute later Emily emerged again, walked down the ramp and joined Mac. She turned to the *Machine* and said, "Follow me." Instantly the ramp began to roll up, merging seamlessly with the body.

"Okay," said Emily, turning to smile at Mac. "Why don't you introduce me to your new friends?"

"Why, I'd be delighted," Mac said in a poor impression of a snooty English accent. He offered Emily his arm, and together they began to trudge through the snow back to where the Norwegians watched from behind their snowcats. The second Emily and Mac began to walk away, the *Machine* started to move. It raised itself slowly to full height and began to follow behind the two humans like it was a well-trained hound, its multiple legs sending up clouds of snow with each footfall. Even over the whoosh of the gusting wind, Emily was pretty sure she heard the Norwegians' collective sharp intake of breath.

They were about twenty meters away when Emily and Mac stopped, the *Machine* towering over them.

"Let's talk," Mac yelled at the Norwegian commander. The soldier had taken cover behind a large snow-encrusted boulder, his sidearm drawn and pointed at Mac and Emily.

"We just want to talk," Emily shouted to the man.

The commander's reply came back in heavily accented English, "You are on sovereign Norwegian territory. Please leave before we are forced to remove you."

It took all of Emily's restraint not to guffaw out loud.

"Are these guys kidding?" she whispered to Mac through the side of her mouth.

Mac said nothing, instead he stepped forward two paces and yelled back. "Look, let's just get real, soldier to soldier; if we wanted to take our men back, we would have told...Fido back there," he nodded in the direction of the alien machine "...to get my men. Now, I believe that you're a reasonable man who values the lives of his soldiers as much as I value those of mine. So, understand something: we are *not* the enemy. While I still have no idea why or how my wife showed up in a freaking alien spaceship, I do know that we need each other. That we can help each other." He paused for a second to let what he'd said sink in. "So," Mac continued, "why don't we just start from the beginning? Pretend none of this happened. What do you say?"

The commander beckoned another soldier over to his position. The soldier handed him the microphone to a backpack-radio he carried. The commander spoke rapidly in his language, listened to the crackly reply, then handed the soldier back the microphone before standing and yelling something to the rest of his people. The Norwegian soldiers moved obediently to each of the snowcats, opened the vehicles' doors and ushered the captive Vengeance crew out.

The Brits were lined up at gunpoint, and for one sickening moment Emily thought they had underestimated the commander's fondness for his own soldiers and that he would use the submarine's crew as a bargaining chip for her surrender. Instead, he indicated for the men to start walking toward Mac. Mac's crew hesitated, their eyes staring in Emily's direction—understandably, Emily thought, given the hulking behemoth that stood guard behind her.

"All right you bloody Muppets," Mac yelled, "did you think you joined the air force? We work for a living, now move your bloody arses. Double quick." The Vengeance crew began to move, still a little reluctantly, toward Mac. "That's it. Welcome back. Form up behind me."

"Sorry, Boss," said Richardson.

"No shame," Mac told him, clapping the man on the back. "Not like any of us had much of a choice." He turned to face Emily. "Now what?"

"Now we go make peace," she said, and started to walk toward the waiting Norwegians.

•••

The Norwegian commander stepped out from behind the back of a snowcat where he had taken cover. His pistol was holstered, Emily noticed. Well that was a good sign, at least. The man seemed as cool as a proverbial cucumber, his attention solely on her and Mac, apparently unperturbed by Emily's machine. His people, on the other hand, seemed distracted by its presence, their masked heads constantly moving to the *Machine* as it lumbered to a stop behind Emily, its tentacles undulating as though blown by the wind.

"What are your intentions?" the commander asked.

Straight to the point, Emily thought, "We come in peace," She said, using her best unassuming smile. "We mean you no harm."

The commander fixed Emily with a stare, before his eyes finally moved up to the Caretaker craft behind her.

"That *thing*, it is alien technology, I presume? So, it follows that you must be an alien, but you look human to me, as do your...associates." He nodded at Mac and the rest of the Vengeance crew. "So, tell me, what *are* you?"

Emily smiled. "We're as human as you and your men. As for the *Machine*, well that's a long and rather complicated story, but I'd be more than happy to explain it to you and the rest of your group." She extended her hand to the officer. "My name is Emily Baxter and this is my husband, Mac. I'd *like* to explain everything, but I think it would be best if I did that in the presence of whomever your leaders are."

The officer regarded Emily's proffered hand for a

moment, then extended his own. "Major Petter Djupvik," he said in his heavily accented English. The man had a strong grip, but he didn't try to crush Emily's hand as a demonstration of his masculinity. Another good sign. He was confident and open, which meant chances were he was willing to negotiate. "You'll need to come with me."

"Okay," said Emily, "We'll follow you to the town."

"No," said Major Djupvik firmly, "if you want to meet our people you will need to come in with us; you and Sergeant Mac. That is all. No other men. No...*Machine*."

Emily looked at Mac for a moment, her eyebrows raised, silently communicating the question of whether or not they should comply.

Mac nodded.

"Okay," said Emily, "we'll come with you. As a gesture of good faith."

"Very good." The major turned and spoke to his people in rapid fashion. The Norwegian soldiers broke cover and made their way over to the snowcats. In the meantime, Mac had walked back to join his men.

"Head to the landing area," Mac said. "If you don't hear from me within two hours, take the Zodiacs back to the Vengeance. Wait another two hours, and if you still haven't heard from me, go home."

Emily didn't have the heart to tell him that the crew of the Vengeance might not be very welcome back in California, thanks in part her and Rhiannon's escape, but she felt confident that it wasn't going to come down to the men having to leave her and Mac behind. *Hopefully.*

"Sergeant Mac and you, Miss Emily, please join me," Major Djupvik held the door to his snowcat open.

Emily and Mac climbed in.

"This brings back memories," Emily said to Mac.

Major Djupvik turned to look at them from the front passenger seat. "I'm sorry?"

"Another long story," said Emily.

The snowcat's engine rumbled to life, then the vehicle lurched forward as the twin tracks engaged. It quickly picked up speed as the driver directed it toward the town in the distance.

CHAPTER 2

The town was called Longyearbyen, according to a sign Emily spotted on the way in. Emily wasn't sure just how she had expected the place to look, considering they were on an island in the middle of a sea in one of the coldest parts of the world—*maybe a few huts*?—but it sure as hell wasn't like *this*. The snowcat rumbled along a main street with rows of houses on either side that wouldn't have looked out of place in New York state, or anywhere along the Upper East Coast. There were larger buildings, too; huge storage units, warehouses, an airport, a dock where she saw several big ships at anchor, and, amazingly, a university campus.

"Before the red rain came," said Major Djupvik, pointing to an architecturally impressive building that seemed to be all glass and angles, "the university was a major resource and education center for teaching arctic studies. Now we use it for other purposes."

"How many of you are there here?" Emily asked, nonchalantly.

The major smiled politely. "I'm sorry Miss Emily but that information is for the Kommunestyret, our community council, to disclose. Ah, here we are, the council halls." The snowcat came to a stop outside the entrance of a large, two-story gray and red building. "The Kommunestyret...our council...used to be fifteen people, but when reports of the red rain reached the island, a lot of them either left to head back to the mainland to be with their families or stepped down. Now we have just five members." The major got out, opened the passenger door, and ushered Emily and Mac out. "Follow me, please," he said. Four of his snow-camo-wearing soldiers took up positions on either side of the major's guests.

Major Djupvik led Emily and Mac to the building, and into a reception area. Once inside, the four-man escort removed the snow hoods they'd been wearing and, much to both Emily's and Mac's surprise, revealed that they weren't men at all. The four women, all in their mid-twenties Emily guessed, saluted the major then walked off together, talking quietly while casting glances back at Mac and Emily.

"I see you've met our Jegertroppen. Impressive, are they not." The new voice was female, and when Emily turned, she saw it belonged to a woman in her mid-forties walking across the reception area. She was dressed in a tight-fitting turtleneck sweater and blue jeans that showed off her athletic figure. "Hello," the woman said, in only slightly accented English. "My name is Magda Solheim. I'm the Governor of Longyearbyen, and, I suppose, this entire archipelago." She smiled warmly, and held out her hand to Emily, then Mac in turn. "Would you like something hot to drink? We have tea, coffee, or perhaps you'd like some hot chocolate? Something to eat, maybe?"

"Tea would be great," said Mac, enthusiastically. "No sugar. Thank you."

"Make that two," said Emily, smiling politely.

Magda turned to a young male assistant standing next

to her and relayed the new arrivals' orders.

"If you would follow me," said Magda, gesturing toward a large wooden double door.

"I've heard of the Jegertroppen," said Mac, "An all-female Norwegian special forces group, right?"

"You are correct," said Magda. "Petter...Major Djupvik...is their commanding officer. We have forty members here under his command." She pushed through the door and ushered Emily and Mac into the expansive meeting room beyond. Four other people sat around the table, three women and a man with a thick gray beard. The major followed behind Mac and Emily, closing the door after them. He moved to a position at the back of the table, casually leaning against the wall. He was a good-looking man, Emily thought. In his thirties, with a head of blond hair and a full beard. Blue eyes watched both her and Mac unerringly, despite his apparently relaxed attitude.

"Please take a seat..." said Magda, as she took a chair alongside the four other council members.

Emily and Mac sat at the table, across from their hosts. In front of each council member was a brass desktop nameplate. The assistant brought their tea and set it down in front of them.

"Please," said Magda, "when you are ready, explain to us why you are here."

Emily took a couple sips of her tea, cleared her throat and said, "I don't know how much you know about what happened after the red rain came, but long-story-short, we were invaded by aliens."

At the end of the table, behind the nameplate Tolline Jørgensen, sat a ruddy-cheeked rotund woman in her late fifties. "We are aware of that," she said. "Several of our community have made exploratory trips back to the mainland and told us what happened out there. About the red vegetation and the creatures."

Emily nodded, and continued, "The aliens responsible

for the red rain were called the Caretakers. We know this because I was captured by them when Mac and I were on a scouting mission to Las Vegas a few years ago. They let me go, but not before they warned us that our group needed to remain where we were in California. They promised dire consequences if we left."

It was obvious from the incredulous looks on some of the councilors' faces that Emily had lost them with that little nugget of information.

"It's the truth," Mac chimed in. "I was there. I saw it happen. I can vouch for my wife."

Perhaps, Emily thought, it was Mac's powers of persuasion or, more likely, it was the way he met each of the councilors' eyes with his own, daring them to call him a liar, that kept their mouths firmly closed.

"As I said," Tolline continued, "we are aware that there was some kind of a worldwide event, probably extraterrestrial in nature, but you're asking us to believe these, what did you call them, these Caretakers, for some reason singled you out? I'm sure you can understand our incredulity."

Emily smiled and leaned forward. "Let me make one thing clear here," she said, "I don't give a damn whether you believe me or not, this is quite simply the reality of how it is. You'll forgive me for being blunt, I hope, but the fact of the matter is that what I am telling you is the truth. Perhaps you should talk to Major Djupvik and ask him how I arrived at your island."

All eyes turned from her to the major. He nodded. "I can confirm that Miss Emily arrived via...unconventional means."

"Explain?" said Norfred, the lone man on the council. He had remained silent until that moment. What followed was a rapid exchange in Norwegian between the major and the council members, with several sideways glances at Emily. When the conversation was over, whatever it was

14

Major Djupvik had said seemed to have made an impression because the council members turned back to Emily and Mac with a cautious respect that bordered on fear in their eyes.

Magda watched Emily for a few moments, then her gaze drifted to Mac, before returning to Emily again. "Major Djupvik has confirmed your story. Now, please tell us what it is you want from us."

"Your help in reclaiming this world," said Emily. For now, she had decided to keep the events that had taken place after Mac left Point Loma to herself. She would need to fill her husband in on everything that had happened (not something she was looking forward to in the least), and, of course, the changes to their son, Adam, after his abduction. Those events were personal and painful; it was going to take time to explain everything in detail to her husband. Right now, it would just confuse the issue for everyone concerned. Emily continued, "We came here because of the seed bank. If what we have heard is correct, it has enough product stored in its vaults to help us kick-start a farm or two. The food supplies we have left are going to run out sooner rather than later, so if we're to survive—if humanity is to have a chance to continue—we *must* become self-sufficient. Will you do that? Will you help us?"

"I think you are leaving something out, Emily," said Magda. "Major Djupvik told us about the craft you arrived here in. He told us that he believes that machine is alien. How did *you* come by it?"

Emily caught Mac turning to face her. She glanced at him. He was wearing an expression that said *Yes, I think I'd like to know that part, too.*

After a few moments, she spoke. "The Caretakers are all dead."

"What?" Mac exclaimed. He stood up. "What? How?"

Emily closed her eyes and exhaled slowly. "It's another long story."

Mac looked at the council then back at Emily, his

eyes wide. "I'm pretty sure we all have the time." There was a note of confusion, maybe even betrayal to his tone that she did not like.

"I was going to tell you," Emily said, addressing Mac, "but I wanted to explain everything later, when we were alone."

"Why? What the *hell* has happened?"

The woman named Yulia interrupted, "I was under the impression the two of you knew what was happening?"

Emily shook her head. "My husband left Point Loma on a submarine to come here to recover seed from the seed bank. I stayed at Point Loma. But there were...complications."

"What *kind* of complications?" Mac demanded.

"Valentine," Emily replied quietly. "Valentine happened. She tried to have me killed, among other things."

Mac's face flushed a bright crimson, and his eyes narrowed. "What? She *what*? *Jeez*-us. What else?"

Emily paused, searching for a way to hold off telling Mac about Adam in front of the council, but she couldn't see a way to do it. It was all too late now, anyway. If she tried to BS her way out of this she would seem disingenuous at best, as though she were purposely concealing information from the council, when she needed them to trust her. *Best if I just come clean*, she decided. "The Caretakers kidnapped Adam," she said, quietly.

"What?" Mac sat back down again. "Bloody hell! Jesus!" He exhaled several expletives over the course of the next fifteen seconds. "Is he—"

Emily preempted Mac, placing a reassuring hand on his knee. "Adam's alive." She saw her chance to at least conceal what had happened to their son until later when she had Mac to herself; there was no need for these strangers to hear more than they needed to, not right now. "He's just fine." God, she hated lying to him, but she didn't want to confuse things for Mac by telling him what had actually

16

happened to Adam, how he had been changed, become the meta-human-biological-machine that called itself Tellus. That she, Emily, had created Tellus, indirectly, by giving birth to Adam and was therefore its mother, too. It was all so damn confusing. But she did not want to tip her hand to the Norwegians. She didn't know whether she could trust them, not yet anyway. "Yes," she continued, smiling as best as she could at Mac. "Adam's fine."

Mac's head sank slowly into his big hands. "Thank God for that. Where is he? What the hell happened?"

Emily took a moment to gather her thoughts, then began to explain how, after Mac and the crew of the Vengeance had shipped out for Svalbard Island, Valentine had begun her attempt to assume complete control of Point Loma. "He's safe," she assured her husband, not wanting to elaborate. "After the Caretakers kidnapped Adam, Valentine had me arrested on charges of murder. Rhiannon busted me out and we stole a helicopter and went looking for him."

Again, Emily saw no reason to inform Mac about the guard who had tried to kill her, or how Rhiannon had been forced to kill him in self-defense, or of their close encounter with the swarm that had led to Rhiannon's current blindness. Not just yet. That would come later. When they had time together.

"We tracked Adam down to a Caretaker ship somewhere in New Mexico. When I got into the ship, all the Caretakers were already dead, except for one. It told me why they had kidnapped Adam—they were fascinated by him because he was the first human child born on the planet since they'd landed—but during their experiments on him he somehow managed to take control of their computer systems and he found..." Emily paused as she searched to find the right words "...He found old memories, hidden so deeply within their system that the Caretakers could never have found them. Those memories showed that whatever entity originally created the Caretakers had intended them to help proliferate life, not destroy it."

Mac looked confused. "If they were originally made to help then what made them destroy our world?"

"Another race of aliens captured the Caretakers at some point and reprogrammed them to do what they did to earth. Ours wasn't the first planet the Caretakers did this to and we wouldn't have been the last."

The Norwegians looked politely confused, exchanging glances across the table. "So...who are these other 'aliens?'" Magda asked.

"We don't know who or what they are. All the Caretaker told me before it died was that the creatures reprogrammed his race to change the worlds they came to in a very particular way. Once the transformation is complete they place a ring around the planet that signifies it's ready." Emily pointed the index finger of her left hand skyward. "Then these other aliens come along and harvest the planet for their own use. They move from planet to planet, following behind the Caretakers."

"Like locusts?" asked Norfred.

"Yes, I suppose so. Just like locusts," said Emily.

"So how long before these...Locusts arrive here on Earth?" Mac asked his wife.

Emily shook her head. "The Caretaker didn't know. It just said that they are on their way."

"And how are we supposed to stop them?" Tolline asked.

Emily thought about the question for a few seconds. "There are around a thousand survivors at Point Loma. If we are going to beat these aliens...these *Locusts*, then we are going to have to do it together. That means we need your help. I don't know how many people you have here but if we're going to stand a chance of winning against what's coming, we are going to have to pool our resources and stand together."

The Norwegians conversed in their native language

for almost a minute, openly looking and gesturing at Emily and Mac.

"Got any idea what they are saying?" Emily asked her husband quietly.

"Oh, I'd guess they're either discussing how crazy we are and they're trying to decide which snow bank to bury us in, *or* they're trying to figure out if we're telling the truth."

"Let's hope it's the latter."

The discussion went on for a few more minutes, then culminated with a lot of head nodding. Magda turned to Emily.

"We will need to discuss this further," said Magda. "If you would like to stay as our guests we will make arrangements to house you for your duration here."

Emily and Mac stood. "Thank you," said Mac, "that sounds perfect."

Magda turned to her assistant, spoke two long sentences, then, as the assistant left the room, turned back to the newcomers. "While we arrange everything, would you like a tour of our facilities?"

It's not like we have a world to save or anything, Emily thought, but said, politely, "That would be great. Thank you."

"I'll need to let my men know to meet me back at the *Vengeance*," said Mac, pulling his radio from his parka.

"Of course. Major Djupvik, if you would escort our two guests, please."

The major nodded and walked around the table to join Mac and Emily. "Follow me," he said.

"Thank you, major," said Emily.

Holding the door open, the soldier said, "Please, call me Petter."

•••

"We have just over three-thousand people here,"

Petter explained to Mac and Emily as they walked out of the administration building and headed toward a group of large warehouses farther along the street, their feet crunching in the snow. A bitter wind blew through the streets, cutting at their exposed skin like a razor, but the major seemed totally oblivious to it. "Most of those people are researchers and scientists, but I have almost a hundred professional soldiers under my command who were ordered here by my government just after the red rain came. Forty of those are Jegertroppen; our female special forces."

They were approaching one of the large warehouse-like buildings. Petter pulled a key from his pocket and unlocked a padlock securing the door. He held the door open and ushered Emily and Mac inside. A wave of warm air washed over them. He unzipped and removed his jacket then gestured to Mac and Emily to do the same, hanging the coats on hooks.

"This way," Petter said. He led them though a second door.

"Wow!" said Mac as they stepped into a massive space that must have been at least six acres in size, if not more. Powerful heat lamps hung from the ceiling, and water gurgled through clear plastic tubing, all to feed row upon row of plants, each row placed with just enough room for a human to move between them. Four people walked between the rows of crops and vegetables, tending and trimming, checking drip lines and lights.

"Are those...? No way...No way! Is that...those are tomatoes," Emily said. She couldn't stop herself from grinning as she reached out a hand toward a plump red tomato hanging from a vine. "Can I?" she asked, looking back at Petter.

Smiling, the major nodded.

Emily plucked the tomato from the vine and bit into it. "Oh my God. Oh my good God." She felt tears slip down her cheeks as flavor—*so much delicious flavor*—filled her mouth. She passed the rest of the fruit to Mac who placed it reverently in his mouth and began to chew with an almost dreamlike look of bliss on his face. Emily looked around the rest of the building. From where she stood she could see rows of tomato plants but also what might be corn, and carrots. There were lettuces, and the deep purple stems of beetroot pushing up from large planters stacked on ziggurat-like wooden benches.

"We grow enough in this one warehouse to feed most of us. We have another four like this around the town growing more herbs, vegetables, and fruit. Follow me." Petter began walking between the rows of tomatoes, past cucumbers and carrots. The smell was like a flash from her childhood, growing up on her parents' farm in Iowa. The musty, pungent scent of earth and plants and water...it was sublime. Intoxicating. *It was life.*

They did a full circle of the facility, walking down one side then back up the other as Petter explained that some of the scientists and researchers who had worked on the island before the red rain had been researching how to produce food in low temperature climates. They had quickly begun converting the warehouses into greenhouses, using seed recovered from the vault. It had proved far more successful than they had hoped.

"It was what saved us," Petter said as they approached the entrance they had arrived through. "Now, if you will come with me, I will return you to your men."

Mac caught Emily's eye. He smiled a wide grin that showed all his teeth, flecked with pieces of red tomato skin. He didn't need to say anything, his expression said it all: *There's hope. Hope for all of us.*

•••

Emily and Mac climbed into the snowcat alongside Petter and his driver. The vehicle's engine was already running. As soon as Emily closed the door behind her, the major ordered the driver to head out.

They traveled most of the trip back to the *Machine* in silence, both Emily and Mac lost in their own similar thoughts. The warehouse-farm changed everything. *Everything.* It offered the first real ray of hope for humanity since the Caretakers had arrived. If the Norwegians would be willing to share their expertise with the Point Loma survivors, it would eliminate one of the biggest threats to humanity's continued survival. Having a sustainable food source was, well, massive. There were other problems, of course, the hardest of which was just how they were going to take back Point Loma from Valentine and her cronies. Perhaps, if they could return with fresh vegetables, fruit, and seeds, they could use that as leverage to persuade the rest of the survivors to turn over Valentine...maybe even Valentine would see the futility of her position and give up. *You can live in hope*, Emily thought, *even if you die in despair.*

The snowcat approached the Caretaker machine Emily and Rhiannon had arrived in. Emily sensed the three men tense as the huge craft came into view. The driver pulled up alongside it, straining his neck out the window to gape open-mouthed at the vehicle.

"Hell of a ride, you've got there," Mac said, his tone hushed. He turned to look at Emily as she opened the door and stepped out of the snowcat. "We'll really have to have a chat about it. *Soon.*" His eyes showed his bewilderment over how *exactly* she'd managed to come by a piece of Caretaker technology, let alone figured out how to pilot it.

Emily smiled, nodded, then said, "I'll meet you back at the Vengeance." They had agreed it would be best for Emily to follow behind Mac so he'd have time to explain to the sub's crew that they had nothing to fear when the *Machine* showed up.

Before Emily could close the door behind her, Mac took out his radio and handed it to his wife. "Take this," he said. "In case of emergencies."

"You really think anything's going to screw with us in that?" Emily nodded at the looming outline of the *Machine*.

"Who said anything about you?" said Mac, half-seriously. "That's in case we need your help."

"We'll be ten minutes behind you," Emily said, as she took the radio and closed the door. She stood for a few seconds and watched the snowcat disappear around a hill, then turned and walked back toward the *Machine*. The walkway was down already. She climbed up the ramp and headed toward the control room where Rhiannon and Thor waited. The room was sparse; no displays or control systems lined the curved walls. Two chairs that looked to have been extruded from the very floor itself sat in the room's center. Rhiannon sat in one, with Thor lying next to her. The malamute got up and padded over to Emily as she entered the room, his tail swishing back and forth. The room's walls glowed a dim red, pulsing slowly. It hadn't been doing that when she had left.

"Welcome back," said Rhiannon. She rose unsteadily to her feet, still acclimating to her blindness. Rhiannon had lost her sight back in New Mexico from the sting she had suffered when the three travelers had battled a swarm of alien bugs; a sting that had taken her to the brink of death and left both her eyes blood-red orbs. She had recovered, but it still wasn't clear at this point whether Rhiannon's blindness was temporary or permanent. But at least the girl was alive; a minor miracle in and of itself given their past experience with the creatures that now inhabited this world. When it had come time to leave Adam and find Mac, Emily had wanted to leave Rhiannon with her son, but the girl had insisted that she was coming along.

Emily walked up to the girl and gave her a hug. Hot tears began to roll down her face and onto the girl's neck.

"What's wrong?" Rhiannon asked, breaking free of Emily's hug, then moving back a step. "Oh my God! Mac...is

Mac okay?"

Emily didn't think her love for this young woman could grow any stronger, but the concern in her voice for Emily's husband was so heartwarming. She felt her heart swell.

"Mac's fine," Emily said, placing a hand on Rhiannon's shoulder while smiling broadly, even though the girl could not see her. "It's all good. Better than I'd hoped for, in fact." She stepped closer to Rhiannon and took her elbow, guiding her back to her chair in the center of the room. "Have a seat. We have to go rendezvous with the Vengeance. I'll explain everything on the way."

"We can't," said Rhiannon. "The *Machine*...something's wrong with it."

Emily cocked her head to one side. "What do you mean?"

"About an hour after you left there was a sound, like an alarm. I heard the ramp drop and thought it was you coming back, but when you didn't say anything, I ordered the *Machine* to retract the ramp, but nothing happened. I haven't been able to make it do anything since then...It just stopped working."

Emily stepped back. Her eyes moved to the red pulsing walls. "Damn!" she said eventually. "It must be the cold." None of the red rain creatures she'd encountered seemed capable of handling the cold for very long. It stood to reason that the same would apply to the Caretakers' machines.

"What are we going to do?" asked Rhiannon.

Emily fished the radio Mac had given her from her pocket. "Looks as though I'm going to have to call AAA."

CHAPTER 3

Mac sent a Zodiac to pick up Emily, Rhiannon, and Thor from the disabled Caretaker machine. He was waiting for them on the deck of the Vengeance as the Zodiac pulled alongside. Emily helped Rhiannon to her feet and guided her to the side of the boat. The tide was gentle but the Zodiac still pitched up and down enough that Rhiannon almost lost her footing a couple of times. If it hadn't have been for Emily's helping hands she would have been in the sea.

Mac stifled a gasp when he saw Rhiannon's eyes. He looked at Emily, confused. "What's going—" he started to ask the question but stopped mid-sentence as Emily shook her head back and forth.

"I'll explain when we're on board," said Emily.

"Hi Mac," said Rhiannon, cheerfully.

Mac smiled back at her. "Hello sweetheart. Let's get you up here shall we." He reached down with his meaty paws and lifted the girl out of the Zodiac, depositing her on the submarine's deck. Then he helped Emily on board before calling to Thor, who had until then been sitting patiently at the bow of the small boat. The malamute leaped over the side and up onto the deck, instantly making his way to Mac. The dog rolled over onto his back and allowed the soldier to rub his belly, his tail swishing back and forth on the submarine's cold metal surface.

Emily placed an arm around Rhiannon's shoulders and guided her over the deck as Mac led them back to the entry hatch. He called down to another seaman inside the Vengeance to make sure he was waiting at the bottom of the ladder, then, one after the other, positioned Rhiannon's feet onto the first rung of the ladder.

"That's it," said Mac, keeping a hand on the girl's wrist as she uneasily began climbing down and he made sure the sailor waiting at the bottom of the ladder had her.

Emily followed behind, nimbly moving down the ladder.

"Sit," Mac told Thor, which the dog obediently did. The Scotsman picked the malamute up as though he were nothing but a big bag of potatoes, cradling him with one arm, then climbed carefully down into the submarine.

"Let's get to my cabin," he said. "This way." He led the three newcomers down a corridor to a tiny room. The only furniture consisted of a bunkbed, a chair, and a small cabinet. The room was so small there was barely enough space for all four of them to fit.

"Sit here," Mac said, taking Rhiannon's hand from Emily and guiding her to the lower bunk. He seemed about to say something, but instead he tapped a couple of the pockets of his Parka with his fingers, then fished out a pair of sunglasses. "Here," he took Rhiannon's hand again and placed a pair of sunglasses into her upturned palm. "Best you wear these, until we let everyone know about your..."

"Cool!" said Rhiannon. She put on the sunglasses. "How do I look."

"Marvelous," said Emily.

"Now," Mac continued, turning to face Emily, "would someone please tell me what the bloody hell is going on? Start at the beginning."

Mac took a seat in an old wooden chair, while Emily stood. She breathed in deeply and began to talk. She explained again how, after Mac had left, Valentine had made a play for power; how the Caretakers had kidnapped Adam; how Valentine had used their son's disappearance to frame Emily; that Valentine had tried to have her murdered; how if it had not been for Rhiannon's bravery in rescuing her, that plan would have succeeded. She told him how they had stolen a helicopter and escaped the camp, following the mental pull of Adam's mind as it acted as a kind of psychic GPS beacon for her. She quickly explained their journey east, their encounter with the swarm of glowing creatures that had been responsible for Rhiannon losing her sight, and, finally, how they had found the Caretakers' ship...and Adam. When she was finished, Emily paused for a moment or two, assessing how best to tell Mac about what had happened next. She decided not to sugarcoat it.

"I told you Adam was safe—" Emily began.

Mac's reaction was instantaneous, his eyes widened and he started to speak, but Emily took his hand in hers, silencing him. "And he *is* safe," she continued, "I just...I just couldn't tell you everything, not in front of the Norwegians."

"Ooo-kay," he said, guardedly, "I trust you. Now, tell me what's going on with my son because I am very, very confused right now."

Emily took a big breath of air and dived right in. "The Caretakers took him because he was different, unique. Before it died, the last Caretaker told me they had never come across someone like Adam...ever! So, they kidnapped him and they...they experimented on him."

"What!" Mac exploded. "What?"

"It's okay, really it is," said Emily. "Please, I know that this is difficult to hear but just let me explain, okay?"

Mac gave an abrupt nod of his head.

"The Caretakers changed him, Mac. He's still our little boy, but he's...he's changed.

A storm of emotion swept across Mac's face; fear, anger, sadness, confusion. He abruptly stood up, sending his chair skittering across the floor. "What the hell do you mean by 'changed?'"

Emily took his hands in hers. He stared intently back at her as she continued her story. "They connected him to a machine, expecting him to die, but he didn't die, he thrived. Somehow, he gained control of the Caretaker ship and its technology and dug into its memory. He found a secret buried so deeply, even the Caretakers didn't know it existed. A terrible secret from their history. The secret was that the Caretakers had been changed by the Locusts from their original purpose as benevolent beings tasked with helping life flourish wherever they found it, into a weapon of destruction. The Locusts follow from planet to planet as the Caretakers reshape each new world to the Locusts' specifications and harvest it for their own use."

"What?" said Mac, stunned.

"Yes, but the Locusts must have planted a self-destruct mechanism deep in the Caretakers DNA, because once Adam revealed the fact that they had been manipulated by the Locusts, it activated, and the Caretakers started dying. It killed them all, Mac, but not Adam. *Not Adam.*"

Mac let go of Emily's hands. His face was flushed bright crimson.

Emily continued, "I...I still don't really understand the science behind it, but the process the Caretakers put him through, it accelerated Adam, he's not a baby anymore, more like a teenager, I suppose, but it also enhanced his mind. With access to all that alien knowledge and technology, it's given him...powers...abilities. He can control aspects of the red world. Emotionally, he's still a child, but his IQ, it must be off the charts, unreadable by human standards. And he's still growing, but his body is unable to keep up with the powers he's been given, doing just about anything tires him out very quickly."

There was a long pause while Mac digested what he'd been told. "But he's okay, right? He's still...human." Mac bent down, righted the fallen chair, and sat back down. Thor got up and moved closer to his master, pushing his head against Mac's hand until he started to stroke him.

Emily nodded. "Yes, he's alive and well, but he's permanently joined with their ship now. He has access to almost all the Caretakers' memories and data. He said he's connected to everything that the red rain changed, like an unimaginably complex version of the Internet. It's through that connection that he can gather so much information. He can even control some of the lifeforms; just the small ones right now, but he thinks that eventually he will be able to possess any life form on the planet."

"Jesus!" Mac hissed. He looked up at his wife, his eyes tearing up. "He's still our boy, right? He's still our Adam."

"Yes, oh God, yes. He's still Adam," Emily said. Stepping in close to her husband she placed a hand on his cheek, "I know it's a lot to take in, but, yes, he's still our Adam. He's just very, very powerful."

"Jesus!" Mac repeated.

"He's able to control their craft, too; at least, some of them," Emily explained. "He's still learning, still discovering what he's capable of. Adam managed to work out how to control the machine Rhiannon and I arrived at Svalbard in. He told it to bring us here. When we left he was trying to gain control of the ship we found him in."

Mac was dumbfounded. "It's all just...I...after everything that happened after the red rain came, I thought there was nothing left that could possibly surprise me. But this...this I just can't get my head around. I'm going to need some time to process it all."

Emily touched his hand. "It's a massive amount of information to take in, I know; I'm still wrapping my mind around it, too. But Mac, he's still our son and he wants to help us."

Mac nodded silently. His face remained stoically calm, but his eyes revealed the storm of confusion that Emily knew must be raging within his body.

"Our real problem, isn't Adam," Emily continued, "it's the Locusts. And if we have any hopes of getting back to Point Loma and enlisting their help, we're going to have to figure out how to deal with Valentine and her cronies."

Mac pulled Emily in, enclosing her with his arms. He cradled the back of her head with one hand and held her to him. When he pulled back, there was a change in his face; her husband, the kind, gentle man that Emily loved more deeply than she ever could have imagined was gone, replaced by the professional, deadly soldier.

"Okay," Mac said, "We'll deal with the Locusts once we find them, in the meantime, I'm going to figure out how I'm going to kill Valentine."

•••

"Honey, wake up."

Mac's voice pulled Emily from a deep, dreamless sleep.

"What is it?" she asked, seeing a fresh look of concern on her husband's face. She cast a brief glance at her watch; she'd been asleep for a couple of hours since she had revealed everything to Mac about Adam.

"It's the Captain, he's taken a bit of a fall," Mac said. "I need your help with him."

"Of course," Emily said. She threw back the thin blanket that covered her and sat up.

"What's going on?" Rhiannon asked, sitting up.

"Captain Constantine's had an accident," Emily said,

"I'm going to help Mac. You okay here for a few?"

Rhiannon nodded. "I hope he's okay."

"I'm sure he will be. Won't be long," said Emily, closing the door behind her and Mac.

Mac led Emily through the sub's innards.

"What happened?" she asked.

"He was top-side, running through some inspections; slipped on some ice and hit the deck hard. Pretty sure he's done some real damage. He's still up top; we didn't want to move him until we knew the extent of his injuries."

The wind had picked up again as they emerged onto the sub's deck. It sliced the air with sword-like gusts of razor-sharp cold. Emily shivered, zipped up her parka, and followed Mac aft along the deck toward the stern.

Captain Constantine was just beyond the base of the conning tower. Two other crewmen stood over him, talking quietly to their commander. Someone had covered him in thick blankets to ensure he stayed warm. Even so, his face looked gray as Emily and Mac approached.

"Oh boy, what have you done now?" Emily said, smiling confidently as she approached.

The captain's head turned in her direction, and, despite his obvious pain, a smile crossed his lined face. "Well, well, well. Mac filled me in on your return, I'd hoped to make time to talk with you after you had gotten some rest. This wasn't quite what I had in mind, though." He tried to keep his smile in place but it was quickly turning into more of a grimace as he fought back the pain. Emily saw he had a nasty gash over his right eye, the trickle of blood running down his cheek already freezing over.

"Where are you hurt?" she asked him.

"Right leg. Just below the knee." The words came out in a hiss.

"I'm going to take a look," Emily said, kneeling at his feet. She lifted the blanket to reveal the captain's legs. Gently, ever so gently, she rolled up the right leg of his pants.

Emily flinched when she saw the obvious outline of a broken tibia bone pressing against the bruised skin just below his knee. There was more bruising closer to his ankle too. "Okay, looks like you've got at least one break," she said. She stood back up and turned to Mac, leading him a few meters away. "That's a really nasty break. Might be a problem with his ankle, too. Do we have anyone on board capable of working on this?"

Mac nodded at the two men standing over the commander. "They're it. Neither of them have the kind of training to deal with something this serious."

Emily thought for a moment. "It's going to be a bastard trying to get him into the sub's infirmary."

"We can strap him to a board and lower him down. It'll be painful."

Emily shook her head. "I'd be really nervous about making his injuries worse. That head wound looks bad, too. And for all we know, he could have a concussion or worse."

Mac exhaled hard, a thick white fog of vapor.

"The Norwegians have a hospital. That means they should have more experienced medical staff and better facilities than we have on board the Vengeance," Emily said, leaving the statement hanging in the air for Mac to consider.

He thought for a few moments, then, "Yeah, let's give them a bell. See if they are willing to help. It'll be a good indication of whether they're really willing to lend us a hand." Mac pulled his portable radio from his belt, tuned the frequency to a nautical emergency channel and spoke. "Longyearbyen, Longyearbyen, this is submarine *HMS Vengeance*, we have a medical emergency. Requesting urgent assistance for our commander. Do you copy, over?"

Several seconds of silence followed, then a voice came back over the radio, "*HMS Vengeance, this is Longyearbyen town, we copy. What is the nature of your medical emergency?*"

Mac quickly explained what had happened.

"HMS Vengeance, *please stand by.*" There was another long pause then, "HMS Vengeance, *we will be sending a medical crew. Please prepare for our arrival.*"

"Roger that. Thank you," said Mac and signed off.

Five minutes later, the sound of an outboard motor echoed across the mountains. A medium-sized boat with a large red cross on its side appeared from the direction of Longyearbyen and quickly closed on the submarine. Pulling alongside the *Vengeance*, the Norwegian crew tossed a line to a waiting seaman who tied it off.

A woman carrying a black medical bag appeared and Mac offered her his hand, helping her aboard.

"Hello," said the woman, in a heavy French accent. "My name is Doctor Renée Candillier."

"I'm Emily and this is my husband, Mac."

"I am happy to meet you both. Where is the patient?"

Mac led the doctor to where the captain lay. Emily and Mac both stayed back and allowed the doctor room to work on her patient. Candillier checked the gash over Constantine's right eye, then his breathing, his eyes, and heart, before examining his leg. She pulled a syringe from her bag, filled it with an opaque liquid and injected it into the muscle of his broken leg. The captain's face visibly relaxed within a few seconds of the injection. She then proceeded to fit a temporary splint to the leg, stabilizing the injured limb with a plastic tie to his other leg.

Candillier stood and walked over to where Mac and Emily waited. "He has a very bad fracture in his right leg. I also believe that he has probably broken his ankle, but the only way to be certain is to get him back to my clinic and x-ray him. The morphine injection I gave to him will help with the pain. Do I have your permission to transport him?"

Mac looked at Emily. Emily looked at Mac. They both nodded.

"Very well," said the doctor. She waved at the two men waiting on the boat. They grabbed a stretcher and climbed aboard.

"I'd like one of my men to accompany the captain," said Mac.

The doctor nodded, watching as the two orderlies set the stretcher down next to the captain and gently began to move his body onto it.

"Billings, front and center," Mac yelled. One of the two men watching the captain jogged over to Mac.

"Sir?"

Mac handed him his portable radio. "Take my radio and accompany the captain. We'll have someone relieve you in a few hours. Any problems, report back to me immediately. Understood?"

"Yes, sir," said Billings, he turned and walked back to help transfer the captain onto the boat.

"Doctor Candillier?" Emily said, stepping over to where the woman was supervising captain's transfer.

The doctor turned, "Oui?"

"We...that is, Mac and I...we have a...our daughter, Rhiannon, she was injured on the journey here. She's become blind. Would it be possible for us to stop by your clinic tomorrow and have you check her out?"

The doctor smiled. "Yes, of course. Say two o'clock tomorrow?"

Emily smiled back and offered her hand. "Thank you."

Candillier shook Emily's hand. "That is what I am here for." She turned to Mac. "Don't worry, we will take very good care of your captain."

"Thank you, doc," said Mac. He helped the doctor back over her boat's gunwales. She followed behind the stretcher as the two orderlies moved through a doorway into the boat's cabin. Minutes later, the engine turned on and the boat pulled away.

Emily and Mac waited on the *Vengeance*'s deck, watching the boat until it disappeared around a bluff.

CHAPTER 4

The next afternoon Emily, Mac, Rhiannon, and Thor boarded a boat brought alongside the *Vengeance* by Petter Djupvik, and headed back to Longyearbyen. The sea was choppy, sending the military assault craft bouncing over two-meter high waves, curtailing all conversation until the group pulled into Longyearbyen's harbor. An SUV waited for them while they climbed out of the boat and quickly set off for the hospital.

"I wanted to thank you for rendering assistance to the captain," Mac said to Petter.

The Norwegian nodded. "I believe you would have done the same were the positions reversed."

"Well, no matter what your council decides, we owe you."

Five minutes later, the SUV pulled up in front of the hospital, a two-level building close to the center of the town.

"When news of the red rain came," Petter said, holding the door of the SUV open for Emily to help

Rhiannon out, "like the council members, many of our medical staff opted to go back to the mainland. We now have only two general practitioners, a physiotherapist, a midwife, and several volunteer nurses. You met Dr. Candillier yesterday when she helped your captain after his unfortunate accident."

"She seems like a nice person," Emily said, closing the SUV door behind Rhiannon.

"She is very competent," said Petter. "She will remain Captain Constantine's primary physician, but regrets that her duties will not allow her to see you today. She has arranged for doctor Johansen to examine Rhiannon."

"Is the captain okay?" Rhiannon asked, pushing the sunglasses Mac had given her further up her nose.

"Yes, little one, he is doing very well, considering. This way please." He ushered them through the main entrance, nodded to a young man behind the reception desk, then led them down a corridor.

"Here you are, Mac," Petter said, pointing to a door on the left side of the hall. "The captain is in there with Doctor Candillier."

"I'll see you back in reception when we're both done," Mac told Emily. He squeezed her hand, ruffled Rhiannon's hair, knocked on the door, then slipped inside the private room when a female voice beyond told him he could enter.

"If you would like to come with me, please, ladies," Petter said, walking farther along the corridor. He stopped five doors down, knocked on the door, then opened it and stepped inside. "Please, come in."

A man, somewhere in his forties sat behind a desk. He looked tired, with the dark bags under his eyes, pale skin, and an unkempt beard matching his receding dirty-blond hair. He smiled broadly as Emily and Rhiannon entered the room.

"Hello. Hello," he said jovially. He stood and took Emily's hand, shaking it enthusiastically. "You must be

Rhiannon," he continued, reaching for the girl's hand, shaking it with as much enthusiasm as he had Emily's, which made Rhiannon giggle. "My name is Dr. Eirick Johansen, and I am going to be your doctor."

Rhiannon smiled at the doctor's contagious enthusiasm. "Nice to meet you," she said.

"Please, come this way," the doctor said, opening a door that led into an examination room.

Petter touched Emily on her arm. "I'll wait for you in the reception, okay?"

"Mind looking after Thor?"

"Of course," said Petter. "Come on, Thor."

The malamute looked at Emily. "Go with Petter," Emily said, handing his leash to the major. "And be a good boy."

Petter laughed. "I am always a good boy," he said, then left with Thor before Emily could figure out if he had misunderstood her or was making a joke.

"Norwegians," Emily sighed. "Not sure I'm ever going to get used to them."

•••

"I've run as many tests as I can with the equipment we have available here, but I can't see any medical reason for Rhiannon's blindness," said Doctor Johansen, an hour later. "Of course, we would need to have her examined more closely at a better-equipped hospital, preferably by a specialist. But, given the current situation, that does not seem probable."

"What about the...discoloration?" Emily said.

"To me, it seems to be just that, a change in pigmentation, nothing more. Structurally, her eyes seem perfectly normal. "

"Will I ever get my sight back?" Rhiannon asked. Her voice was quiet, small.

"It is possible that what you are experiencing might be...ummm, what is the word...imaginary?"

"Psychosomatic?" Emily offered.

"Yes, psychosomatic. It might all be in your head." Johansen tapped gently on Rhiannon's temple.

Rhiannon blinked. "You think I'm crazy? I'm not crazy."

"No, no, no. It might be that your blindness is caused by the stress of what you went through, rather than the venom. It's hard for me to think of a reason for why a predator would want to blind you rather than kill or paralyze you. You understand? So, it is possible that your mind is playing tricks on you, that it just expects you to be blind, for whatever reason. That is why I think it could be the shock of what happened to you."

Emily shook her head. "I don't think so. She was stung by a kind of alien bug. She was unconscious for a long time."

Doctor Johansen shrugged again. "I am sorry, Emily. I have done everything that I can with what I have available. Other than the blindness, I can find nothing else wrong with Rhiannon."

Emily smiled and offered the doctor her hand. "Thanks anyway, doctor." She placed an arm around Rhiannon's shoulders and guided her out to the waiting room.

"I really am very sorry I could not be of more help," Johansen said, sitting back down behind his desk.

Emily nodded. "Thank you again."

They followed the corridor back toward the reception area. "Don't worry," Emily said. "We'll find someone who can fix this. There has to be someone." Her mind drifted back to the few days she and Rhiannon had spent in the Caretaker ship while Adam built the original machine to transport them here to Svalbard, Adam had made no mention of being able to heal Rhiannon's blindness. But when the machine was finally revealed to them, he had instructed Rhiannon to take the helm within the sparse control room. When she sat in the command seat, the girl had given out a gasp of surprise. "I can see!" she had said. "I...I..."

"What? How?" Emily had exclaimed, taking the girl's hand in hers.

"It's...amazing! I can see so much more than before I lost my sight."

Emily had jumped as, from nowhere, Adam's voice had resonated within her head, despite him being buried deep within the bowels of the Caretaker ship, some hundred meters or more away from them. She hadn't been sure if she was ever going to get used to that.

"*I have linked the machine's intelligence to Rhiannon, he had explained to his mother. She will be the one to control it. It will listen to you, Mommy, protect you always, but its operator must be Rhiannon. It is an extension of her now, the best that I can do to fix her wounds at this point.*" Adam had made no mention of whether he would be able to make Rhiannon whole again, but the implication was there that he might. And that was something for Emily to hold on to. Adam had switched his attention to Rhiannon, but his voice still echoed in Emily's mind. "*The machine will follow your commands, Rhiannon. You will see on frequencies you never dreamed existed.*"

"How do I make it go?" Rhiannon had asked aloud, a childlike excitement in her voice.

"*It is you, Rhiannon. Simply think a destination or action as you would for your own body, or say it aloud. It will do your bidding. Take you wherever you wish to travel.*"

"Run," Rhiannon had said without warning.

Emily had screamed aloud as the craft had suddenly raised itself on its multiple legs and begun to run, quickly picking up speed. Like some barely tamed stallion, it had galloped across the land at a breakneck pace, leaping over hedgerows, and brush, dodging between the trunks of Titan trees.

"Oh my God, be careful," Emily had yelled, grabbing at the seat's armrests, as the craft dodged left and right through the forest. "*Careful*!"

"I'm not telling it what to do," Rhiannon said, her words barely audible behind her unrestrained laughter. "It's avoiding everything itself."

It had quickly become apparent that piloting the vehicle was a mainly passive experience. Its innate intelligence allowed it to avoid any obstacle that it was presented with while it attempted to carry out whatever command Rhiannon ordered of it.

"Take us back to Adam," Rhiannon commanded. Obediently the *Machine* had described a wide arc through the trees, and run back to the ship, stopping almost exactly where it had begun.

Now, as Emily and Rhiannon walked to the hospital's reception area, Emily wondered whether Adam had specifically given Rhiannon control of the craft for that exact purpose; to keep her spirits high, to give her the ability to participate within the coming struggle, because he knew that there was little or nothing he could do to restore her sight to what it once was. If she was correct in her assessment, then it meant her son was a compassionate soul. And that was just fine by her.

Of course, now that the *Machine* was to all intents and purposes dead, that hope had been torn away from Rhiannon and her spirits had noticeably sunk. That was why Emily had asked for this appointment, in the hopes that maybe there was *something* human medicine could do for her, but that hope too had been denied the girl.

Mac and Petter were already waiting in the reception area, sitting on a comfortable sofa talking like old friends, Thor resting comfortably on the floor at their feet. Both men stood when they saw Emily and Rhiannon approaching. Thor got up and greeted them as well.

"How's the captain doing?" Emily asked, reaching out

to scratch the malamute's head.

"Considering he has a double fracture, he's pretty chipper," said Mac. "Course that might be down to the pain meds he's on. Good drugs these Norwegians have."

Emily was glad to see some of the concern for the skipper had left Mac's face. The two men had a close friendship that went beyond their professional interaction, almost a father-son relationship. "I'm glad the old man's doing well," she said.

"He's going to be out of commission for several months though. He's given me temporary command of the *Vengeance*."

"Well, okay. Congratulations on the promotion."

"Petter was just telling me that the council has prepared that apartment they mentioned for us here in town. We can stay there while they make their decision. Petter says it's big enough for all four of us."

Rhiannon gave a little whoop. "Thank goodness. I hate being stuck on that submarine."

"I'll radio the sub and let them know we'll be living it up on the island for a couple of days," said Mac.

"Well," said Emily. "I guess that's decided."

All three adults laughed.

•••

Petter escorted them from the hospital. He seemed more relaxed, happily chatting about the island's history as they crunched through the snow toward their apartment.

"Did you know this town was named after an American businessman?" he asked Emily.

Emily shook her head. "Really? It seems like such a distant place for an American to turn up in."

"John Munroe Longyear owned one of the companies that first began coal mining here in the early twentieth century. So, I suppose we have you and your country to thank for our continued existence."

Emily smiled at the nugget of information. "It just seems so inhospitable. It's hard to imagine what would draw people here under normal circumstances."

"The people here are good people, brave, good-hearted," he said. "Scientists, mostly, but there are some poets and writers. It attracts...what is the word?...dreamers. I think maybe we are all dreamers here."

"You sound as though you love this town very much," Emily said.

"I do, yes. You don't come to this kind of a place unless you are dedicated, loyal to the search for what it is that you are looking for. Or maybe I should say, you don't come here and stay unless all that is true."

Thor was happily running ahead of the four humans, tail wagging furiously, bounding through the drifts that had collected along the side of the road. The last time she had seen him this happy was in Alaska, on the way to the Stockton Islands to meet Jacob. Back then, she had not been able to appreciate the malamute's pure joy, her focus squarely on surviving the deadly environment to try to reach the perceived safety that Jacob had said he offered. Now, relaxed, and out for what amounted to an afternoon stroll, she could simply enjoy him enjoying himself.

As if he had sensed Emily's thoughts, Thor, his nose suddenly high in the air sniffing furiously, gave a short, deep bark, and took off running toward the space separating two nearby houses.

"Hey, Thor, get back here," Emily yelled after the dog.

Thor stopped momentarily and looked back at Emily, barked once, and took off again.

"Well, shit!" said Mac, his eyebrows raised as he watched the dog run between the houses. "This is a first."

Emily was stunned. In all the years she and Thor had been together, he had never once disobeyed her, that she could remember. "Thor!" she yelled again, but the dog did not stop. He disappeared around the back of a house.

Petter apparently found it amusing. "Perhaps he does not want to leave the snow just yet?" he said, smiling.

"Uh huh," Emily replied. "Can I go get him?"

"Of course," said Petter. "We will wait here for you to return."

Emily followed Thor's tracks between the houses, calling his name as she trudged through the deeper snow that had piled up there. "I swear to God, mutt, if you make me follow your ass halfway around this—" Emily rounded the back of the house and stopped dead in her tracks.

"Wow!" she said, eventually.

A chain link fence that came up to Emily's waist cordoned off an area at the rear of the house. It extended about ten meters from the back door. Thor stood on his hind legs, his front legs resting on the top rail of the fence, his tail moving back and forth furiously.

And he had found a friend.

A German Shepherd, as white as the snow that surrounded her mirrored Thor, her tail moving just as frantically as his. The two were almost muzzle to muzzle, sniffing each other cautiously, but happily.

Emily was stunned. She watched the two dogs grow acquainted over the next couple of minutes, still not believing what she was seeing.

"It looks like love," a voice said.

A woman, somewhere in her fifties stood in the doorway of the house where the white Shepherd lived, watching her with an amused look on her face.

"I...we thought Thor was the only dog left on the planet," Emily said. "This is unbelievable."

The woman looked confused. "Why would you think that?" She stepped down into her backyard, walked to the fence and stood next to her dog. She scratched her dog behind the ears, then did the same for Thor.

"It never crossed my mind that any dogs were left alive elsewhere. And to find one, I mean that's huge."

"One?" the woman said, suppressing her laughter. "Well if one makes you happy you will be ecstatic when you find out that there are several hundred here in town."

"What? Really?"

"Oh yes. And cats, too. I'm more of a dog person myself, but each to their own. There are even chickens, sheep, and pigs at the university still, if I'm not mistaken. Oh, and some goats." The woman held out her hand to Emily. "My name is Edith Vikra, and this young girl is Samantha."

"Thor," said Emily, walking to the fence and shaking Edith's hand. "The dog's name is Thor, not my name." She felt her face going red as the word salad spilled from her mouth. "I'm Emily."

"Ahh, yes, the *alien*," Edith delivered the last word with mock gravity. "You are the talk of the town."

Emily smiled and shook her head. "I can assure you, I'm as human as you are. There's nothing to be frightened of."

"Oh, we are not frightened. When you have lived out here for as long as most of us have now, fear becomes frozen just like everything else."

Emily pulled the glove from her right hand and allowed Samantha to sniff it, then ran her hand over the dog's silky white fur. "She's beautiful."

"She is my...what is the word? Darling? Yes, she is my darling girl." An involuntary smile lit up Edith's face. "Would you like to come in and have a cup of tea?"

"I would love to, but I can't. My husband and Major Petter are waiting for me to bring our wayward son back to them. Maybe another time?"

"Yes," said Edith, "maybe. And please bring back Thor, I think Samantha has become partial to him."

Emily smiled broadly. "I will, thank you." She turned her attention to Thor. "Okay, you," she said, taking his collar in hand and pulling him gently down from the fence. "Say goodbye to your girlfriend. Get down off there."

Thor gave the Shepherd a last sniff before obediently returning to Emily's side. With a final wave to Edith, she and Thor walked back to where she had left Mac, Rhiannon, and Petter.

"We thought maybe you'd gotten lost," said Rhiannon as she heard Emily's boots crunching toward them.

"You didn't tell us there were dogs on the island," Emily said, addressing Petter.

"What!" Mac and Rhiannon echoed in almost perfect unison.

"I just met one of them, courtesy of Thor's nose, apparently. Her owner said that there are hundreds here on the island."

Petter looked honestly taken-aback. "I am sorry, it did not even occur to me until now that that would be important to you. Of course, we have many dogs here on the island. Some are pets, most are working dogs. I am sorry, I should have realized."

Emily touched his arm. "It's okay, it's good news for us, and for him in particular." She nodded at Thor. It was only then she noticed Rhiannon was crying. Emily reached out and wiped the tears away from the kid's face before they could freeze.

"Hey," said Mac. "What's the matter?" He stepped in and placed a protective arm around her.

Rhiannon gulped a few times as she collected herself. "I'm okay," she said, her voice strained by emotion, "but you realize what this means; if there are dogs then that means there are going to be puppies. The world still has puppies."

No one spoke for several seconds. Emily took Rhiannon in her arms and squeezed her gently. "Puppies," Emily whispered, looking at Mac, who returned a smile just as big as his wife's.

And suddenly, despite the freezing weather and snow-bound land surrounding them, the world seemed just a little bit warmer.

•••

The apartment was on the third floor. Emily and her family were the only residents, according to Petter.

"Most of the tenants were off island when the red rain came," said Petter. "Now we have more room than we know what to do with." He handed Mac a slip of paper with several numbers written down on it. "The phone system works. I've written my personal number on there, along with the council members' and the number for the hospital. Feel free to call if there's anything you need. I've had some food brought in for you."

"Thank you," Emily said, as Petter handed her the apartment key. "Really, you've gone above and beyond for us. It's so very much appreciated."

Petter dipped his head. "If what you say is true, and we are all that is left of the human race, we should treat each other accordingly, no?"

Emily smiled back at him. "If everyone had had that attitude to begin with, maybe we wouldn't be in this mess."

"Perhaps we will learn our lesson this time around. Now if there's nothing more you need from me?"

"No, we're good," said Mac. "Thank you again." He offered Petter his hand.

"Have a pleasant afternoon," the major said, shaking Mac's hand vigorously, then he turned and walked back to the stairs. They could hear him whistling some melody as he descended the stairs to the waiting SUV.

"Okay," said Mac, rubbing his gloved hands together. "Let's get inside before we freeze to death out here."

•••

"Not too shabby," said Mac as he walked from room to room. The apartment had three bedrooms, a living area and a kitchen.

"Hey, look at this," said Emily, "the place even has a balcony." A sliding glass door led out from the living room onto a snow-blanketed balcony. There was a small fire pit with a couple of chairs placed around it; a pile of sticks that, in a previous life, had been a wooden shipping pallet was set near the door.

"I'm starving," said Rhiannon.

"Well let's have a look at what goodies Petter left us. Here, take my arm." Emily led Rhiannon through to the living room and sat her down on the sofa.

"Emily, you're going to want to come and see this" Mac called from the kitchen.

Emily joined him at the open fridge door. "Wow!" she exhaled, then added another "Wow!" The fridge was stocked with fresh produce; potatoes, onions, carrots, celery, broccoli, tomatoes. She opened a couple of cupboards, found spices and some condiments, a couple cans of soup, and some canned beans.

"Oh. My. God. Is that bread?" Emily said. Her eyes had wandered to a loaf of brown bread wrapped in cellophane sitting on the kitchen counter. "They have a bakery...? Are you sure we didn't all die and this is heaven?"

Mac grabbed a large knife from a metallic strip over the stove, tore off the cellophane and cut three thick slices of bread. He sniffed the slices deeply, like he was inhaling the bouquet of the finest wine. "Wow! Just wow," he said. He handed a slice to Emily, grabbed the two other pieces, and together they walked to the sofa. They sat down on either side of Rhiannon and placed a slice of bread in her hands. For the next several minutes the only sounds any of them made were *mmmm* or *ahhhh* as they savored the bread.

"I never thought I would ever taste something so

awesome again," said Rhiannon, voicing what the two adults were thinking.

"How about I make us one of my world-famous stews?" said Mac.

"Really? World famous, eh?" Emily said.

Mac laughed, "Give me a couple of hours and prepare to have your minds blown."

•••

Emily swallowed the last of her stew and let out a long sigh of contentment. "Husband of mine, you were not kidding. That was out of this world."

Mac gave a little bow. "My pleasure. How about you, Rhia? What do you think?"

"Can't talk. Eating," the kid said as she shoveled spoonful after spoonful of Mac's stew into her mouth.

"What about you, big dog? Was that good?" Mac said, smiling at Thor who lay on the floor next to a now empty bowl. The dog's tail swished back and forth, and he gazed at Mac in eager anticipation of more food.

"I'd say that was a yes," Emily said, chuckling gently.

"The secret's in the soy sauce," Mac explained from behind a broad grin. "Always a good replacement if you don't have any chicken stock."

"Well I guess we know who'll be doing the cooking from now on," Emily said.

Mac smiled proudly. "More?" he asked.

Both women nodded, yes. Ten minutes later, the bowls were again empty and their bellies were full.

"I'm going to explode," Rhiannon said. She made a show of undoing the top button of her jeans, which made both adults laugh. "Can you show me to my bedroom?" she added.

"Sure thing," said Emily. She helped Rhiannon to her feet.

"Good night, sweetheart," Mac said, planting a loud kiss on the top of the girl's head.

Rhiannon hugged him hard, then allowed Emily to escort her to her new bedroom.

When Emily came back out, Mac was on the balcony, a fire taking shape in the fire pit. He'd pulled the two chairs together so they could sit next to each other. Emily sat while Mac stoked the fire with a large metal poker, then tossed another handful of sticks onto it. He slumped down into the second chair with a contented "Ahhhhh!" as the fire took hold. The snow on the balcony and around the foot of the fire pit was already beginning to melt from the growing flames.

"A girl could get used to this," said Emily, curling her legs up under her, she leaned against her man's shoulder. She was happy, she realized, a genuine, honest-to-God sense of contentment having wrapped itself around her like a warm blanket on a cold morning.

"I can't remember the last time everything felt so *normal*," she said. "I didn't think we'd ever get to experience something like this ever again."

Mac nodded. "Would you look at that view."

To the west, the sun was setting, driving orange shards across the ocean, turning the snow a fiery orange. It was stunning.

They sat together for the next hour, talking quietly about nothing at all, holding hands, smiling until the sun had finally sunk beyond the horizon.

"Brrrr," said Emily, turning her face toward Mac's, "it's gotten a bit cold? I think we should head inside and warm up."

"You want me to put another log on the...*ohhhh*!" Mac's eyes met Emily's and he saw the unspoken invitation in them. "Yes, yes indeed it is a bit on the nippy side. Best we get you in before you catch your death." They stood as one. He placed his hands on her hips, kissed her gently on the mouth, then turned her around and ushered her back into the living room. Entwined in each other, they stumbled their way to the bedroom, pieces of clothing describing a trail behind them.

•••

The next morning, they were awakened by the sound of the bedside telephone ringing.

Emily rolled over on her side and picked up the receiver. "Hello?" she answered, her voice slurred from sleep.

"Good morning, this is Petter. The council would like to see you in one hour. I will pick you up, okay?"

"Okay," said Emily, suddenly awake. "We'll be ready. Thank you." She hung up, shook Mac awake, threw on her blouse then headed to Rhiannon's room and woke her too.

"Will you be okay here with Thor for an hour or two?" Emily asked her.

"Is there more bread?"

Emily laughed, "Yeah, we saved you some."

"Then we'll be fine."

Mac and Emily showered, grabbed a bowl of leftover soup, then, after saying their goodbyes to Rhia, headed out the door.

CHAPTER 5

The questions started as soon as Emily and Mac sat down at the conference table.

"I'm sorry, would you mind explaining who this Valentine person is again?" Magda Solheim asked.

"She was one of the survivors from the McMurdo science outpost in the Antarctic. To put it bluntly, Valentine's a power-hungry bitch who thinks that every other human survivor is taking up space in her world, and that that entitles her to do exactly as she pleases with those lives, including having anyone who stands in her way murdered," said Emily. She looked at her husband. "Does that sound about right?"

Mac nodded. "Sounds spot on to me, love."

"But all we have is your word that that is so," Magda said. "You want us to send our people to help you, but for all we know, this Valentine could be an elected and beloved leader and we would be helping you with a coup."

Mac answered. "We understand your position. All we

want from your people is backup. The survivors at Point Loma outnumber us, so if we go in and start making demands then we need to be able to back those demands up with some muscle."

"Could you not just use the craft Emily arrived in? Surely that would be enough to make them surrender." This came from Jørgensen

"Would you have surrendered if Emily had waltzed in here in that thing?" Mac asked.

"No," said Petter, "we would not have."

Mac nodded. "Exactly! And neither will Valentine. She'll happily sacrifice all of the other survivors until only she's left."

"And besides," Emily chimed in, "I don't believe the majority of the Point Loma group supports Valentine's actions. I think they are just scared of her and her goons."

Mac finished Emily's point for her. "Chances are that if the camp sees Valentine outnumbered or arrested they'll feel confident enough to switch sides. We don't want any bloodshed, if it can be avoided. What we hope to be able to do, with your permission, is to take a sample of the vegetables and fruit you're raising here as proof that we can return the world to a semblance of what it once was. Valentine is a consummate politician; she uses fear to control the people. Fear of her. Fear of your neighbor. Fear of the 'other'. It's textbook authoritarian stuff. I'm confident that if we can give the survivors hope of a normal life, they'll come over to our side willingly and without a shot having been fired."

"And, if your plan doesn't work?" Jørgensen asked.

"Most of the survivors at the camp are either civilians or military who haven't ever had to fire a shot in anger. I don't anticipate much in the way of resistance. It'll work," Mac said, no doubt in his voice.

Petter stepped forward. "And how would we get to Point Loma?"

"You'd travel with us in the *Vengeance*. It'd take several weeks to get back to Cali, but that would provide us with the best opportunity to sneak in unannounced."

Norfred spoke next. "And what would be in it for us? This deal seems one sided to me." His response drew glares from several of the female councilors.

Mac responded. "Fair question. When we've taken care of the Valentine problem, there will be an open invitation to any of you and your people to join us at our Point Loma community. You'll have the protection of our military, access to all of our knowledge about this world, homes with an ocean view, great weather, and the chance to start over again."

Emily spoke up, "As far as we know, we are it...your group and ours. The last of humanity. Sure, there could be others, but I don't know how they could have survived this long. So that just leaves us. We are humanity's last, best hope for a future. Will you help us?"

Still, Norfred seemed unconvinced, but said nothing more.

"Any other questions?" Magda asked, looking from councilor to councilor. She was met with shakes of the head from everyone. "Very well. Mac, Emily; if you will excuse us while we discuss this further." The governor turned back to her colleagues and began to speak in her native tongue.

For the next ten minutes, Mac and Emily sat silently watching the council animatedly discuss their request between themselves and Major Djupvik. Apart from an occasional word in English, neither of them had any idea what was being said or whether the discussion was going in their favor or not.

"Remind me never to play poker with these guys," Mac whispered to Emily.

Emily smiled in return. This was a long shot, she understood that. These people did not know her, had only basic information and experience of the red world to go on.

But their help would tip the balance in taking back Point Loma with as little bloodshed as possible.

Finally, a show of hands, split four to two, signaled that the discussion was over.

Magda stood, smiled politely, and spoke, "We are willing to allow twenty of our military, volunteers, to accompany you back to California. Major Djupvik has already volunteered to go, but it will be with the understanding that he retains complete command over our people. Is that acceptable?"

Mac stood, nodded, said, "Thank you, that will work just fine."

Truth was, Emily thought, they had hoped for more, but had expected less. With this additional force they should have no real problem taking back the camp.

Best laid plans of aliens and men, Emily reminded herself, then stood and thanked the council too.

CHAPTER 6

"How would you like to proceed?" Petter asked, as he, Emily, and Mac exited the council building and began walking back to the couple's apartment. The weather was warmer, maybe even above zero, Emily decided, the knife-wielding wind having faded away to virtually nothing.

"Do you have your volunteers yet?" Mac asked.

"Not yet," said Petter, "but I will be addressing my people as soon as our conversation is over."

"My suggestion is that once you have them, we'll get together and we'll formulate a plan. Your people all speak English, I presume?"

Petter nodded. "Most speak at least three languages. English is one of them."

"Well now I feel inadequate," said Emily. "Most I ever learned was a little Spanish, back in high school."

Mac checked his watch. "Why don't we get together in three hours back in the council office. Will that work for you?"

Petter nodded. "We will see you there." He saluted, and headed off.

"Well, that went better than I expected," Mac said once Petter was out of earshot.

"Will twenty volunteers be enough?" Emily asked.

"Between our blokes and what Petter can muster, we should be good. Valentine and her lot aren't going to be expecting any kind of assault from outside of the camp. If we're quick and quiet, we should be able to take back the camp with very few casualties."

"And when we do, what about Valentine and her collaborators?"

"I think there has to be a trial," said Mac.

"And then...?"

"Jail? Banishment? Execution? You know what my personal preference would be, but it's going to be up to the people to decide what course of action to take. It ain't my circus and those aren't my monkeys."

They reached the apartment building and were halfway up the stairs when Emily felt the familiar tingle at the back of her skull that signaled Adam had made a connection with her. She stopped, placed a hand on Mac's arm, then sat down on a step. "Hello Adam," she said aloud.

Mac looked at her quizzically, his head slightly cocked to one side.

"*Hello, Mommy. Hello, Daddy.*"

Mac's mouth dropped. He looked around checking that he wasn't the recipient of a practical joke.

"You can hear him?" Emily asked.

Mac looked at her, not saying anything, his eyes wide with surprise. "Yes," he said finally. "I..." His voice trailed away to nothing.

"*It's okay, Daddy, you don't have to be scared.*"

Mac sank down next to his wife on the stair. He reached out and took her hand in his own. "Hello, son. You sound so grown up now" he said, quietly. Emily saw tears

56

welling up in the corner of her husband's eyes. It was true, Adam's voice sounded like a twenty-something man's. But even though his masculinity was obvious, his words were carried on a tone of gentleness; soft, melodic, calm. *Kind*, but also with an underlying strength that only came from certitude. Like a young priest comforting the bereaved, his voice had an intimateness to it that made her think he was at total peace. Emily squeezed her husband's hand gently, smiling reassuringly.

"*I have news for you,*" Adam said. "*I have moved deeper into the memories of the Caretakers, searching for information on the creatures that caused them to deviate from their assigned pathway.*"

"Locusts," Emily said. "We call them Locusts."

"*Locusts, yes, a suitable name for these creatures. The Caretaker memories I have identified are old, deteriorated, but I have studied them and recovered knowledge that may help you. While not as old as the Caretakers, these creatures have existed for millions of years longer than humanity. But like the Caretakers, I believe that they are not a natural product of the universe, rather they are a construction of some older race, perhaps built as a tool or a weapon. And while they are undoubtedly intelligent, they appear to have no use for physical technology, simply relying on their innate ability to reprogram other lifeforms to become their tools or to carry out their bidding. While I cannot be absolutely sure of it, I believe these creatures to be comprised of energy, shedding their physical forms once the resources of the planet they occupy have been consumed, then occupying new bodies on the next, traveling via the hidden lanes that run throughout this universe.*"

"Hidden lanes?" Mac said.

"*There are pathways running through and between galaxies, connecting stars and planets. If found, those lanes can move matter and energy over unimaginable distances in very little time. The Locusts utilize these lanes to travel from one world to the next, just as the Caretakers used them to bring their ships here to Earth."*

"Wow!" said Emily.

Adam continued. *"The Locusts' needs are simple; they consume everything. They do not seek enlightenment. They do not look to improve theirs or any other species' lot. They merely consume...and move on."*

"Do you know when they will come?" Mac asked.

"I do not have the ability to track them finitely, the Caretaker technology is vast and complex and, even with my heightened abilities and capacities, it will take me many hundreds of years to fully comprehend and utilize all that it has to offer. But I am able to sense...disruptions within the energies that encompass the lanes connecting our world."

"And?" said Emily, leaning forward, squeezing Mac's hand tightly.

"And I believe they will be here very soon. You must prepare for their arrival. I detected the demise of the entities that sacrificed themselves for you. More lifeforms have agreed to help you."

Mac looked at Emily, both bewildered by what their son had just said. Emily voiced their confusion, "Adam, I don't think I understand what...Oh!" Her mind connected the dots of what he was trying to tell them. "You mean the *Machine*, don't you?"

"*Yes*," Adam continued. *"The entity you called the 'Machine' was a collection of creatures that volunteered to help you. They understood that their lives would be lost once you reached the island, their temperature tolerance being limited to only a short duration within colder climates, but still they volunteered."*

"Wow!" Emily said again.

Mac said, "You're telling me that the craft that Emily arrived here in was...alive? That it wasn't something that you made, it was built out of other creatures? And that they willingly volunteered?"

"*Of course. I have others now who have agreed to render their assistance to you, they are aware of the danger the Locusts pose and will help.*"

"This is beginning to hurt my brain," Mac said, shaking his head in disbelief.

"*You must meet the new craft here...*"

Emily felt a new memory form in her mind. She gasped as she recognized the location.

"*If I am able, I will tell you when the Locusts arrive, but it will be up to you to find them. You must locate them and you must destroy them before they can shed their corporeal form and move on to the next world. There will not be another chance to stop them. The possibility of another being such as I existing is now beyond improbable. Countless other worlds, other civilizations will fall to the Locusts. It is not only the fate of this planet that now lies in your hands, but innumerable others.*"

"How are we supposed to destroy them?"

"*I will provide you with a solution once you have located them.*"

"Son, are you all right?" Mac spoke quietly. There was a suggestion of desperation in his voice that Emily had never heard before.

"*I am...depleted,*" Adam said. "*The constant absorption of knowledge that flows to me is a drain on my human mind. The systems that preserve me are attempting to adapt my body to accommodate these extra physical stresses, but the growth process is both gradual and painful. Nonetheless, I go on. I persevere.*"

"Is there anything we can do to help?" Emily asked, automatically, already knowing the answer.

Adam's voice became tender. "*Thank you, Mommy, but there is nothing you can do to alleviate these changes. The pain is bearable. The outcome inevitable.*" Adam paused for a second. "*Now, my time is done. You must be at the location I have given to you within the next two days. Farewell."*

"I love you, son," Mac whispered, but Adam was already gone.

•••

"Are you okay?" Emily asked, trying but failing to hide the concern from her voice. In all the years she had known her husband, not once had she seen him anxious...until now. His eyes were wide, blinking only occasionally. Sweat ran down his forehead, mingling with a stream of tears and snot. He wasn't bawling, his features remained as stoic and rugged as they ever had, but his emotional distress was as obvious as the sun in the sky.

"Jesus!" he whispered for what must have been the fifth time. "Our son, he's...Christ!...What the hell is he exactly?"

"Still our son; that's what he is."

"But...Jesus!"

Emily took her husband's hand. "I know. I do, really I do. It's an incredible amount to take in. This is all so overwhelming, so God-damned unfair, but Mac, I tell you now, he *is* still our son. He's *still* Adam."

Mac squeezed Emily's hand tightly, then released it. He used the sleeve of his tunic to wipe the tears and snot from his face. He took in a deep breath, puffed it out.

"Better?" Emily asked, smiling sympathetically.

Mac nodded, leaned in, took her head in his hands and kissed her on the forehead. He released her and leaned back. "So, where is Adam sending us to pick up the new transport?"

"New York," Emily said. "We're going back to New York."

•••

Emily had a distinct sense of déjà vu as she waited on the concrete dock, watching supplies and personnel being loaded aboard the *Vengeance*. Rhiannon and Thor stood beside her. The *Vengeance* was docked at Longyearbyen port, as close as was possible in the shallow water, supplies ferried out to the sub in a flotilla of small watercraft.

"You ready?" asked Mac, crunching through the snow to Emily.

"As we'll ever be," Emily replied. She smiled at her husband. Even in the subzero temperature, she could see beads of sweat on his forehead, a testament to how damn hard a worker the man was.

"Let's get a move on, then, shall we?" Mac helped Rhiannon into a dinghy moored nearby. Thor leapt in too, curling up at Rhiannon's feet. Of all of them, the malamute seemed to be the most at home here on this desolate, frozen island; Emily felt a pang of guilt at taking that away from her four-footed friend.

Mac reached a hand out and helped Emily down into the slowly rising and falling dinghy. He nodded to a Norwegian on the dock. The man untied the mooring line from the metal bollard, then tossed the line into the dinghy. The outboard motor coughed into life and Mac edged the boat out into the choppy water, making a beeline for the *Vengeance*, the dinghy dipping and rising as it bounced across the water. He pulled alongside the sub and proceeded to reverse the process they had just gone through, tossing a line to a waiting sailor, then helping the women and Thor on deck. The Norwegian sailor who had caught the rope climbed into the dinghy, wished them all luck, and headed back to land.

"Well, this is just like old times," said Emily, smiling at Mac as he walked with his family toward the sub's main access hatch. As they approached it, Mac pulled something that looked like a large piece of folded cloth attached to a coil of paracord from the inside of his jacket.

"What's that for?" Emily asked.

Mac smiled, and rather than answer, called Thor over to him. Mac unfurled the cloth and Emily had to smile when she saw it was a dog harness. He slipped the harness over Thor's head and then fastened it behind his back. "This'll make things a little easier for the old man," he said.

Emily leaned in and kissed her husband on the cheek. "Well you just think of everything," she said.

"I aim to please," Mac replied, with a grin.

Holding Rhiannon's hand, Emily maneuvered the girl to the access hatch, then climbed onto the ladder and down a few rungs until her shoulders were just above the deck of the submarine. "Okay," she said to Rhiannon, "Now just move your foot forward a bit...that's it." She reached out and took Rhiannon's left ankle in her hand. "Now just step forward slowly...perfect." She guided Rhiannon's foot onto the first rung, then repeated the action with her right foot. Emily urged Rhiannon to step down a couple more rungs until the girl was safely between Emily and the ladder. "Now, one foot at a time."

Emily and Rhiannon slowly descended the ladder. "Step off now," Emily said when they were safely inside the sub. Emily guided Rhiannon a little farther into the corridor then stepped back into the pillar of light shining down from the deck access hatch.

"Okay, lower him down," she called up.

In the circle of sky still visible at the top of the ladder, Emily first saw Thor's tail appear then the rest of the malamute as Mac slowly, carefully, lowered the dog down to Emily's waiting arms. Thor seemed completely unfazed by the whole experience, waiting quietly while Emily removed the harness. When she was done, she yelled up to Mac that he could drop the rope. Emily collected the rope as Mac started down the ladder, sealing the hatch behind him.

"This way to our rooms," Mac said, when he had both

feet on the floor. He took Rhiannon by the elbow and moved her along the corridor. "Duck your head," he told her as they stepped through the opening of a watertight door.

Their room was at the end of the corridor, near the sub's galley. It was large enough for two people and, as Rhiannon could not be left by herself, Emily would share it with her while Mac would take the berth next door. A number of pieces of fresh clothing, donated by the Norwegians, lay neatly folded on the two beds. There were enough for a week's change of clothes for both Emily and Rhiannon, which was a godsend, as far as Emily was concerned.

Emily guided Rhiannon into the room then spent a couple minutes helping her navigate around it by touch until the girl was confident she could maneuver in the tight confines of the barely three-meter wide cabin.

"I'll arrange for some food to be brought down as soon as we're under way," said Mac.

HOME

CHAPTER 7

A cool breeze blew off the choppy water of the Hudson River as the *HMS Vengeance* cruised across its surface into the Upper Bay. The submarine adjusted course slightly until it headed toward the west side of Manhattan. The three figures standing on the observation deck of the sub's conning tower stood in silence; just looking. Before them, what had once been the pinnacle of humanity's engineering skills and striving for a better tomorrow now lay obscured behind a tangle of red jungle.

"My God," Emily gasped, unconsciously gripping Mac's forearm. To the sub's left, the unmistakable outline of the Statue of Liberty was still visible rising into the air, hidden beneath a red shroud. Vines had wound around the statue's base and grown upward, twisting their way up the symbol of freedom. Lichen and other vegetation covered every centimeter, until nothing of the original statue was left visible other than its blood-red silhouette.

"I had always imagined that I would visit New York one day," said Petter, "but not like this."

Jersey was nothing now but rolling hills of red, the vast bulk of buildings devoured, Emily imagined, by the same strange fungus that had dismantled the hotels in Las Vegas. Brooklyn had fared a little better; the skeletons of buildings were still visible through the gently swaying cover of red leaves, thick boughs of Titan trees, and tall grass. Gone was the iconic landscape of New York City, the towering skyscrapers vanished, supplanted by alien Titan trees. The human-jungle of buildings and roads replaced by an otherworldly jungle that had obliterated most of the buildings and landmarks. But dotted across the landscape. the remains of an occasional skyscraper still peeked out from behind the jungle like bleached bones; the eviscerated cadaver of humanity's greatest social achievements.

"Engines to one-quarter," Mac said quietly into a microphone.

Emily exhaled a short breath, knowing she was not the only one that felt as though they were entering an ancient sepulcher, her silence an emotional reaction born out of respect for the millions that had been consumed by the red rain in these cities. She was, she realized, quite possibly the only person left on Earth who had ever set foot in that great city, and that weight was a terrible, painful burden to her.

The *Vengeance* cruised upstream, leaving a v-shaped wake behind it.

Governor's Island was little more than a blood blister floating on the Hudson. To starboard, the wharfs of Red Hook were still visible, the red jungle having stopped about fifty meters from the shoreline, leaving a long gray concrete scar along the river's edge. The rusting hulk of what had once been a huge cruise ship now lay half-submerged in the water, its prow pointing skyward, its once-pristine white paint flaking and dappled with orange. A half-bat half-bird-like creature flew into the air from one broken, rusted porthole on the side of the cruise ship's upper deck, its wings glinting in the afternoon sun as it flapped high into the air then glided out over the remains of Brooklyn.

"There," said Petter, pointing ahead, past the ship's sunken remains.

Emily strained her eyes against the glare of the sun bouncing off the water to see what the Norwegian major was pointing at. It was a large concrete berth, free of any ships or watercraft.

Mac moved a pair of binoculars from around his neck to his eyes and studied the dock for a good minute before speaking. "It looks clear of any debris above water," he said. "Let's give it a shot." He quickly spoke directions into his microphone and the submarine almost immediately began to slow, then angle toward the open mouth of the dock. Mac continued to scan the water ahead of them, looking for any signs of submerged hazards, but within a few minutes the *Vengeance* edged slowly alongside the dock.

"Engines, all stop," Mac ordered.

The sub came to a complete stop. Within a minute, the deck hatches opened and a group of burly sailors hefted a large metal gangplank from below deck then quickly maneuvered one end over the four-meter gap between the *Vengeance* and the dock. Another group of sailors jogged over the gangplank onto land, weapons drawn as they fanned out before dropping to one knee. They scanned the open ground between the dock and the edge of the jungle. A third group of sailors followed behind, quickly tying mooring lines from the sub's stern, center, and bow to rusty bollards dotted along the crumbling edge of the pier.

When the sailors were done they retreated onto the deck.

Mac turned to face Emily. "Okay, now what?" asked Mac.

"Now," said Emily, "I guess we wait."

•••

Emily stood alone on the deck of the *Vengeance*, staring across the jungle in the direction of Central Park, a slight breeze ruffling her hair. Her mind was running back over the events of those first few days after the red rain had come and the change it had brought with it. Those changes were completed now; the old world—humanity's world—was all but gone, buried beneath the carpet of red. The ruins of man's greatest achievements consigned to the same chapter of history that contained the world's other vanished civilizations.

"*Mommy?*"

Adam's voice startled Emily from her reverie.

"Adam. I'm here," she said to the empty air in front of her. Although she could not see her son, all her other senses told her he was right there, beside her.

His voice floated to Emily again, "*I'm sending the transportation to you and Daddy. Tell the others with you not to be afraid.*"

Emily nodded, "When will it be here?"

"*Soon,*" was the reply.

Emily thought she detected a hint of tiredness in her boy's voice. "Honey, are you okay?" she asked but there was no reply. Adam was gone.

•••

Emily dropped below deck and headed to the command room. Mac was going over a duty roster.

"Adam says the replacement transport is on its way," Emily said as she ducked into the room.

"Do we have an ETA?" Mac asked.

Emily shook her head. "He sounded really tired, Mac."

Mac stepped in closer and put a hand on Emily's shoulder. "Well, when you think about it, it stands to reason that he would be exhausted. I mean, he's learning all this new stuff. It's going to take its toll on him, right? Nothing to worry about, I'm sure love." He smiled reassuringly at his wife. Emily knew he was just trying to make her feel better and that he had no more of an idea whether what he said was the truth or not. For all they knew, the mind-bogglingly complicated system their son was at the center of might slowly be killing him.

"Well, he said that—"

Emily's sentence was cut short by the sound of the sub's intercom demanding attention. Mac unhooked the microphone and said, "Go ahead." A voice, buzzing with either an edge of excitement or panic, Emily could not tell, crackled out of the speaker. "Topside lookout reporting, sir. We have movement in the jungle. Multiple contacts heading our way."

Mac pressed a button near the intercom and instantly a klaxon began to reverberate through the submarine. He turned a large black switch on the intercom then spoke clearly and without a hint of panic. "All hands to battle stations. This is not a drill."

Immediately the crew began moving to their emergency stations. Mac took Emily by the arm and headed out of the command room. At first Emily thought he was taking her back to her cabin but instead he took her to the ladder leading up to the deck and began climbing. She followed behind. Mac pulled himself up onto the deck. "Where?" he yelled to a young sailor standing in the conning tower with a pair of binoculars staring wide-eyed down at Mac and Emily.

"There," the sailor yelled back, while simultaneously pointing due west toward the border of the jungle. Both Emily and Mac shaded their eyes against a sun that was now just an hour or so away from setting.

"I don't see anything," Emily said to Mac, but almost as soon as the words had left her mouth, the trees near the edge of the jungle began moving, swaying as if they were being buffeted by a rogue wind.

"What the...?" Mac said.

From the edge of the jungle, a swarm of creatures moved out of the trees and began to walk, slither, and crawl over the open ground toward the submarine. There were long-limbed animals that looked like malnourished giraffes that stood a good ten meters tall; pig-sized bundles of limbs that would have been easy to mistake for sea anemones; much smaller multi-eyed rodents that dodged and weaved between the larger creatures' feet; huge bugs that hopped ten meters at a time. There were, Emily estimated, a good two hundred or more performers in this weird alien carnival moving toward the sub.

More sailors joined Emily and Mac on the deck. They were all armed with automatic weapons; a few, Emily saw, had grenades too. Mac unslung his own weapon from his shoulder and held it ready. Emily pulled her pistol from the holster on her hip and chambered a round.

The creatures continued to advance. Their pace was slow, almost methodical, Emily thought. It was as though they were all out for an evening stroll together, with no sign of aggression between the various species.

"Get ready to cast off," Mac yelled. Sailors moved to where the mooring lines were attached to the sub. The lines would have to be abandoned because there was no way the sailors could get to where the lines were secured to the bollards on the quay.

"You sailors," Mac shouted at a group of men gathered nearby. "Get your arses into gear and grab that gangplank." He pointed at the metal bridge between the submarine and the shore. "Well move it," he yelled when the sailors did not budge. They jogged over to the gangplank and began unlocking the ties securing it to the sub.

Emily continued to stare at the advancing wall of creatures. They all seemed oblivious to each other, as though each species had reached some semblance of detente.

The sailors were getting nervous. While many had seen any number of the weird and wonderful fauna the red rain had produced, this was something new. And it was, Emily admitted, quite terrifying.

Abruptly, the front row of animals stopped about fifty meters from the submarine. As the slower creatures behind them caught up, they too slowed to a halt, all waiting patiently until the final straggler had joined them.

"What in God's name is going on?" Mac said. He directed the question at Emily, as if she would know.

"Don't look at me," Emily exclaimed.

"Hold your positions," Mac called out to the sailors poised at the mooring lines.

The animals did not advance any farther, even as others joined them. Then, in a bizarre ballet, they began to climb on one another, their tentacles and legs and arms and claws tangling with their neighbors.

"What in the world?" said Mac.

Seconds later, the creatures began to melt.

•••

Maybe melt isn't the correct word, Emily thought as she watched with an oddly detached fascination. *Meld*, that was what the animals were doing. Fusing together. Where one animal connected with the other a dim but discernible band of white light burned. Where there were spaces, smaller creatures climbed over the larger animals' bodies and slipped into the gap, combining with the others. Emily's mind flashed back to the first day after the red rain, when she had left her apartment and encountered the spider-like aliens in Central Park. What she was seeing now was eerily reminiscent to what she had witnessed in the first days after the red rain had first swept across the planet. The creatures that had once been living, breathing human beings had fused with each other to make the huge tree-like structures that had in turn gone on to spew the red dust that had transformed almost every living thing on the planet.

Now, as each new layer of creatures formed, the one below began to shift, stretch, reform, taking on a new shape. A crackling, popping sound reached the human watchers. To Emily's ears it sounded like fresh cut logs burning in a fireplace.

The sailors and soldiers on the deck muttered nervously but held their positions.

Petter climbed up on deck and made his way over to where Emily and Mac stood. He said something under his breath that was probably a curse.

"Christ!" said Mac. "What the hell are they doing?"

Emily was about to say that she had no idea but at that very moment she recognized the shape the lower level of animals had transformed into.

"Oh my God. It's the *Machine*. They're recreating the *Machine*," she blurted out.

"What?" said Mac. He turned to look at her, flabbergasted.

"That bottom part," she pointed at the transformed lower section that just ten minutes earlier had been a row of beasts. "It's the same shape as the body of the vehicle we traveled to Svalbard in."

Mac looked again and brought the binoculars up to his eyes. "You're right," he said after a brief pause. "Bloody hell!"

Emily turned to look at Mac. He was watching her intently, an expression of utter disbelief on his face that probably mirrored the one she thought she wore. "This is Adam's doing," Emily said. "Somehow he's commanding those creatures to become a copy of the *Machine*. A *living* vehicle."

A slow but continual flow of animals emerged from the jungle, adding themselves without hesitation to the self-assembling craft. Over the next hour, everyone on deck watched with a morbid sense of fascination as the unmistakable outline of the twin of the vehicle Emily, Rhiannon, and Thor had traveled in gradually formed in front of their eyes. By the time the sun set below the horizon, the *Machine*'s multiple legs and the lower section of the main body was already clearly defined. As darkness settled gently over the remains of New York and its boroughs, the white glow of the constant fusing of one creature after the other created an otherworldly light show in the darkness beyond the *Vengeance*.

"Let's get some of these men below decks," Mac said to Parsons. "Pull anyone who isn't part of the security detail," he ordered.

Gradually, the men began dispersing below decks until only three two-man security teams were left.

"You and Emily should get some rest," Petter said, joining Mac and Emily in the sub's conning tower. "I will watch over the *Vengeance* through the night."

"Are you sure?" Mac asked.

Petter nodded and smiled. "I would not have offered if I was not."

●●●

The following morning, a fiery red sunrise greeted the first humans to set foot in New York since Emily had left. *Was it really only three years ago?* Emily wondered, as she stared out across the water.

Mac joined his wife on the deck of the *Vengeance* carrying two cups of weak but hot coffee, a shield against the day's early-morning chill. Rhiannon was asleep in the cabin, Thor standing watch over her.

"Not much left to go," said Mac, offering Emily one of the cups of coffee. He was referring to the automaton that now stood almost three-quarters complete on the shore.

"Thanks," Emily said, as she took the coffee. "If I had

to guess, I'd say it'll be finished before this afternoon."

Sipping at their coffee, they watched new animals make their way from the jungle then add themselves to the slowly growing mechanism assembling itself before their very eyes.

"Do you miss the place at all?" Mac asked, nodding in the direction of Manhattan, after the silence between them had stretched into a minute.

Emily considered the question before she answered. "You know, I haven't really given it that much thought, been kind of busy for the last few years. But who doesn't miss their old life? I mean, it was all so easy by comparison to this one. We had no idea just how good we had it. So, yeah, I miss it, but you want to hear something weird?"

"What?" said Mac, taking another sip from his mug.

"I'm kind of glad it happened, now. I mean, it's not like we can go back. So, we get this second chance, a chance to make things better. To do the *right* thing. I'm grateful for it. Is that wrong of me?"

Mac put his free arm around his wife's shoulder, leaned in and kissed her on the top of the head. "It is what it is love, and no amount of wishing is ever going to take it back to how it was. Which is probably for the best, like you said." The silence returned between them; not an uncomfortable one, but the type of silence that makes the moment better, purer.

Eventually, Mac did a slow one-eighty turn, his eyes taking in the landscape that, despite his knowledge of the history of desolation and death that lay broken and decayed beneath its red covering, was stunning and beautiful in its own alien right.

"Always wanted to see the Statue of Liberty," he said eventually, pointing with his mug, his eyes lingering on the red outline of the statue across the water from where the *Vengeance* was moored.

Emily turned and looked across the river too.

"You know," she said, "in all the years I lived in Manhattan, I never visited it. The statue."

Mac looked at her sideways. "You're pulling my leg, right?"

Emily shook her head slowly, smiling.

"Wow! Really?"

This time she nodded. "Really."

"Hmmm!" Mac said, then, nonchalantly added, "Want to take a tour?"

Now it was Emily's turn to look sideways at her husband.

"Now *you're* joking?"

"Nope," Mac said. "I mean, it's not like we'll ever get the chance again. And besides, we'll probably be the last two humans who ever get to see it. So, you up for a bit of exploring?"

"Okay," said Emily, surprised at how excited she felt. "When?"

"No time like the present," Mac said, through his Cheshire Cat grin. "I'll go make the necessary arrangements."

•••

Ten minutes later, Emily and Mac were skipping across a kilometer or so of gray Hudson River water in the sub's Zodiac.

"My God," Emily sighed, as the boat drew closer to Liberty Island. "She's still so beautiful." There was no mistaking the emotional impact of the massive statue, even though only the outline of it remained visible behind the blood-red covering of vines and vegetation. The sheer power of what that landmark once stood for still undeniable.

In that moment, staring up at the monument to ideals that had been left in her and the Earth's other survivors' hands, it hit Emily just how much her life had changed since that fateful day the red rain had fallen. She had lost so *very* much that day, but gained so much, too, despite the end of the world ruining any chance she would have had for a nice, 'normal' life. She had not given it much thought over the years since she had left New York, but now that she was back, it hit her like the proverbial sledgehammer. She had gone from being a journalist riding her bike through the streets of the city that now lay in ruins just across the water, to travelling to the farthest northern reaches of Alaska and then back again in a submarine, of all things. She had done things on that journey north that she profoundly regretted; the death of little Ben, Rhiannon's younger brother, a scar that would remain with her forever. But, she reminded herself, there had been no other choice she could make back then.

And on the journey that led her to this moment in time, she had taught herself how to drive a car, then a snowcat, and, eventually, with Mac's help, a helicopter. *A freaking helicopter!* She had battled monsters that had once been human and humans who were little more than monsters. She had made and lost good friends. She had fallen in love, married, become the mother of a fantastic kid whose chance at a normal life had been so unfairly snatched from him, only for Adam to become the powerful being who held the very future of this world in his hands.

Emily realized none of these things would have happened had the Caretakers not found this small, blue planet that she called home, forcing her to become something so much more than she had ever dreamed she could be. But her achievements, in the face of so much adversity...well, their magnitude had caught her off guard.

"She's magnificent," Mac said, staring up at the statue, breaking Emily's moment of self-assessment.

Emily looked up at the statue, then back to Mac. "She certainly is," she whispered, allowing her eyes to drift back to the statue as Mac swung the boat parallel to the shore, looking for a place to land.

They moored the Zodiac at the end of a dilapidated

wooden jetty on the southeast corner of the island, grabbed their weapons and backpacks and walked to shore.

The island was covered in waist-high grass and the occasional small tree. The base of the plinth the statue stood on, easily twice as tall as Mac, was now a wall of crimson. Here and there, the wall had crumbled, revealing the original stone beneath the covering of red lichen.

A broken path, cracked and overgrown in places but still visible, curved around and behind the statue. Emily and Mac followed it until they came to what had been a souvenir shop and perhaps a restaurant, it was hard to tell, the place was so overgrown. The glass walls of the building, shattered long ago, lay in shards and pieces on the ground, the souvenir shop's merchandise broken, rotted, and rusted, strewn across the floor.

Mac knelt, picked something up from the ground, brushed the dirt and pieces of lichen still clinging to it away, and looked at it for a few seconds before handing it to Emily. It was a small ceramic replica of a plaque that Emily knew was somewhere on this island. Inscribed on the ceramic was the poem *The New Colossus* written by Emma Lazarus.

Emily read it silently, tears forming slowly at the corners of her eyes.

"A mighty woman with a torch, whose flame is the imprisoned lightning, and her name Mother of Exiles," said Mac, reading over her shoulder. "Never truer than it is today." He caressed Emily's shoulder.

His wife smiled at the inference. She wiped her tear away with her sleeve, then placed the ceramic plaque in her jacket pocket. When she spoke, it was with reverence, as though she stood in a great cathedral. "It's easy to forget what this stood for; the promise that it held for this country, for the world. And now, it's buried beneath all this red shit. It's just not right, is it? Christ! I just want to burn it all down."

Mac looked lovingly at his wife, while she stared up

at the statue.

He touched her hand.

"Mmmm?" she said, her eyes unable to leave the colossus.

"Don't move. I'll be right back." He was gone before she could say a word, his broad back disappearing along the path that had brought them here. A few minutes later he reappeared, an object held in each hand. "Here," he said to Emily, holding both hands out to her.

Emily looked at the objects he held; one was the Zodiac's spare red plastic jerrycan of gasoline, the other a flare gun from the boat's emergency kit. She had learned from their experience clearing the ground around Point Loma that the red vegetation was particularly susceptible to fire, and Mac must have sensed what she was thinking.

"The gas is to make sure we get the job done right," he said.

Emily nodded and took both items from him.

"I'd suggest we get a little closer to the statue," Mac continued. "Just to be sure."

Wordlessly, the two humans walked to the base of the statue until a metal security fence blocked them from getting any closer. Emily pulled the cap off the spout of the gas can and began to shake its contents over the bushes and tall grass covering the ground and building. The vegetation was so thick and ubiquitous it formed a continuous sheet of red, beginning at the base of the statue's steps, rising upward to completely obscure the stone woman's message beneath its ruby-red feelers. *If the fire is going to take*, Emily thought, *this is the place to start it.* She emptied the entire contents of the gas can out, then tossed the empty container away.

"Best we put a bit of distance between us and here," said Mac. They walked back to the path.

"You do the honors," Emily said, offering Mac the flare pistol.

Mac nodded gratefully, took the pistol and aimed at

the gasoline-soaked area. "Ready?"

"Do it..."

There was a click, a flash, and the flare arced out and over fence, landing in the middle of the gas-soaked redness. There was a bright flash and whoosh as the gasoline ignited. Orange flames swept out across the base of the plinth, spreading quickly. The vegetation was dry enough that within thirty seconds of the gas igniting, the fire had caught and spread to the building at its base and now moved up the plinth toward the foot of the statue, spreading across concrete steps and walls.

"We better move before we're cut off," said Mac.

"In a moment," Emily said, her eyes unable to leave the sight of the fire roaring toward the hem of the statue's robe, hungrily devouring any red it came into contact with. Black smoke poured into the sky, but where the fire touched red it burned away all signs of the alien life that had usurped this symbol of humanity's need for freedom.

Emily felt Mac's hand on her elbow. "Time to go, love," he urged, and she allowed him to guide her back toward the jetty and their waiting boat off the island. By the time they reached the Zodiac, the plinth was completely aflame, and the flames were reaching ever higher up the statue herself.

They climbed into the boat, threw off the mooring lines, and started the engine. Emily placed herself at the front of the boat, her back toward their destination, her eyes fixed on Liberty Island. Orange embers, caught by the hot air of the inferno, floated skyward. Here and there along the Jersey shore those embers touched off smaller fires. Those new fires grew quickly, spreading into the jungle's interior. By the time the boat pulled up alongside the *Vengeance*, a line of fire nearly a kilometer long burned on the opposite shore, sending a plume of black smoke into the air that drifted slowly toward the corpse of New York city.

But through the haze of smoke and fire, the now-unmistakable visage of Lady Liberty burned brightest of all.

CHAPTER 8

"Made yourself a bit of a bonfire?" asked Parsons, cheekily, as Mac and Emily pulled the dinghy alongside the *Vengeance*. He caught the mooring line Mac threw to him and tied it off.

"Long story," Emily said, taking Parsons' offered hand and leaping onto the sub's deck. Mac climbed up behind her. All three stood on deck, entranced by the conflagration. Liberty Island was a tower of flame and smoke, as was a long stretch of the mainland, too.

"Let it all burn, I say," Parsons mumbled.

"Couldn't agree more," said Mac, giving the Welshman a friendly slap on his back.

They continued to watch as the fire spread down the coast until nothing could be seen of the west and northern shores but billowing black clouds of smoke and the orange glow of the fires within.

"Sir?"

Mac turned to see a sailor waiting for him.

"What have you got for me?" Mac asked.

"Sir, the shore-lookout asked me to report that he thinks you should take a look at the, uhh, transport. The...animals have stopped coming."

Emily, Mac, and Parsons all turned to look in the direction of their transportation.

"He's right," said Emily. All signs of movement around and on the *Machine*, had ceased. "We *should* go take a look."

"It's just nonstop adventure with you," Mac sighed.

Emily got the impression he was only half joking. "Well it keeps life interesting," she replied.

Mac turned to face Parsons. "Fancy a look inside?"

"Lead the way," said Parsons.

The three of them walked down the gangplank and on to shore. In the hour or so that Emily and Mac had spent on Liberty Island, the construction of the *Machine* had been completed. It stood now, gray skin glinting in the noon sun, with no hint as to the living material that had gone into its construction.

Mac stopped and turned to Emily as they drew closer. "What now?" he asked. The replacement *Machine* stood upright on all six legs, with no obvious means of entry.

"If it functions the same way as the last one, then master control of it is going to be keyed to Rhiannon's voice and presence, but it will still follow commands from me," said Emily. "Adam said that it's sentient, has its own intelligence so it will recognize me." She split from the group and approached the *Machine*, walking between its legs, she moved to the front.

"Open, please," she said. Instantly, a large panel in the front of the vehicle folded back on an unseen hinge. A long walkway extended down to the ground through the opening, stopping near Emily's feet.

"I'll be right back," she said, "I just need to check it out." She took the walkway up into the belly of the *Machine*.

While the exterior looked identical to the first

transport, the interior had been changed, quite radically, Emily saw. Gone were the walls that had encapsulated the control room Rhiannon used to guide the *Machine*, opening up more space. Beyond the command chair, the new space was taken up with three rows of seats that looked like molded plastic. They were very basic, utilitarian, but they would be better than standing for the trip. She counted them quickly. There were enough for every one of the crew, more than enough actually. A second room accessed through a doorway behind the last row of seats was large enough for them to stow a significant amount of gear and supplies.

Emily reached out a hand and laid it gently against the curved wall in front of her. In the rush to get to Mac, she had not thought to ask how Adam might fabricate the machines—not that the truth should have come as a surprise, given the history of Caretaker technology. Now, after witnessing this machine's creation, she felt a new respect. The wall felt warm against the palm of her hand and—and she was sure she wasn't imagining this—she thought she felt a faint *thud, thud, thud.* Like a heartbeat, deep within. The vehicle, if it was even appropriate to call it that, had become a new, living creature, made up of the animals that had sacrificed themselves in its creation, just as those creatures had been born from the people and animals that had lived around the city on the day the red rain spread across the planet. There was a certain poetry to it all, she thought, albeit a dark one. It was as if in some small way, those people were now reaching out from oblivion to lend a hand in taking back this planet; ensuring that life, *human life*, would have a chance at survival.

"Emily? You okay up there?"

Mac's voice echoing up the entrance ramp broke Emily from her reverie. "I'm fine," she yelled back. "Come on up."

Mac and Parsons appeared at the entrance of the control room, their eyes moving over the interior of the craft.

"Not exactly how I envisioned it would look," said Mac after a few moments.

"Storage area is through there." She pointed at the second door. The two men stepped into the storage room, gave it a quick once over, nodding as they discussed how much equipment the room could store then rejoined Emily.

"Isn't much to write home about," said Mac.

Parsons nodded his agreement. "I was hoping for something a little bit more...Star Trek-y."

"Sorry to disappoint," Emily said, laughing gently.

Mac stood with his hands on his hips, surveying the control room. "Well, I suppose now's as good a time as any. What do you say we get this show on the road?"

Emily nodded her agreement.

They filed back down the walkway, Emily ordering it to close behind them, and began to walk back toward the dock where the *Vengeance* was moored.

•••

"Looks like we're just in time," said Mac, as the three of them walked from the newly birthed replacement *Machine* back toward the submarine. While they had been inspecting the interior, the wind had changed direction and smoke was now billowing across the Hudson in the direction of the *Vengeance*. "Best we don't hang around too long," Mac said. "Mr. Parsons, would you get the lads and ladies, together and start loading supplies into the transport?"

"Aye, Aye, sir," said Parsons. He gave a quick salute and angled off toward a group of sailors who stood on the deck staring at the *Machine*, while Emily and Mac headed below.

•••

Four hours later, all the provisions and equipment had

been loaded into their new transport. The crew, standing in the waning light of the New York afternoon, waited in line two-abreast near the feet of the *Machine* for orders. Mac appeared from inside and walked halfway down the ramp. "Alright, you Muppets, in you get. Move it. Fast as you can now." The soldiers quick-marched up the ramp and into the belly of the craft where Emily waited to direct them to the seating area.

"Just take a seat and wait," she said, pointing to the entrance of the control room. She couldn't help but notice the nervous glances the men and women gave as they entered. It wasn't hard to figure out why, of course. All the crew had spent some time on deck since they'd arrived and had seen how this machine had been assembled. The Brits didn't seem too worried, but the Norwegians, with their limited exposure to the changes wrought on the world, seemed especially nonplussed.

"It's okay," she said, smiling and using as reassuring a tone of voice as she could. "I can vouch from personal experience that it's not going to eat you." She had meant it as a joke, but she wasn't sure it had done anything to help improve the mood.

"Did anyone ever tell you you'd make a great flight attendant?" Mac said with a smirk, as he followed up behind the last two men in line.

"Very funny," said Emily, lightly punching the Scotsman on the arm. "Are you ready?"

Mac nodded, "Just need a minute to double-check we left nothing behind." Mac headed back down the ramp. Emily followed after him, knowing the real reason he wanted that extra time. At the bottom of the ramp, he stopped and looked back at the *Vengeance*. It was a black shadow within the smoke now. "Breaks my heart to leave her behind like this," he said, eventually. "When this is all behind us, I'll be back for her."

Emily said nothing.

"Okay," said Mac a few seconds later, turning to face his wife. "We're ready to roll...or walk...or whatever this thing does." Mac jabbed a thumb at the *Machine*.

"Let's go home," said Emily and headed back up the ramp.

Mac stood for a few more moments, then turned smartly and joined the rest of the crew.

CHAPTER 9

Emily stood at the front of the *Machine*'s control room facing the seated soldiers. She was trying to channel the inner flight attendant Mac had jokingly commented on earlier. She smiled and spoke as calmly and confidently as she could, "Okay, everyone. I just want you all to relax. This next part is going to be...a little weird, but there's nothing to be afraid of. Just sit back and enjoy the ride." She smiled and nodded a final time, then took her own seat next to Rhiannon. Thor was already lying next to it, relaxed but alert. Rhiannon sat in the center chair, Mac seated to her left. "You ready, sweetie?" Emily asked, turning in her chair to face Rhiannon.

"If this trip is anything like our last ride, I'm glad I'm still blind," Rhiannon said in an overtly loud voice, then smiled mischievously when she heard a collective nervous questioning chatter from the seats behind her.

She's just kidding, Emily mouthed to Mac. She faced forward again. "Okay, ready when you are."

"Machine," Rhiannon said aloud—in response to the girl's voice a slight tremor ran through the walls and floors, like the haptic feedback from a game console controller— "Take us to Point Loma, California." A large section of the wall in front of the seated humans seemed to dissolve, revealing a one-hundred-and-fifty-degree section of the smoke-covered Hudson River and the outline of the *Vengeance.*

"Don't worry, it's just a view-panel," said Emily.

There was a hissing noise, followed by a few exclamations of surprise as all the seats began to extrude a foam-like substance around each of the passengers until they were cocooned in its gentle but unrelenting grasp. The seats held their passengers firmly enough to keep them safely restrained, while still able to move their fingers and turn their head a degree or two to the left and right, but that was about it. Even Thor was covered by his own personal cowl.

"It's okay," said Emily, "It's for our own protection. We'll need it for when—" Her words were cut off as the reasoning for the safety bubbles became abundantly clear to everyone on board. Stomachs lurched and there were gasps of surprise from almost everyone as, through the view panel, the remains of New York dropped out of view as the *Machine* raised itself up to full height. Then there were actual yells of fear from the men and women as the craft began to move rapidly toward the edge of the dock, accelerating quickly. Rhiannon, on the other hand, was laughing hysterically, apparently enjoying every second. The *Machine* turned in the direction of the mouth of the Hudson River, leaped high into the air, and dove into the river. Once in the dirty water, the craft began to accelerate at terrifying speed, pushing the passengers into their seats like a fighter pilot pulling a High-G turn. It continued to gain more and more momentum, the force on its passengers' chests growing from an unpleasant push to an almost crushing pressure. Then, as suddenly as it had begun, the pressure evened out.

There were an equal number of expletives yelled and prayers muttered in both English and Norwegian, but eventually the noise died away as everyone slowly relaxed.

Everyone except for Rhiannon that was, she continued to laugh until she was red in the face.

•••

What followed was a roller-coaster ride through the ocean's depths. The *Machine* ducked and swerved around submerged mountain ranges, followed the contours of long sunk landmasses, and roared past dozing volcanoes. Occasionally, through the view-port, the crew caught fleeting glimpses of monstrous sea dwellers, animals that Emily was sure had not existed before the red rain had worked its changes on the creatures that lived on land.

About three hours in, Emily felt the craft begin to slow, rapidly, again pushing its human passengers back with incredible force as it decelerated. Then, through the view-port, land appeared. The *Machine* maneuvered itself up onto the rocky shore. It nimbly climbed across the boulder-strewn beach before scaling an almost vertical cliff face. It ran across the ground in giant leaping bounds, maneuvering through the red jungle so quickly that the trees and vegetation became nothing but a blur of red that forced most of the passengers to close their eyes to avoid vomiting.

Emily could not say for sure where they were *exactly*, but if she had to guess she would estimate that they had made landfall somewhere in the Gulf of Mexico and were now heading across country toward the Pacific. The *Machine* always seemed to take the most direct route to a location.

Eventually, the ocean once more came into view, and the craft dove into the water. People grunted loudly as, yet again, they were forced back into the padding of their seats, but this time there were no yells of surprise or fear. Two hours later, the *Machine* began to slow as it gradually rose toward the surface.

Emily looked at her watch. It was just after two in the afternoon, local time. "Make landfall about ten kilometers south of Point Loma," she said to Rhiannon, who repeated the order to the *Machine*. There was no point in them just showing up at Point Loma, she and Mac had reasoned; that would terrify all the survivors while placing themselves at a strategic disadvantage. They needed the element of surprise on their side, especially if they wanted to limit the risk of armed confrontation between themselves and Valentine's cadre of thugs and supporters.

Through the view-screen, Emily saw land appear then rapidly grow larger as their transportation moved toward it. A few minutes later, the *Machine* pulled itself from the water onto a beach and came to an abrupt stop. The padding around each of the passengers retracted with a burbling hiss, vanishing back into the seats as though it had never existed.

Mac was the first to his feet. "I want everyone to remain where you are," he said. "Major Djupvik, if you wouldn't mind joining Emily and me."

Petter nodded, climbed to his feet and stretched. Emily joined him, her muscles tight and tingling with pins and needles after being restrained for such an extended period of time. The three of them walked to the exit. "Let us out," Emily said, waiting for the portal to open and the walkway to descend before following the others down onto land. Mac and Petter, squinting hard against the afternoon sun, quickly scouted around the perimeter of the *Machine* to ensure there were no obvious dangers.

They had come to a stop on a sandy beach that stretched inland for about thirty meters before turning into a rocky stretch of open land. In the distance was the red jungle. Emily wasn't particularly worried about an attack from there; Adam had explained that the *Machine* had an automatic defense system that would activate if it or its passengers were threatened. Emily assumed the same went for this new one, too. She hadn't seen it in action, but she was confident the imposing automaton was more than an adequate deterrent to attack from all but the largest creatures that hunted in the jungle.

"Let's get everyone off," Mac said.

Emily nodded. The ride had been uncomfortable, but swift. She was quite sure the men and women would be happy to get their feet back on land after what she was confident must have been the wildest ride of their lives.

Mac disappeared back inside the craft. Less than a minute later, the first of his men began to file down the walkway.

"Stay within twenty meters," Mac ordered as his personnel fanned out across the beach, some jogging back and forth, others just stretching. The Norwegians, on the other hand, nervously milled about while never leaving the *Machine's* shadow. They seemed absolutely fascinated by the transformed Californian landscape. Emily had to remind herself that this was still a new experience for them. It was going to take some getting used to.

Mac and Petter walked back over to her. Mac held a long stick in his one hand, and a couple of pieces of short driftwood in the other. Petter carried some hand-sized stones, and a couple of shells.

"Are we going to be making sandcastles?" Emily asked, genuinely curious as to what the two men had in mind.

"Only if you promise you can rustle me up a ninety-nine," Mac said.

Petter looked curiously at Mac but Emily had been with her husband long enough to know that one of the top items on his 'things I miss since the end of the world' list was a British 'delicacy'—his words, not hers—that involved putting a stick of chocolate in an ice-cream cone, often consumed when on holiday at the seaside.

"It's a Scottish thing," Emily said, by way of explanation to the bemused Norwegian officer. Petter shook his head, then carefully dropped his handful of beach detritus into the soft sand at his feet. Mac dropped what he was carrying alongside it, all except for the long thin stick.

"No, my dear, dear love, we will not be making sand castles, as I forgot to pack my bucket and spade," he said smiling at his wife, "what we will be doing is planning our attack and I will be using these"—he tapped the bits of wood, rock, and shell with the tip of his boot—"to help us create a map of Point Loma base."

•••

With Emily's help Mac spent the next ten minutes recounting the layout of Point Loma from memory, while drawing an outline in the sand of the base. Mac identified the sentry towers with driftwood, highlighted the sleeping quarters of Valentine and her close supporters with pieces of shell, and drew in the roads and other buildings using his stick.

"We go at oh-one-hundred-hours," Mac said to the twenty men and women crowded in a semi-circle around his sand drawing. There would be five teams of four personnel who would move to secure key locations, while Mac, Emily, and Djupvik would be tasked with taking Valentine in her quarters. The crew members who were not going to be taking part in the raid would wait with Rhiannon in the *Machine*.

"Why don't we just take Emily's machine and walk right in there?" a soldier said.

"Well, for one, it makes a hell of a racket; they'd be ready for us. Second; we want to take the ringleaders alive. That means keeping any engagements to a minimum, preferably to zero if possible. We're confident that if we grab Valentine, any resistance will crumble."

"How do we get across from Coronado to Point Loma?" someone asked.

Emily answered the question, "There are two Zodiacs

stored here on the island, in case any of the Point Loma scavenger teams get into trouble or suffer a problem with their own transportation. We can use them to ferry you all across."

"Rules of engagement?"

"Most of these folks are unwilling participants in Valentine's plan," Mac said. "They are going to be very surprised when we show up back at camp, so non-lethal force where you can."

"And if they resist?" another soldier asked.

"Then you do what you have to, to ensure the safety of yourself and your team," Mac said, stone-faced.

CHAPTER 10

The assault team set off an hour later, following the curve of the beach along the southern flank of Coronado Island. Just before dark, they reached the ruins of the North Island Naval Air Station, and immediately hid in what had once been a storage shed, but was now just an overgrown ruin. It would suffice, though, giving the team a place to stay out of sight of any of Point Loma's sentries.

"I'll be right back," Mac said, he grabbed a pair of night-vision goggles then disappeared out through the door-less exit.

About fifteen minutes later he was back.

"Zodiacs are where we left them," he told Emily and Petter. Mac had given the two boats a detailed inspection and declared both seaworthy. Each boat could hold up to fifteen passengers and equipment. Rather than use the outboard motors, the attacking force was going to have to paddle across the estuary separating Coronado Island from the mainland, and Point Loma. "We lay up here until oh-one-hundred hours," Mac continued, keeping his voice low, checking his wristwatch. "In the meantime, get some sleep if you can. I'll keep watch."

It seemed to Emily that everyone but her managed to get some rest in the hours that followed. She was nervous, antsy, and sleep refused to come to her. This close to home—as that was, she realized, *exactly* how she felt about Point Loma—the memory of those final days before she and Rhiannon and Thor had (quite literally) flown away, came flooding back. The memory of Adam's abduction; how Valentine had used it to have her arrested; how that bitch had tried to have her murdered; and how Valentine surely would have succeeded, if it had not been for Rhiannon's timely intervention. She regretted the deaths of the two men that had followed (well, she regretted one of them, but the other, the man who Valentine had ordered to rape and murder her, *that* man she wished could be killed all over again). And now, the hour was fast approaching that she would finally be face-to-face with Valentine again. But this time, if luck and surprise and good planning were all on her side, the tables would be turned. She hadn't given much thought to how the confrontation might play out before this moment, but now she wondered how she would react when Valentine was within punching distance. Emily's base desire was to simply put a bullet in the woman's brain and be done with it, but that would make her no better than Valentine, and if there was to be a reunification of the other survivors with an eye to moving forward, then there would have to be a trial. A fair trial and a fair verdict. But that opened up the possibility that Valentine would get off, be set free, and Emily had met enough people like Valentine in her life to know that she would never change. Not ever.

Emily's thoughts were interrupted by the touch of someone's hand against her shoulder.

She turned and saw Mac illuminated by the dim glow of a flashlight covered by a piece of thin cloth that allowed just enough light to see him by but not enough that it would betray their presence.

"Almost time," he said, smiling at her. "You ready, love?"

Emily nodded.

"Okay, let's wake the rest of these Muppets up and get on with it."

He squeezed Emily's shoulder gently, smiled, then began moving from sleeping body to sleeping body.

Emily took a second to gather herself, then she too set about waking the rest of the team.

•••

If anything, this was the exact opposite of what the Zodiacs were designed for. Rather than zipping across the water with their powerful motors, the boats performed a slow, methodical crawl across the strait separating Coronado Island and Point Loma's dock, which lay three hundred or so meters away. Six of the occupants in each boat paddled in unison toward the shore, timing each downward sweep of their paddles with the next oncoming wave that lifted the boat. Their progress was made even more difficult by the rough seas that insisted on pushing the Zodiacs farther up the channel, in the direction of the remains of San Diego. Clouds obscured the moon, the darkened sky providing perfect cover for their covert approach, but lights glowed across the Point Loma base; floodlights had kicked on automatically at dusk, illuminating the compound, and here and there, despite the late hour, light shone from windows.

They angled the boats toward the concrete dock, night-vision-assisted eyes scanning the area for any sign of a sentry or patrol. None were visible, so they maneuvered the two Zodiacs alongside the wharf. The boats' sides scraped loudly against the concrete for a moment, the sound swallowed by waves smacking against the walls, before coming to a stop, rising and falling on the waves' swells. Two men from each boat leaped to shore and quickly tied them off. The rest of the assault team climbed up onto the wharf, then with a go-signal from Mac, silently moved off toward their assigned targets.

Mac, Emily, and Petter watched as the other teams disappeared into the darkness. With a nod from Mac, they moved toward the nearest building and began to quickly make their way through the compound aiming for the apartment block where Valentine was, hopefully, sound asleep and blissfully unaware of the wrath that was about to come crashing down on her head. Mac's plan was to take Valentine and her cohorts alive. He figured that once they had Valentine in their hands, any resistance would quickly fade.

They came up from the south, managing to stay in the shadows until they reached Valentine's apartment building. But now they would have to negotiate an exposed eight-meter stretch of ground that would leave them fully visible during the few seconds they needed to get across, thanks to the light from a lamp above the apartment building's entrance.

"Emily, you go first. We'll cover you," Mac said softly, crouching next to Emily in the darkness, his head swiveling as he continuously checked for movement.

Emily gave a sharp nod.

"Go," Mac whispered.

Emily took a deep breath then sprinted toward the building at a crouch. She reached the apartment building entrance, held her breath that the door would not be locked, grabbed the handle and pulled.

The door swung open. She breathed a sigh of relief, ducked her head into the interior and quickly scanned the entrance. It was empty. She slipped inside, double-checked that she was alone, then turned back and gave Mac and Petter a thumbs-up. One after the other the men ran to Emily and slipped through the door she held open for them.

"Second floor," Emily whispered. "Room 2a."

The two men nodded and moved toward the stairwell. Emily winced at the sound of the door creaking loudly as Mac held it open for her and Petter. They made their way up the stairs, opened the door to the second floor and stepped out, their weapons swinging back and forth. The floor was empty, no sleepwalkers or guards in sight.

"This way," Emily said, nodding to the left. The three figures moved silently and quickly along the corridor until they reached Valentine's apartment.

Mac reached out and tried the door. "Locked," he whispered. He motioned for Petter and Emily to move away, then stepped back and in one swift movement, stomped his foot with all his considerable weight against the door just above the lock. The door almost broke free on Mac's first kick, the lock hanging on to a few pieces of splintered wood which flew away as Mac shoulder-barged through into the apartment. The door slammed back against the interior wall loud enough to wake anyone else asleep on the same floor. Mac, then Petter, then Emily ran inside. They raced into the main bedroom, weapons ready.

The bedroom and its bed were empty.

Emily caught Mac's perplexed look before he turned and ran out to the living room. Emily followed him, noting that there was no sign of anyone there either, then moved into the kitchen. It was also empty, but there was a plate on the kitchen table. It was impossible to tell what the food that still sat on the plate had been, as it was now nothing more than mold. A knife and fork lay on the floor near the feet of a chair that lay slightly askew, as if whoever had been sitting here had suddenly stood up, dropping the cutlery.

"*Mac, do you copy?*" The sudden sound of the walkie-talkie was startlingly loud in the silent apartment.

Mac raised the microphone to his mouth. "Go ahead."

"*We're at the north sentry post. It's deserted.*"

Another voice cut in: "*This is Team Two, we're at the south post. Not a sign of anyone here, either.*"

Mac's forehead furrowed, his eyebrows drawing closer together. He paused for a second then spoke into the microphone. "Team Three and Four, are you at your target locations?"

"*Team Three, here. Can't be completely sure but there doesn't appear to be anyone around, sir. The place...it feels...deserted.*" Team Three had been assigned to the main apartment area to ensure that if an alarm was sounded, they would catch any potential responders before they could exit the building.

"*Team Four reporting, main gate security booth is empty, sir. The barrier is up. No sign of anyone.*"

Mac announced into the radio, "All teams, hold your positions until you hear back from me."

Emily walked back to the door they had broken down and stepped out into the hallway. There were several other apartments along this hall and, given the amount of noise they had made busting down the door to Valentine's apartment, she would have expected that someone would have come to investigate what the hell was happening. She waited in the corridor for a few moments and just listened.

Not a sound. Not even a creak.

"What do you think's going on?" Mac's voice startled Emily.

"I have no idea," she said, "but whatever it is, I don't like it."

•••

"Knock it down," Mac instructed Petter.

Petter nodded and kicked open the door to the apartment next to Valentine's with a single hard thump from his booted foot. Mac dodged inside, his rifle swinging left and right as he moved through each of the rooms.

"It's clear. Come on in," he said twenty seconds after entering. Emily and Petter followed him inside.

"You turned the lights on?" Emily asked as she walked to where Mac stood in the center of the living room.

"No," said Mac, with a shake of his head, "They were already on when I came in." He paused for a second, slowly turning left then right, surveying the room. "There's something just not right about this."

Emily followed suit, allowing her eyes to roam over the living room they stood in. An open book lay cover up on a coffee table. She glanced at the title; Toward Yesterday, written by some author whose name seemed vaguely familiar to her. A mug of congealed liquid which at some point might have been coffee, sat next to it. She stepped into the bedroom. The bedsheets had been thrown back as though someone had gotten out of the bed and not bothered to make it. Emily slid back the closet door; inside there was a selection of men's and women's clothes hanging neatly from plastic hangers.

She rejoined Mac and Petter in the living room. "It's like they just up and left," she said. "They didn't even take their clothes." After food and shelter, clothing was one of the most precious supplies the Point Loma survivors had. After all, it wasn't like they could walk into a mall and just buy new ones. There was no way whoever lived in this apartment would have walked out on a closet full of clothing unless they had absolutely no choice.

"Do you think they knew we were coming?" Petter asked, looking suddenly wary, as if an assailant might leap from a cupboard or from behind a sofa.

Mac shook his head. "If they spotted us earlier in the day, they would have had more than enough time to set up an ambush. They could have hit us as we landed on the beach. They outnumber us massively. We wouldn't have stood a chance."

"I agree, this is something else," Emily said. Her

mind went back to the night the Caretakers had come for Adam. She turned to the two men. "Before Rhiannon and I left Point Loma to go search for Adam, I had a dream. Except it wasn't a dream, it was Adam, showing me what the Caretakers were doing to him. His way of trying to warn me, I suppose. He was sharing with me how the Caretakers kidnapped him. If it wasn't for that 'dream', and the telepathic ability that Adam uses to communicate with me over distance, I wouldn't have had any idea how or where my son had been taken."

Both men looked at Emily, neither saying anything.

"Soooooo," Emily continued, "Maybe something like that happened here, after we left."

"But you told us the Caretakers were all dead," Mac said.

Emily gently gnawed at her bottom lip. "I know," she said, "that's what Adam told me, but maybe he's wrong. Or maybe the Caretakers came back to Point Loma while Rhiannon and I were still searching for Adam."

Mac stepped in close to his wife and laid a hand against her arm. "Can you reach Adam now? Ask him if he knows what's going on here?"

"I'll try," Emily said. She closed her eyes and allowed herself to relax, searching her mind for the strand, that psychic connection to her son. But it wasn't there. She opened her eyes, shook her head. "Nothing. He must still be recovering. Adam said he would establish communication with me when he was strong enough again."

"So, we're on our own then," said Mac.

"But, maybe this is something else, unrelated to these Caretakers you talk about," said Petter.

"Like what?" Emily asked, turning to face the Norwegian.

"Isn't it simply more likely that they just left? Maybe moved somewhere else?"

"Where?" Emily asked. "There isn't an intact city for

thousands of miles, maybe none at all, for all we know."

"And all three submarines were still in their bays, we passed them on the way in. We know they didn't leave in them."

The subs. Emily hadn't thought about the three submarines still docked on the waterfront. "Maybe they're in the subs," she said.

"Why?" asked Mac. "Why would they leave a perfectly good, undamaged building to take refuge in a submarine? That makes no sense."

Emily considered the question for a few seconds. "Maybe a storm? Or something...else."

Petter shook his head. "I don't think so, we saw no signs of storm damage on our way in. Both of these apartments look like they were abandoned suddenly, and without much of a struggle."

Mac stroked his chin, rubbing his fingers over his stubble for a good ten seconds or so. Then he took up his radio and spoke. "All teams. Rendezvous at our location. Copy?"

"Copy!" came the reply from each of the team leaders.

Within five minutes the rest of the assault team rolled into the apartment. They all looked nervous, Emily noted, as they filtered inside what had been Valentine's apartment.

"Find a place to make yourselves comfortable," Mac said. "We're going to bed down in here for the night. Johnson, Wilkinson. You two have first watch. Stevens and Richford; you're on second watch. Four hours. Got it?"

The men nodded, then Johnson and Wilkinson stepped back out of the room and took up position in the corridor.

"The rest of you, get some shuteye. We're going to do a bit of exploring come morning."

•••

Emily woke surprisingly refreshed. After the teams had arrived the previous night, she had settled in on the sofa with Mac. They had talked quietly for a few minutes until the sound of the others' snoring had gotten both her and Mac giggling like a couple of silly teenagers. Then she had simply settled silently against him, feeling the warmth of his body seeping through his fatigues, the smell of his skin and sweat in her nostrils, the whisper of his breath, rhythmic and full against her hair. She had eventually slipped into a deep sleep. When Emily awoke, she was stretched out fully across the entire sofa, a comforter had been spread over her at some point while she slept. As her sleep-blurred vision cleared, she saw the rest of the crew were up and moving around. A delicious aroma filtered through the apartment and drew her to full consciousness. Mac was talking with Petter and another soldier near the kitchen.

"Is that coffee I smell?" Emily asked, standing and stretching.

"Sure is," said Mac, smiling back at his wife. "We found Valentine's stash. Liberated it for a higher cause. Don't think she'll mind." He smirked, took a sip from the cup he held in his hand then walked over to Emily and handed the steaming mug to her.

"Thanks," she said, planting a kiss on her husband's cheek.

"I was just outlining a new plan with Petter."

Emily nodded and took a sip of coffee, savoring the flavor and texture and heat against her tongue.

Mac continued, "So, we want you to bring the *Machine* up to the base so we can offload the rest of the crew. At that point, we're going to do a thorough building-by-building search and make sure that the complex really is empty."

Petter took over. "And if it is empty, we will try and understand where your...colleagues went."

"I can do that," Emily said. "Can I have your radio?"

Mac passed her the handheld. "Emily to Parsons. Do you copy?"

After a short pause, the Welshman's voice came back loud and clear. "*I copy, Emily.*"

"We're going to need Rhiannon to shuttle the rest of you to Point Loma. Can you arrange that with her?"

"*Will do. We'll be there in thirty. Anything else?*"

Emily said there wasn't and handed the radio back to Mac.

Mac turned and faced the room. "Okay, everyone quiet down and listen." He waited for the soldiers to fall silent and turn their attention to him. "As you have probably realized, the rest of the Point Loma survivors have turned up missing. As all of us but our new Norwegian friends know, the idea of them pulling up sticks and buggering off the reservation is pretty dubious. So, that leaves two possibilities: someone or something has taken them against their will, or they are still here at Point Loma, hiding from us, or incapable of or unwilling to communicate with us. Rhiannon is bringing the rest of the team here in the *Machine*, for backup, then we are going to conduct a thorough search of all the buildings, including the submarines. Understand?"

The soldiers all nodded or called out that they did.

"Well then, what are you waiting for? Breakfast in bed? Let's move out."

CHAPTER 11

The *Machine* and the rest of the crew showed up a few minutes after Emily and the rest of the landing team arrived at the assembly point, just outside the camp's main gate.

"Wow!" said Emily as the *Machine* strode across the beach then cut inland toward her group. This was the first time she had seen it in motion from the outside, and only now did she realize just what an imposing—*no, scratch that*—what a *terrifying* sight it really was with its spider-like legs and tentacles. It strode toward the gathered humans then stopped about fifteen meters from them. The ramp unfurled, and its passengers began to file out, one after the other. Last, guided by a tall blond Norwegian soldier who could not have been more than twenty if he was a day, came Rhiannon. Thor trotted alongside her, but when he saw Emily and Mac he gave a quick bark of excitement and ran to them, moving from mistress to master, unable to contain his happiness at seeing them.

Emily ran her hand over Thor's head, scratching around his ear and under his chin. "Missed us did you, boy?" She buried her face in the ruff of his neck. "Well, I missed you too."

"Did you miss me, as well?" asked Rhiannon. The Norwegian soldier was still at her side, her hand resting on his right forearm.

Mac stepped in close and took the girl in his arms. "Like a hole in the head," he said, laughing.

Rhiannon punched Mac lightly where she thought his arm should be. He had to move his shoulder into position to make sure she connected.

Mac straightened up. "Okay, soldier," he said, turning his focus to Rhiannon's Norwegian escort, "you're dismissed. You'll find your comrades that way." He nodded to where Petter and his team waited, talking animatedly. The young Norwegian saluted sharply, then turned and headed off to where the rest of his group waited. But not, Emily noticed as he turned away, without a puppy-dog-eyed lingering gaze at Rhiannon.

"So, is he as cute as he sounds?" Rhiannon whispered, loud enough for only Emily to hear.

Emily leaned in close to Rhiannon's ear. "Totally," she whispered back.

"If you two ladies are quite finished," said Mac, walking up behind the women and throwing his arms around their shoulders, "we have some lost survivors to locate." He guided Emily and Rhiannon over to where the rest of the soldiers waited. "Okay, for those of you who are just joining us, you can probably tell by the lack of new faces amongst us that the Point Loma survivors are not home. That's because, well, we have no idea why, to be honest. So, we're going to split up into multiple groups and make sure they aren't hiding out somewhere in the base. I'm sure I don't have to remind you ladies and gentlemen that most of the people in this camp are innocent participants in what happened to my wife and..." he paused momentarily to place his hand against Rhiannon's back, "...and my daughter. So, if you should find anyone, go easy on them. Alert your team leader and they will notify either myself or Major Petter. Any questions?"

There weren't.

"Alright then. Team leaders, take your people and see Mr. Parsons. He's going to give you all your search locations."

Mac began to walk away, then paused and turned back to face his people again. "And I know I don't have to remind you all, but be careful out there."

•••

Mac assigned himself, Emily and four other sailors to search the *Le Terrible*. They stood on the deck of the French submarine, the morning sun shining down warmly on their skin. But Emily didn't feel warm. A cold chill ran down her spine as she waited next to Mac for one of the sailors to open the midsection entrance hatch. Maybe it was just her, but as Emily's eyes moved over each of the men, she saw a tenseness in their faces. Their brows were furrowed, their eyes focused intently on the hatch. No, she was definitely not imagining this. For all any of them knew, this entire submarine could be nothing more than a giant coffin full of the dead. Or worse, maybe it was full of things that were still very much alive. As far as she was aware, none of the other survivors had experienced events after the red rain the way she had. They had all either been at the bottom of the ocean or ice-locked on some distant piece of rock. So, maybe it was just her anticipation of the unknown that had her so spooked, but she didn't think so.

"You feel that, too, don't you?" she whispered close to Mac's ear.

His only reply was a curt nod and the words, "Stay close to me." That was enough for Emily to know that he was nervous. And that made her even more nervous.

A sailor lifted the hatch leading down into the sub, it rose on a hidden hinge that creaked and groaned ominously. The sailor shined his flashlight into the darkness, then maneuvered himself onto the ladder and began to climb down. The rest of the men followed behind him, Mac and Emily the last to descend into the submarine's cold body. At the bottom of the ladder, they found themselves in the main corridor that ran fore and aft of the submarine. There was no light, save for the team's flashlights.

"Looks like there's no power at all," said Mac as he flipped a light switch on the wall of a nearby room off and on several times.

"Well *that* doesn't make this any less creepy," Emily muttered.

"Okay, you're with Emily and me," Mac said, pointing at a nervous-looking sailor. He turned his gaze to the remaining sailors. "You three take the aft section. We'll work our way forward. Stay in contact, and let me know if you encounter..." he paused almost dramatically as he searched for the right words, "*anything* out of the ordinary. Got it?"

"Yes, sir," said the three men in unison, but their replies were subdued, barely more than a whisper, as though they did not want to draw attention to themselves. They turned and began making their way toward the rear section of the submarine.

Mac did a quick check of his assault rifle, then, satisfied, he turned back to Emily and the sailor. "Let's move out," he said, his demeanor all business now, but he still managed to throw a reassuring smile in Emily's direction.

•••

"What the hell is that smell?" said Mac.

Emily's eyes watered as she made the gut-wrenching

mistake of taking a deep inhalation of air through her nose. She grimaced, "Oh my God! It smells like an open sewer on a summer day," she said.

They were twenty minutes into their search of the submarine, and so far, there had been no sign that there was anyone or any *thing* on board.

"Might be a problem with the bilge system," Mac said. "This boat's been at dock for how many years now? It's not like we've kept up to date with the monthly service. Besides there's always—" Mac stopped talking as he crossed the threshold into a small room just off the main corridor.

Her eyes elsewhere, Emily walked into Mac's back, bouncing a step backward after the collision. She peered over his shoulder and saw empty cans of food lying discarded across the room's floor, along with a scattering of crushed plastic water bottles. In the corner of the room was a pile of disheveled dirty blankets; obviously someone's bed. In the opposite corner was a bucket where the stink emanated from. Whoever had been living here's makeshift toilet, she realized.

"Nothing creepy about this," said Emily, her words a sardonic whisper.

Mac brought the microphone of his radio to his lips. "Be aware, at least one possible survivor on board. Use caution," he whispered.

Mac nodded at the sailor, subtly indicating that he should enter the room. The sailor slipped past Emily and Mac, and moved cautiously inside, his weapon moving across every possible hiding place that might conceal whoever had been staying here. Not that there were many places to hide. The room had been a storage area at some point; apart from the detritus scattered over the floor, there was only a wire-frame shelf unit and a metal cupboard that came up to Emily's waist. A smaller recessed area sat just off the room, it had another shelf unit that held various metal objects in plastic bins that Emily assumed must be spare parts for some mechanism within the submarine.

"It's empty, sir," the sailor said, lowering his rifle to his side. "Whoever was here must have bugged out when they heard us come on board."

"Maybe," said Mac, "but that doesn't mean they aren't still on the boat somewhere. We keep our eyes open. Understood?"

•••

Both Emily and the sailor nodded that they did indeed understand.

"Okay," Mac continued, "let's check the rest of this boat."

They moved out into the corridor and continued toward the sub's forward section. The communication room was clear, the rack where the sub's radio system should have been now empty, the equipment transferred to Point Loma long ago. The crew's living quarters seemed similarly empty, which left only the torpedo room, but a quick sweep of that turned up nothing either.

Mac spoke to the second team on his radio. "The forward area looks clear, rendezvous back at the entrance hatch."

It was as they were moving back through the crew's living quarters that Emily spotted something they had missed when they came through just minutes earlier. Halfway down the row of bunk beds, she noticed one of the bottom beds had several blankets hanging loosely over its side. No one had thought to check under the bed, and no one would have on the way out either if it had not been for the hint of movement Emily's flashlight caught as they made their way back to meet the others. She wasn't one-hundred-percent sure but for a brief second, she thought she saw a flash of skin, maybe a foot, before it was pulled out of sight into the darkness beneath the bunk.

Emily placed a hand on the crook of Mac's arm.

"What's—" he started to say then fell silent as Emily moved a finger to her lips. She pointed to the bed and the crumpled pile of linen. Mac moved his flashlight to the area Emily was pointing at.

"Cover me," he whispered to the sailor, then began to move toward the bed. If there was someone or *something* hiding beneath the bunk, Mac's approach would be blocked to them by the blankets. He reached down and slowly pulled the blanket up.

A woman screamed.

The sailor yelled a warning, his finger moving off his weapon's guard to the trigger.

"No!" Emily said, knocking the barrel sideways. "It's a woman. Don't shoot. She's human." Emily stepped in front of the weapon, blocking the sailor's line of fire.

From beneath the bed came the sound of whimpering mixed with sobbing. Mac had instinctively stepped back from the bunk, his rifle trained on the darkness beneath. His free hand was reaching toward the blanket, but he stopped when Emily stepped in behind him and touched him on the shoulder.

"Mac, she's terrified. Let me do this," Emily whispered into his ear, gently pulling her husband back. In the second the shadows beneath the bunk had been illuminated, Emily had caught the unmistakable outline of a woman in the flashlight's beam. Emily knelt, reached for the blanket and drew it gradually back, just enough that she could see the woman beneath the bed but not so much that whoever this survivor was would feel totally exposed.

The woman was curled up in the fetal position, her knees pulled tightly up to her chin, obscuring her face. She was wearing a dirty t-shirt, a stained skirt, and no shoes on her feet, just socks that could have been white at some point but were now an oily black. The exposed parts of her skin were dirt-smeared, her hair a tangled mess.

"It's okay," Emily said, "we're not going to hurt you."

She reached out her hand and laid it against the woman's ankle.

The woman squealed, pulling her legs even closer to her, squeezing herself up against the sub's bulkhead.

"No, no, no," Emily cooed, "It's okay. It's okay." She kept her hand against the woman's trembling leg and waited, speaking in a low, measured tone, reassuring her. Minutes passed. Slowly the woman's crying subsided and, finally, Emily felt her begin to relax. "That's it, you're okay," Emily said. "Can you look at me, hmmm?"

The woman slowly dropped her hands and raised her head.

"Lynda?" Emily asked, suddenly recognizing the woman despite the layers of dirt that streaked her face. Lynda Hanson had been a botanist in her previous life. In this new life, she sat on the Point Loma council. She had always appeared to be a smart woman to Emily, but now, in the white glow of the flashlights, she seemed like little more than a frightened child.

Emily reached out a hand to her. "Why don't you come on out of there and let's get you looked at? Can you take my hand?"

Gradually, ever so gradually, Lynda's hand edged toward Emily's. When, finally, the two touched, it was as if Lynda had been afraid that Emily might have been a ghost. Her eyes widened and her hand grabbed onto Emily's as though she were a drowning woman who had just found the last piece of floating wreckage. She began to scramble out from beneath the bunk, so fast that Emily could not back away quickly enough. Clear of the bed, Lynda threw her arms around Emily, the two toppling to the floor as the woman once more broke down into tears. This time though, they were tears of relief rather than fear.

"It's okay. It's okay," Emily repeated, gently rocking the woman back and forth in her arms. "You're safe now. It's all going to be all right."

•••

Mac carried Lynda in his arms from the submarine, Emily walking right alongside him. Emily had wrapped the woman in a blanket to keep her warm, and now she lay silently against Mac's chest as he stepped through Valentine's apartment doorway and walked straight to the bedroom. He placed Lynda gently onto the bed.

"Can you bring some water for her?" Emily asked, raising her eyebrows as she ushered Mac out of the bedroom past several gawking sailors.

"Sure thing," said Mac, taking the hint. He closed the door gently behind him.

Emily turned back to Lynda. She lay silently on the bed, the covers pulled up to her chin. Her eyes seemed a little brighter to Emily, just a little more *alive*.

"How are you feeling?" Emily asked, walking back across the room. She sat on the edge of the bed and smiled.

Lynda's eyes widened a little, her lips moving but forming no words, as if she had not spoken in such a long time she had forgotten how. Eventually, she said, "Better." The word was spoken so quietly Emily wasn't sure she had actually said anything at all. It was only when the woman croaked "Thank you," her hand emerging from beneath the bed covers to grasp her own, that Emily was sure.

There was a light knock against the bedroom door.

Emily slipped her hand from Lynda's grip and walked to the door. Mac stood outside with a bottle of water which he handed to her.

"Any progress?" he asked, looking over Emily's shoulder.

"Some," said Emily, "can you give me a half hour?"

Mac nodded. "We need to find out what happened as quickly as possible, love."

"I know, but just let me bring her back before we

114

interrogate her."

Mac nodded again. "Do whatever you have to do." He stepped back and pulled the door closed behind him.

"Here you go," said Emily, turning back to Lynda. "Can you sit up?" She held the bottle of water out to the woman. Lynda pushed herself to a sitting position, but, Emily noticed, she pulled the blankets up with her too, cocooning herself in them. "Here." Emily pulled the blanket down on one side, freeing Lynda's hand, then placed the plastic bottle of water between her fingers.

Lynda drank deeply. "Thank you," she said after she had emptied half the bottle.

Emily smiled. "Better?"

Lynda nodded, a brief, sad smile parting her lips

It was all Emily could do to refrain from asking Mac's question. Truth was, not knowing what had happened here at Point Loma while she was gone was burning at her insides. But, she had to play this carefully. Lynda had obviously suffered some form of a mental break with reality, caused by God knew what. And Emily instinctively knew that if she pushed too hard for answers, she risked forcing Lynda back inside her own head, and this time she might lock that mental door behind her.

"Here, have a little more," said Emily, offering Lynda the bottle of water again.

Lynda drank the remaining water and handed the now-empty bottle back to Emily with a more sincere smile.

"Are you hungry?" Emily asked.

Lynda nodded.

"Well, how about we get you cleaned up and into some fresh clothes? Then I can see about rustling up some food for you. Does that work?"

Again, Lynda nodded.

Emily helped Lynda to her feet, then escorted her to the adjoining bathroom, sitting her on the commode. She turned on the shower and ran the water until it was nice and warm, marveling at the fact that they at least had this one basic luxury, courtesy of the nuclear generator Parsons had hooked Point Loma's electrical system to.

"Let's get you out of these," Emily said, as she began to help Lynda out of her dirt-crusted clothes, while trying not to turn her nose up at the woman's body odor. Lynda had lost probably twenty pounds since Emily had last seen her, her ribs were clearly visible through her skin. Lynda had no shyness about standing naked before Emily, not through any sense of confidence, Emily thought, but rather because the poor woman had no energy to expend on being embarrassed. Emily understood this. She had gone through a similar time back when she had been trapped in her Manhattan apartment when the red rain first fell. She knew only too well the effect prolonged stress and fear could have on both a person's psyche and body.

"In you get," said Emily, guiding Lynda into the shower.

Maybe it was the simple comforting feeling of hot water cleansing her skin, or maybe it was subtler, perhaps the exercising of a normal everyday routine, but as the water washed away the dirt from Lynda's body, Emily thought she saw life flow back into the woman. Her posture straightened, and she leaned against the glass wall of the shower, her head pressed against her forearms as the water beat against her skin. She let out a long sigh. "My God," she said, "I never...I thought..."

"I understand," said Emily. "Just take your time. Let me give you some privacy. I'll be right outside."

Emily sat on the side of the bathtub, hoping that allowing Lynda to clean herself in private would help accelerate her recovery process. Fifteen minutes passed before Lynda turned off the shower. She pulled a towel that Emily had slung over the shower door for her, and when she stepped out, it was wrapped tightly around her.

Emily smiled, almost saying what she was thinking:

you look human again, but caught herself. Instead she said, "Feeling better?"

Lynda smiled broadly, honestly. Her eyes looked brighter, though her face still looked haggard.

"Let's get you those clothes?" She led Lynda out into the bedroom and opened the closet. "There should be something that fits."

Lynda found fresh underwear and slipped them on, then pulled out a pair of jeans and a blouse, checked their length and fit then put those on, too.

"That's much better," said Emily.

"Thank you," said Lynda. She took a second and looked at herself in the wardrobe mirror. "Oh my God, I look like crap," she said, but her observation was curtailed by yet another smile.

"You've been through a lot," said Emily. "Now, how about we go find you some food?"

•••

Lynda ate in silence.

Emily had expected Lynda to wolf down the contents of the MRE Mac had prepared for her, but instead she seemed to be savoring every bite, taking her time. It was just the three of them in the apartment now, Mac having sent the rest of his men out to perform some make-work duties to allow them the privacy to talk.

When she was done, Lynda belched loudly, apologized, and smiled, embarrassed.

Mac gave a deep chuckle, "Don't worry about it. You should hear some of the noises my men make after they've eaten."

"Do you feel up to talking about what happened, now?" asked Emily, placing a reassuring hand on Lynda's.

Lynda nodded and took a large gulp from a glass of water. "After you and Rhiannon left," she began, "Valentine was livid. She was sure that someone else within the camp had helped the two of you escape. She blamed it on Hubbard, although he denied it. But Valentine wasn't listening to anyone, and, looking back on it now, I think it was all just a part of her plan to consolidate her power-base, and Hubbard was the one person who seemed to have no problem standing up to her. Valentine put him through a sham trial and then she had him shot."

"What!" Emily exclaimed. Wallace Hubbard had been the camp's doctor. He had been kind to her, and news of his murder reinforced her hatred for Valentine.

"It was a warning to anyone else that thought they could question her authority. Anyone who disagreed with her or objected to her orders got a visit from one of her goons who convinced them with their fists to change their mind."

"So, where did everyone go?" said Mac

"About five days after you escaped, one of the lookouts reported a strange light to the northwest. We all looked at it; it was green flashes in the sky; like meteors. Very bright. Silent. There were hundreds of them. It went on for hours. Some of the men wanted to go investigate, but Valentine forbade them. I walked down to the dock and boarded the submarine to get a better view of the light show, and fell asleep in the conning tower's observation deck. The next morning, when I came back, everyone was gone. Everyone! I went to all my friends' apartments, checked them all, but everyone had just vanished. I found plates of breakfast food on the tables, showers still running. Whatever happened, it happened quickly and, I think all at once. I...I went back to the submarine, because whatever had taken all the others, obviously hadn't thought to check there. And that's where I stayed."

Emily and Mac exchanged glances.

"After a time, I began to doubt that there had ever *really* been anyone else. That maybe I had imagined everything, *everyone*, and that I was the only survivor. The idea that I was all alone, well..."

Emily squeezed Lynda's hand. "It's okay," she said, "we understand."

"When I heard you all entering the submarine, I thought that maybe whatever had taken everyone else had finally come back for me. I was terrified. That's why I hid."

Mac spoke next. "Did you see anything unusual? After everyone disappeared?

Lynda shook her head. "Just the weird lights in the sky the night before everyone vanished. But I didn't leave the submarine again after that first morning, so I don't really know."

Mac caught Emily's eye and said, "Let's talk."

"We'll be right back," said Emily.

The two of them walked out of the apartment and stood in the corridor, talking in low tones.

"What do you think?" said Mac.

"Those strange lights in the sky she described; think it could be the Locusts?"

"Maybe," said Mac, "or maybe it was the Northern Lights or any number of other things that could account for it."

"Right," Emily said, "but it can't be just a coincidence that the next morning everyone had vanished. It's not like they'd just up and leave without her. And I've seen what alien tech can do; the Caretakers lifted Adam right out of our bedroom. If these creatures are even half as technologically advanced as the Caretakers were, it's not out of the realm of possibility that they could do the same thing."

Mac breathed in slowly and deeply. "My biggest concern, right after finding out what happened here, is if something really *did* abduct around a thousand people without anyone putting up a fight, then what are we going to do if they come back for us? Better we locate *them* first. We'll need to find out exactly where these green flashes Lynda saw in the sky were. Take a little look-see at what we can find out there."

Emily nodded. "I'd like to say that that many people can't just up and vanish off the face of the Earth, but after everything that we've experienced since the red rain came, well, let's just say that I'm keeping an open mind. When do we leave?"

CHAPTER 12

"I would like to volunteer myself and my people's help," Petter said, after Emily explained that they intended to try and track down the source of the green flares in the sky.

"Thought you might," said Mac, with an approving nod.

Petter looked at his watch. "Give me forty-five minutes for us to grab our gear and supplies, and we will be ready to roll and rock."

"You mean rock and roll," said Emily.

"Yes, indeed," said Petter, smiling broadly.

Mac shook his head in mock confusion. "It's too late to set off tonight. We don't want to be traipsing around the jungle in the dark. How does dawn tomorrow sound to you?"

Petter nodded. "We will be ready."

"Okay," Mac continued, "we'll rendezvous at the north gate."

"Yes," said Petter. He gave a sharp salute to Mac, turned and went to find his people.

•••

A bank of gray clouds greeted Emily and the others in a dawn sky that looked heavy with the potential for heavy rain. The morning air was oppressive, and Emily felt the throb of a headache above her eyes thanks to the storm's approaching low-pressure front.

"Everyone ready?" Emily asked, as Petter and four of his Norwegian fighters joined her, Thor, Mac, and his three-man security team at the north gate. Rhiannon had been charged with remaining behind in the *Machine* to watch over the base, despite her objections.

"As we'll ever be," Mac said. He gave a long look at the clouds, still distant for now. He checked his weapon one final time, cradled it in his arms, nodded to his men, then looked at Emily.

"Lead the way," Emily said, falling in behind her husband as the team ducked under the arm of the security gate and moved toward the jungle. Lynda had said the green flashes appeared to be north of Point Loma, but she couldn't estimate how far away the lights had actually been, so Mac had made sure everyone brought enough supplies to last them six days. If they hadn't found any evidence that linked the flares to the Locusts by the third day, they would turn around and head back.

"Here we go again," said Mac, as they crossed from open ground into the red jungle. The transition was always an eye-opener; the line of Titan trees and tall brush that delineated the edge of the jungle gave only a taste of the alienness that lay beyond.

Petter said something in Norwegian to his people and the five of them exchanged a quick succession of short sentences. Emily couldn't understand a word they said, but the meaning behind them was obvious from their faces: awe, fear, wonder, astonishment, and a bit more fear for good measure.

"It's something else, isn't it?" Emily said, stepping closer to Petter.

"It is unbelievable. Beautiful, in its own way."

Emily nodded. "Yes, I suppose it is. Prettier than the rows and rows of houses that were here before, at least." The skeletal remains of those houses lay all around them, still visible even beneath the plant growth. Most were now little more than rubble and jutting pieces of frame, or the occasional lonely brick chimney stack that still stood upright, defying gravity and the jungle.

"Mac told me that you saw all of this happen," Petter said. "That you saw the rain...change everything."

Emily nibbled on her lower lip for a second. "Yes, I saw the transformation. I lived in Manhattan when the red rain came."

"You saw the people transformed?"

"Yes, even the people," she said. "I thought the rain had killed everyone, but now, now I'm not sure they were really dead. I think that maybe, the rain placed them in a state that kept them all barely alive, just alive enough that the transformation could take place. They became...monsters. But they were monsters that had a purpose; they became...well, everything you see."

Petter stopped mid-step. "You mean that these," he tapped his hand against the curling root of a Titan tree that stretched across their path "were all...human?"

Emily nodded. "Maybe. Or any of the other animals that lived around here. But yeah, that tree might have been several hundred people before the red rain."

"My God," said Petter, slowly removing his hand as he gazed up the twisted trunk of the Titan tree toward the canopy. "It is like magic. Beyond my understanding. What kind of technology can do that?"

"Perverted," Emily answered flatly. She stopped walking. Looked up and began to turn away.

"Everything okay, love?" Mac asked, stopping next to her.

Emily said, "The Caretaker told me that they were supposed to help us, that their original programming was to enhance life, to make sure that it thrived wherever they found it. That purpose was perverted by the Locusts. It's just now dawning on me what might have been. How...beautiful this planet could have been for us, if only the corruption of the ideals of whatever species created the Caretakers had not taken place."

"Ooo-kay," said Mac, "not really sure where this is going."

Emily turned and looked at her husband, placed a hand gently against his cheek. "Suppose we win this fight. Suppose we beat the Locusts, drive them from the planet. And it's all ours again. What then? What do we do then?"

"We start over," said Mac. "We get a second chance in this world. So, we start over. And this time, we do it *right*."

•••

"Well, we're not getting across that," said Mac.

They stood on a raised berm running along the bank of a wide inlet that, to Emily's eyes, looked man-made. The inlet ran from the Pacific Ocean on their left, inland to the east for as far as she could see, which, admittedly was not that far thanks to the dense jungle on either side of the inlet. The tide was high and the inlet was flooded, which put about three hundred meters or so of seawater between where she and the team stood and where they needed to be, on the opposite side. Mac pulled out his map, did some quick referencing, and then announced, "This, apparently, is the San Diego River." He pointed across the inlet at the remains

124

of some large mostly-intact buildings, visible despite the jungle that sprouted up around them. "And that's what used to be SeaWorld across the other side. If we follow the inlet farther inland we should find a couple of bridges we can use to cross."

"Assuming the bridges are still intact," said Emily.

"They'll be intact," Mac said, encouragingly.

"Uh, huh," said Emily, and began following the inlet's trajectory east.

The first bridge they came to was nothing more than a row of pier-columns rising from the water. The actual deck of the bridge had collapsed completely into the river, so the group kept walking until they came to the second bridge. This was in better condition but not by much. Large sections of the deck lay in crumbling piles just below the surface of the water. The third and final bridge was in the same state.

"Told ya," said Emily.

Mac made a face at her. "Okay, well I guess we keep walking east then."

About two hours later, they found what had once been the 5 freeway. It appeared out of the jungle with no warning, the blacktop cracked and broken, but, for the most part, in pretty good condition, protected from the elements by the thick canopy of red far above it. It would cut down their travel time significantly.

They followed the 5 north until they came to another bridge. This one looked to be in almost perfect condition.

"Looks good to me," said Mac, after he had taken out a pair of binoculars and cast its glassy eyes over the bridge. He checked his watch. "We've got maybe three hours of light left. Let's cross here, double back to SeaWorld, and find somewhere to pitch a camp for the night."

The bridge held up...just. They were taking their time moving across it, using the west side of the four-lane span, chatting quietly amongst themselves when a sound like twisting metal filled the air. Everyone turned to look back in the direction they had come in time to see a section of the bridge they had crossed just twenty meters behind them, break away and crash into the water below with a whoosh of spray.

"Well, shit!" said Mac. "Double time across the bridge. Now."

They jogged the rest of the way.

"This way," said Mac, pointing at a section of the bridge's sidewall that had crumbled away. One after the other, they jumped the meter and a half down onto the embankment that lay beyond, creating a natural step back down into the jungle. At the bottom of the embankment, they found themselves wading through a stinking swamp of stagnant water as they continued back in the direction of the ocean.

"What do you know," said Mac a few minutes later. "Looks like luck is on our side for a change." Ahead of them was another road running east to west, following the shape of the inlet. The hardtop was bumpy and broken, but far easier to travel than slogging through the jungle and swamp.

They continued along the road for twenty minutes before they came to an open expanse of concrete off to their right. Like the road, the concrete was cracked and broken in places, red weed and bushes having taken root within the fissures. But there was nothing larger than some tall grass pushing up through the cracks.

"Parking lot for SeaWorld," Mac said. The travelers could see straight across the open lot to what Emily guessed had been the famous (or infamous, depending on who you asked at the time) marine theme park.

Mac looked at the sky. Evening was still distant enough, but the clouds they had seen when they first set out earlier that day now filled the sky, sucking up the light. Mac pulled out his binoculars and scanned the distant ruins of the oceanarium. "It seems quiet enough. We should have enough time left to give the grounds a quick once-over; try and find somewhere we can bed down for the night. Let's move."

•••

The security wall encircling the sea-park had crumbled and collapsed in multiple places around the perimeter, allowing Emily and the team to easily slip through. Ahead of them, fallen pieces of what had once been a giant waterslide littered the ground. Beyond that, a large building lay enshrouded in red plants.

"It looks like it's still intact," said Petter, nodding at the building.

"At least from this angle," Emily added.

"Let's go see what we can see then, shall we?" said Mac.

They walked across the open ground to the building, then followed its edge until they found a door hidden behind a growth of thick, scaly vines. The door opened with only a creak of resistance when Mac pushed against it. "See," he said, "told you luck was with us today." He led the group inside, following a corridor until he found what had once been offices.

"This will work for tonight. We'll stash our gear here for now, then we'll go explore the park while we still have some light. Okay?"

Everyone agreed, stowed their backpacks, headed back out into the corridor, and then out into the warm evening air.

"We should split up," said Petter, "it would make covering the ground faster."

Mac thought about it for a second, then said, "Tomorrow, maybe. Right now, I just want to make sure there are no surprises waiting for us. We'll do a quick reconnoiter around these buildings then head back to base camp. Take a better look in the morning."

They moved quietly through the remains of the park.

Several lagoons and ponds marked where the animals had been housed. The water was stagnant now, covered with a red algae that floated on the surface.

Something was niggling at Emily; had been for the last hour or so since they had left the road and entered the park. Even Thor seemed to have noticed; his ears erect, up in the air instead of to the ground. Now it finally hit Emily what it was.

"Hey, everyone. Could you all just hold up for a second, please," she said.

Everyone stopped.

"What's up, love?" said Mac.

Emily put a finger to her mouth. "Listen."

Everyone listened.

"I don't hear anything," said Mac after twenty seconds had passed.

"Exactly," said Emily. No signs of life at all? Throughout their walk here, there had been a constant background hum of noise, of a jungle filled with life that, while born from this planet, was not truly of the planet. Here, though, in the park, that background chatter had ceased. A pall of silence had settled across the area.

Mac's brows furrowed. "Yeah," he said, drawing the word out as he glanced around. "You're right."

"Maybe there's just nothing living around here," said one of Petter's Jegertroppen.

Emily and Mac both looked at her, eyebrows raised. "Trust me when I say," Emily said, "that there's always going to be something that calls this place home. And the chances are it wants to eat you...or worse."

The Norwegian's eyes widened, and Emily could not help but smile. "Don't worry, all you have to do is remember to run faster than the rest of us."

Mac looked up at the setting sun, blurry through the cloud. "We'll give it fifteen more minutes then we'll head back."

They walked north, past derelict buildings and the occasional large tree, but nothing on the scale of a Titan. *In fact*, Emily thought, *there seemed to be less growth in the park than outside its walls, almost as if any available biological material had been diverted elsewhere.*

"Looks as though this is as far as we go," Mac said a few minutes later, when they stepped around the side of what had been a concession stand but was now little more than a bundle of firewood. Ahead of them was an open body of water, a bay, that stretched north. Several large islands dotted the bay. A bridge, several kilometers long, started just west of where the group stood. It consisted of several curving spans that leapfrogged to each of the islands in turn before connecting with the distant mainland to the north.

"That bridge looks like it is still intact," said Petter. He brought a pair of binoculars to his eyes and moved them across the bridge. "I can see no structural damage. Yes. I would say it is safe for us to cross."

"Great," said Mac, "that'll save us some time. We'll check it out tomorrow morning. Right now, we need to call it a night."

•••

Light streamed in through the dirt-stained window at the back of the office the team spent the night in. The group prepared and ate breakfast, packed up their kit and left. They spent the first two hours of the morning reconnoitering the sections of the park they had missed the evening before, but found no sign of the lights Lynda had said she had seen fall anywhere nearby.

"We'll take the bridge we spotted last night and keep heading north," Mac said, after taking a long drink from his canteen.

The bridge in question was technically two bridges; two double-lane spans that sat alongside each other, one for southbound traffic coming to the park, the other for north bound travel. A four-meter gap separated the north and southbound lanes. A rusted metal-and-concrete guardrail ran along the sides of each span.

They set off in single file across the bridge. The day was already warm, but a breeze blowing in off the bay cooled the air comfortably. Dark rainclouds to the north loomed ominously. Peeking over the guardrail into the gap between the two spans, Emily saw nothing but the water of the lagoon far below. The bridge's humpback design meant the travelers could see no more than a hundred meters or so farther ahead of them. If any section of the bridge was damaged to the point that it was impassible, they would either have to turn around or figure out how to get across the gap to the southbound span. Ahead, the bridge dipped down as it connected with the island.

Emily saw it first. She jogged up to Mac and tapped him on the shoulder. "Look," she said, pointing east into the bay, toward another island, far larger than the one that lay ahead of them.

"What am I looking for?" said Mac, shading his eyes from the early morning sun.

"There," Emily said, pointing to a disturbance in the water just off the island's beach. "Do you see that?"

"Yes," Mac said, after a second. "What the hell *is* that?" He lifted his binoculars to his eyes, adjusting the focus. "It looks like a lot of bubbles. Maybe there was an underground gas release or some—" His words faded away.

"What?" said Emily.

"I can't really...oh, shit!" The binoculars dropped from his hands, swinging like a pendulum from the strap around his neck. Emily took them from him, glassing the distant commotion in the water.

"You have *got* to be kidding me," she hissed.

A gargantuan form was rising from the bubbling, foaming lake, its gray, pock-marked skin dripping water as it pulled itself up onto the distant island's beach. It was colossal in size, like nothing Emily had ever seen. *It must be at least thirty meters in height,* Emily thought, mentally comparing the creature to a ten-story building. Emily zoomed the binoculars in for a better look. It was snake-like, with a bulbous, almond shaped head as big as two SUV's. The head was eyeless. A tongue several meters in length extended from between a set of jaws lined with white-teeth. It had two powerful arms near its head which it used to heave itself up onto the beach of the island. It pulled itself farther up the beach, and lay there, obviously sunning itself.

"Well, that answers why there was so little wildlife in the area," Emily said. "This thing has either eaten it or scared it away."

"At least it hasn't seen us," said Mac. "We need to beat feet before—"

His words were cut off by an ear-shattering screech that came from beneath the bridge.

Mac grabbed Emily and Thor, and pulled them with him behind a rusty station-wagon as, from the island that lay ahead of them, another creature, identical to the first appeared. The second creature's elongated body slipped and slid in the sand of the beach, its tail flicking left and right kicking up waves of sand and rock. The message was obvious: it was pissed off.

"Take cover. Now!" Mac yelled at the rest of the team.

Emily's eyes darted back to the first gigantic creature, but it had vanished, replaced by a v-shaped wake that ripped through the water, heading in the team's direction.

"Shit!" Mac hissed. "It's coming this way."

The second creature roared in anger and dove into the sea. It swam out into the lagoon until the waves lapped against its midsection and stopped, directly below where Emily and the team hid. It raised itself up to full height, its head and narrow shoulders above the metal guardrail. It swayed back and forth, its tongue flicking in and out of its mouth, teeth bared in a snarl. *If it turns around now*, Emily thought, *it'll 'see' us, or sense us by whatever this creature's equivalent of sight is.* This close, the thing's skin looked like that of a dolphin's; thick, slick, leathery, but with pock-marks and dimples scattered randomly over its body like a leopard's spots.

The first creature rose from the water, within striking distance of the second. It adopted an identical posture to the first, hissing and screeching. Both creatures swayed back and forth for a few moments, then the first gave a gut-twisting cry and dove at its adversary. A wall of water rose into the air behind it, crashing across the bridge, soaking everyone as the two titans collided, jaws snapping at their opponent, arms locked around the other as they wrestled for an advantage. More waves flooded over the deck of the bridge, dislodging one of the Norwegian soldiers, sending her sliding out into the open. She scrambled back to where her compatriots crouched behind an abandoned car. The noise was deafening as the two creatures roared their anger, their bodies slapping together like thunderous claps. Each time they hit, it sent another huge wave of displaced water smashing into the bridge.

"We've got to get out of here...*now*," Mac yelled. "On three we make a run for the island. Stay low. Ready? One. Two—" But before Mac could finish his countdown, one of the creatures—it was impossible to tell them apart now, Emily noted—violently thrust the other away. It swayed, then tumbled backward, crashing into the section of bridge that lay between where the humans cowered and where they wanted to be. The bridge shrieked in complaint. Then, as the aggressor pushed its advantage, lunging after its adversary, the bridge began to buckle under their immense weight. A section of road gave way, fracturing into huge, irregular slabs of concrete and rebar. The chunks of concrete, each as large as the station wagon Emily, Mac, and Thor hid behind tumbled into the bay. An entire lane of the bridge ahead vanished in the space of three heartbeats.

Mac jumped to his feet, his hand wrapped around Emily's, her hand holding tight to Thor's leash. But before they could take a step, the creatures rose again, their bodies tussling in the broken space they had just created. One of the titans howled in pain as the other gained a momentary advantage and sank its teeth into the arm of its opponent. Thick green gobbets of blood dripped from the wound. The injured creature fell backward, shrieking in pain and anger, and hit the rough edge of the broken span of bridge, sending more pieces of the road down into the water.

Now there was only a two-meter-wide section of the bridge left.

The injured titan, spurred on by its pain, lunged at the other, pushing it back into the water of the lagoon.

"Now!" Mac yelled. He yanked Emily to her feet, yelled "*Run!*" and began to sprint toward what was left of the road ahead, Thor running alongside. Emily thought Mac would slow down, but he apparently had other ideas. The Scotsman sprinted across the narrow sliver of concrete that still connected the two pieces like a tendon hanging from a severed arm, not giving Emily or Thor a chance to hesitate. Emily glanced down into the sea below and saw the two creatures battling in the water; a green slick of blood floated on the surface from their wounds.

Then they were across. Mac aimed for another abandoned car, and pulled Emily toward it. Only then, breathless and panting, did he turn to look behind him. The Norwegians and the rest of his men were a few seconds slower. Petter was across, followed by his people, then Stevens and Billings, while Richford followed up the rear.

"Come on!" Mac yelled.

Richford was almost across when he was abruptly lifted into the air as the bulk of the two titans collided with the underside of the bridge. Chunks of concrete exploded into the air like shrapnel. One landed on the roof of the car Emily and Mac sheltered behind, crushing the metal roof down to the faded leather seats within. Another struck one of Petter's Jegertroppen in the back of her head. She dropped to the ground, the back of her skull a crushed, bloody mess. Richford, his arms waving frantically as he was launched ten meters into the air, flew in a slow backward arc, and disappeared into the space between the north- and southbound sections of the bridge, his scream lost in the tumult of the battle.

The injured titan was weakening, a steady stream of green blood flowing from the huge gashes inflicted by its opponent. It screeched in pain as the second creature locked its jaws on its throat and bit down, sending a gout of green arcing through the air. Emily heard a crunching sound as the victorious titan ripped through its enemy's flesh. She wasn't sure if it was the bridge buckling or the titan's bones breaking.

Wordlessly, Mac waited for the remaining team members to catch up, then he grabbed Emily's hand again and they rushed the remaining distance to the island. Not slowing, they ran across the island and onto the second section of the bridge that led directly to the mainland. They were halfway across when Emily, breathless, her heart pounding in her chest, insisted that she had to stop and catch her breath. Mac slowed to a jog. Emily shook her hand free of her husband, bent over and rested her hands on both her knees as she sucked in deep lungfuls of air, trying not to vomit.

When she looked back the way they had come, both of the titans had vanished beneath the lake.

•••

They moved across the northern section of the bridge at a jog, continuing until they had penetrated the mainland jungle a hundred meters. Not once in Emily's life in this new version of the world, had she thought she would be glad to be in the red jungle, but she welcomed it now; the thick, lush fronds, trees, and stalks of the plants blocking the team from the sight of the titan in the bay.

"Fuck!" Petter, still panting, yelled when finally they stopped to rest, his hair plastered to his forehead by sweat. He was grim-faced, his remaining Jegertroppen looked shell-shocked. "I know you told me it would be dangerous, and we are soldiers, we understand that we might die...but this...I never imagined this."

Emily placed a consoling hand on the major's shoulder. Petter straightened, sucked in a deep breath or two. "Do we turn around? Head back to Point Loma?" he asked.

"No," said Mac. Like the rest of the team, he was taking this moment to catch his breath. "We carry on. No matter what."

•••

A couple hours later, the storm that had threatened them since they left Point Loma finally fulfilled its promise. Fat drops of rain began to splatter all around the team as they pushed north. Twenty minutes after that, the downpour became so heavy the ground beneath their feet quickly turned to thick mud, slowing the party to a crawl.

"We need to find somewhere to wait this out," Mac said, yelling into Emily's ear to be heard over the thunderous roar of rain against the canopy overhead. They were, if Mac had read his map correctly, somewhere in La Jolla, and the ruins of what had once been suburban homes lay all around. Most had been obliterated by years of red jungle growth; none were in a fit enough state to offer shelter from the storm, so they slogged on.

"There, up ahead," said Emily, pointing through the veil of water and mist that had descended across the landscape at a house that still looked to be mostly in one piece, other than missing half of its roof. The team moved as quickly as they could to it, the mud sucking at their boots. The front door was locked, so Mac kicked it down, and they all stumbled inside, Thor shaking water from himself. Petter and his people did a quick reconnaissance, their flashlights lighting up the two-story home as they moved from room to room.

"Upstairs is a mess," said Petter coming down the staircase, "but there's no sign of anything having lived here. I think we are safe."

"Okay," Mac said, "let's set up camp in the living room and kitchen. We'll hole up here until the storm passes." The living room had a fireplace and Mac set about breaking apart a couple of chairs for fuel. He used the wood to light a fire that brightened the room with its orange glow, adding a welcome sense of warmth and security to the drenched, shivering, travelers.

"I'll get a cuppa going," said Billings. He broke out a couple of portable pans from his backpack, filled them with water from an extra canteen, and balanced them carefully on the fire.

"Get out of your wet gear and dry it off," Mac said, stripping off his top layers of clothing and laying them out on the hearth. Everyone else did the same, positioning them as close to the fireplace as possible to dry. Thor had already curled up near the fire, the smell of wet dog beginning to permeate the room.

Emily moved out into the kitchen and checked the cabinets.

"Hey, Mac. You should come and see this," she called out after opening a door labelled pantry.

Mac followed the sound of her voice. "What's the...oh!"

The pantry was filled with canned goods. Additionally, there were several boxes of spaghetti that looked to be intact.

"Think any of them will be good?" asked Emily.

"Only one way to find out." Mac grabbed a couple cans of baked beans. They had pull-tab tops. He opened them up, cautiously sniffed at them, then smiled broadly at Emily. "Smells like dinner to me."

They ate well that afternoon, warming the food in the pots over the fire.

Later, Emily stood at the window in the front room and stared out at the drowned jungle beyond.

"How you doing?" Mac asked, stepping up behind her.

Emily turned slightly toward her husband and smiled at him. He stepped in and put his arms around her, pulling her into him. She closed her eyes, reveling in the feeling of him against her. "If I keep my eyes closed, I can almost forget where we are," she said. "It's almost...normal. But then, it all goes away when I open them again. And to be honest, that's all I really want; the chance for everything to just be normal again. It doesn't have to be the way it was, I just want the world to stop throwing problems at us."

Mac laid his cheek against the top of his wife's head. "I know, but one day all this will be behind us, and we'll be able to get on with our lives again."

"When?" Emily whispered.

"The day after we defeat the Locusts," Mac said, matter-of-factly. "When that's all over and done with, then we can start rebuilding something that resembles our old life. A normal life."

Emily turned around to face her husband, his arms still encompassing her. "When did you get so optimistic?"

Mac laughed. "I've been striving to have a brighter outlook," he said.

Emily wasn't sure if he was making fun of her or not.

"No, really," Mac continued, sensing her incredulity. "Sometime, all this...this shit is going to end and we need to think about that day, because it's as important, if not more, than our day-to-day survival is. We need to be ready to just live again. I mean, that's what we're fighting for, right? A chance to start over. To have that normal life we want."

"And not make the same mistakes," Emily added.

"Yes," said Mac. "And not make the same mistakes."

•••

After the day's exertions and losses, the warmth of the fire, the constant thrum of rain against the house and their full bellies, gave more than enough cover to the weariness that snuck up on the travelers. Heads lolled, eyes closed, and breathing slowed, as one by one, they fell asleep. Emily, curled up on the double sofa, her head in Mac's lap, stared at the fire burning brightly in the hearth and felt her own eyes grow heavier and heavier. She tried to fight it, but her body could not resist the inexorable pull of fatigue, and a minute later, she too was asleep.

•••

Emily could not feel her heart beating.

Neither could she feel her lungs when she tried to take a breath. Those basic human sensations, hidden from our second-by-second perception until they stutter or fail us, had vanished entirely. In their place, Emily felt a new, alien sensation grip her body, like the pores of her skin opening and closing in a disconcerting asynchronous beat.

I must be dreaming, she thought. But that did not feel right; she was simply too aware of her surroundings, of the strange *not-my-body* impression that her brain was trying to process. She looked around. Her 'vision' was unlike anything she had experienced before; it felt as though she were receiving input from multiple organs at once. Organs which her human body did not possess, which might, she thought, account for the weird spectral glow that permeated everything within her field of vision.

She was standing on a brick path. Wherever this place was, it was dark and wet. She could feel the dampness against her naked feet. To her right, a stream of water ran quickly past, gurgling and foaming as it flowed into the darkness. Above her, was a tunnel, obviously man-made judging by the red brick it was constructed from. She looked down and, had she still possessed her lungs, would have drawn in a sharp breath of surprise. The body she now possessed was not human; it was tiny; a rodent-esque creature that lived in the cracks and fissures of this tunnel. It observed the world through six tentacles and the information it relayed now was, to Emily's human mind, an elevated sensory combination of sight and sound remixed into a greater awareness of her surroundings than she had ever experienced. But even though Emily knew she was probably miles away from where this creature's tiny body huddled in the shadows, she still felt a shudder of apprehension.

Mommy.

The single word was spoken as if by someone standing right next to the little creature.

Adam! Emily wanted to say, but the creature who now possessed her consciousness had no lips to form words. Not that it seemed to matter, because her son heard her thoughts.

Yes, Adam's voice continued in her head, *there is not much time, my energy is low. The information continues to flow to me and I find it harder and harder to tear myself away from it. The universe is so very beautiful, the layers of information folded within existence are...exquisite.* Adam paused for a moment. *And so very addictive. I feel that I may not find my way out from the ocean of knowledge and understanding I am swimming in. Each time, it becomes harder than the last to surface.*

Sweetheart, Emily thought, *what do you mean? I don't understand.*

There is no need for you to understand. I...I will be consumed by the knowledge soon, and after that...

Adam's words trailed off.

What? What do you mean consumed?

There is no time for me to explain. The focus required to communicate with you is so very demanding and I am already depleted. You must listen. They are here...the Locusts. I have successfully identified the area they have claimed as their own. The energy buildup in the area is limiting my ability to see clearly, so you must find the entrance to their lair. And when you have found them, you must destroy them. Do you understand?

Yes, yes, Emily thought. *But how? How are we supposed to destroy something so powerful?*

When you have found a way in, I will send a weapon.

What kind of a weapon?

Adam ignored the question. *You have the cube the last Caretaker gave to you?*

He was referring to the cube the dying alien had given to her when Emily first entered the ship in New Mexico. The first time she had seen the Caretakers use the device had been right before she was captured by them in Las Vegas. She had no idea what the cube was, not *exactly*, other than the Caretakers had seemed to utilize it as a multi-tool, of sorts; able to analyze their surroundings and, Emily suspected, they had used it to transport her to their ship. She had left the cube in the safest place she knew of; the *Machine*, back at Point Loma.

Yes, I still have it.

You must take it to the Locusts' lair. You will need to find the energy reservoir they use to feed. Place it as close as you can to the reservoir. When you have done what is required, you must leave quickly. There will be little time available before events are set in motion that I will have no control over.

I don't understand.

You will understand, but now you must use the link I have created between you and the host creature you inhabit. Find the entrance to their lair. Do it quickly, because I do not know how long I will be able to sustain the link between you.

As quickly as she had sensed her son's presence, it was gone again.

Adam? she thought. But there was no reply. Adam was no longer there. Her son had sounded so tired, and yet...there had been an almost blissful tone to his words. As though he welcomed whatever heightened existence it was that he found himself enveloped in. Emily forced herself to abandon the thought. Adam had said that he was unsure how long he could sustain the connection between her and the creature she now inhabited; she needed to utilize the time she had and find the entrance to the Locusts' lair.

Emily commanded the creature to leave the shadows. She looked around. She was underground, that was for certain. It took her a few more moments to realize she was in a sewer. Ahead of her, a stream of light flowed down from above. She ordered the creature to move toward it. A portion of the tunnel, and the house that had once sat atop it, had collapsed, completely blocking the sewer. A hill of rubble reached up to a hole in the sewer's roof. Emily mentally nudged the creature to climb upward. It scrambled out of the hole and into the remains of the home's kitchen. It then moved from the kitchen out into the front room, leaped up onto the sill of a glassless window and dropped down into a pile of bushes.

Unlike human sight, the creature whose body she now controlled possessed senses that seemed keyed toward detecting multiple energy emissions of a different kind because the red jungle that surrounded her now seemed to glow and thrum with vibrant energy. Each plant, tree, building, life form (and there were many of them moving across the floor and within the branches and roots) appeared as a pattern of energy that to human eyes would have been nothing more than a jumble of swirling colors and indecipherable patterns. But through the lens of her host's mind, Emily understood that these shifting waves of light were indications of the energy's vitality and power. She ran forward, ducking under roots and over rubble, but saw no hint of where the entrance to the Locusts' lair Adam had spoken of might be. She slowed her host to a stop, looked left and right but saw nothing. *There must be a way to figure out where the lair is*, she thought, a clue that she could use.

The sky above Emily's host was sullen, swollen with rain clouds, and growing darker still as day's end approached. It wasn't like she could just ask the creature she occupied where it lived, it had no way to communicate other than through the images and emotions it experienced. To her host's right, the gnarled roots of a Titan tree dug deep into the ground, the twisted trunk rising high into the air, towering above the rest of the jungle.

That was the answer. *Up*, she needed to go upward.

Emily commanded her host to head up the tree, hoping that the creature was capable of climbing. It was. In fact, the higher the creature moved up the Titan tree's trunk, the more at home it appeared to be. Up, up, up it scrambled, until the canopy of the rest of the jungle lay meters below it. It clambered out along the longest branch Emily could find. Below her, the canopy of the jungle, its undulating waves of fronds and branches and leaves spread out like the surface of a roiling red ocean frozen in time. Sheets of rain fell from the gray sky. To the south, she could see the remains of SeaWorld, the bridge they had crossed running like a scar across the landscape. To the east was nothing but more jungle. To the west...

About five kilometers northwest of where she perched, the jungle had been laid bare. The trees and foliage were gone, as if they had never even existed. The eviscerated carcasses of tract homes were clearly visible, their bleached wooden skeletons unmistakable, even at this distance. The welt of deforestation was a perfect circle, about a half-kilometer in diameter, but expanding outward from a center that, to Emily's host's senses, was painfully bright. At the circumference of the welt, the border glowed bright white in a ring of energy as bright as its center. And the circle was growing, expanding, albeit by a small amount; the movement was still perceptible as the ring of white gradually increased in size, revealing more of the skeletal remains of humanity's existence from before the red rain.

Emily memorized the position of the welt, marking it in relation to where it lay to the ruins of SeaWorld. She ordered her host to climb back along the branch, then down the trunk toward the ground. Her intention was to try and get closer to the energy source. She would investigate the area and report back to Mac with as much information as possible. She and her host were halfway down the trunk when, with a suddenness that made her gasp in surprise, the connection between her and the tiny creature snapped, and Emily was jolted back to reality.

•••

Momentarily staggered, Emily's head swirled at the sudden disconnection from her host. Her own human senses flooded her mind, blinding her with light and sound and feelings. Her body momentarily forgot how it was supposed to function, but then her lungs inhaled, and her heart began to beat.

"Emily! Emily, are you okay? Speak to me." Mac's voice was distant, indistinct beneath the thumping of Emily's heart. "Love, wake up. You're having a bad dream."

And then she was back.

Emily opened her eyes and saw Mac leaning over her,

concern stitched through every muscle of his face, his eyes gazing down at her, deep pools of worry. She lay in his arms. On the periphery of her vision she saw the equally worried faces of the rest of the team, and Thor standing at wary attention nearby.

"I'm...okay," Emily said. Her lips felt dry and cracked. She croaked, "Can I get some water, please?"

Mac handed her his canteen and she drank deeply. When she was done, she sat upright, touched her husband's cheek lightly with her hand and reiterated, "I'm okay."

Gradually, the worry melted from Mac's face. "Must have been a hell of nightmare," he said, placing his own hand on Emily's.

"It wasn't a nightmare," Emily said. "It was a message from Adam. I know where the Locusts are."

CHAPTER 13

"All set?" Mac asked.

Emily nodded. A half hour had passed since she had awoken from her vision and quickly explained to Mac and the team what she had seen. Mac had had questions, which she had answered to the best of her ability, but eventually she had said, "It's going to be much easier for me to just show you where the lair is."

They picked up their packs and headed out, Thor trotting happily in the lead.

"Northwest?" Mac asked.

"Yup!"

Petter spoke, "How far do you think?"

"It looked like a couple of kilometers at most, but it's hard to be sure because of the difference in scale, the creature I inhabited wasn't much bigger than a mouse. All I know is that it is in this direction." She sliced the air with her hand like she was performing a karate chop.

"How can you be so sure?" Petter asked bluntly.

"I can't explain it," Emily replied, "other than I just know. It's like...a little beacon pulsing in my head. It's the same thing that happened to me when I was looking for Adam, and it led me right to him."

Petter tipped his head in acknowledgment, apparently satisfied with the description of her psychic GPS.

It was slow going. The terrain was dense with vegetation, mud, and the ruins of tightly packed tract homes which made it even more difficult to keep a straight path.

"At least it's stopped raining," said Mac, as they diverted again, their path ahead blocked by a thicket of red vegetation that had sprung up between the ruins of two homes. While it had technically stopped raining, water still fell from the vast canopy overhead, and the ground was still muddy and treacherous. Several times they had to double back and try a different route because the way was either blocked by dense thickets or collapsed and rotting buildings. So, what should have been a two- or three-hour trek, turned into five exhausting hours, but eventually they found what they were searching for.

"Heads up, we've got company at two o'clock," said Billings, pointing to a glowing white light that permeated through gaps between the trees and bushes ahead of them. Mac dropped to his knee and brought his rifle up; the others did the same, dispersing to whatever cover they could find.

Emily remained where she was. "Guys, it's okay. I think this is the edge of the ring I told you about in my vision." She stepped forward, climbing over a fallen tree.

"Emily," Mac hissed.

Emily ignored him, pushed aside a large bush and stepped through the space. After a few seconds elapsed, she turned back to face the men. "I'm right, come on and look at this."

The soldiers moved from their positions and joined Emily and Thor, who had already slipped past the bush to join his mistress.

"Jesus!" Mac exclaimed. Ahead of them lay a stretch of ground between where he and the team stood and a convex line of bright light that ran horizontal to the ground; the light pulsated from bright to blinding every four or five seconds. The ground between the humans and the light was covered with the same spread of vegetation and detritus that they had labored through for the past couple of days. But on the opposite side of the light's boundary, the ground was barren of all life, leaving behind only a layer of gray dust, all that remained of the vegetation and trees that had grown there. Scattered across the circular welt of dead ground were the husks of destroyed homes, rusting carcasses of automobiles, and other remnants of humanity's lost civilization, apparently immune to whatever this effect was. It was a jarring scene, to see so much land without even a hint of what had been a ubiquitous land of red for so long now.

"It's...it's like the light is eating everything in its path," said Petter

"That's exactly what it's doing," Emily said. "A couple of days after the red rain fell, every plant, animal, human was...transformed. I watched it happen, and it was similar to this except plants, trees, animals...humans, they were all changed to what we have now. But this is different, everything is being consumed. Look, the ring of light is slowly expanding."

The group watched silently for several minutes.

"Look at that branch." Emily pointed at a meter-long tree limb that had fallen perpendicular to the expanding line of energy. As they continued to watch in disbelief, the light moved centimeter by centimeter over the branch. Everything seemed normal this side of the light, but where the light touched the branch, it glowed just a little bit brighter, and on the opposite side, the branch had become a gray husk, that crumbled to nothingness under the light breeze that blew in from the west. "It's consuming everything in its path. That's what the Caretaker warned me would happen; it's converting everything to some other kind of energy."

"Okay, but where's the energy going?"

"To the Locusts. Adam said they have a storage facility for the energy they'll collect."

"But why would they go to all this trouble?" asked Petter, "to first convert the life on this planet to this..." he waved his hand around at the red jungle, "only to suck it dry later?"

Emily considered the question for a second. "It makes sense, when you think about it. The Locusts sent the Caretakers ahead of them, had them do all the hard work of subduing the population and converting them to an easily consumed form of matter. The new life the Caretakers left behind is self-sustaining, and wouldn't put up any kind of a fight when the Locusts finally showed up. They could've taken a million years to get here and life on the planet would still look pretty much like it does today. All they would have to do is start whatever the harvesting process is and convert everything into the energy they require. If they store it away, they could live off it for millennia."

Petter nodded slowly. "That sounds...plausible."

"The question now is," said Emily, "if we cross that line of energy will we still be in one piece when we get to the other side?"

Before Emily could let out more than a gasp of surprise, Mac took five long steps, hopping over the white line of energy.

Emily started to go after him, her sudden anger almost at boiling point that he would put his life at risk so quickly, but she stopped again as Mac put up his left hand.

"Hold on just a second," Mac said. "Give it some time."

Emily's anger faded almost instantly, replaced by a burning fear. "Are you okay? Is something wrong?" she blurted out.

"Not that I can tell," Mac said, "but we don't all want to jump across the line and find out there's a delayed effect, do we?"

"Screw that," said Emily, and walked briskly across the line to where her husband stood, shock and fear in *his* eyes now. She had made a reasonable supposition that whatever process was being employed by the Locusts to harvest the red matter would have no ill effect on people when she saw that anything built by humans was still intact; still, she did not appreciate her husband's recklessness. "Not much fun, is it?" Emily said, then punched her husband hard on the meat of his shoulder. "Come on, Thor, at least you listen to me."

Thor rose from where he had been sitting next to Petter and trotted toward Emily. When he reached the line of energy he paused for a second before leaping across it. The rest of the humans followed behind him.

"Which way now?" Petter asked.

"This way," said Emily, and started to follow the pull she felt tugging at her mind.

•••

The going became much easier this side of the energy line. The eradication of anything alien meant the team only had to avoid the newly exposed human trash that still littered the now denuded landscape.

"It's kind of disconcerting, to see it all exposed like this," said Mac.

Emily understood what he meant. The transmutation of the flora and fauna had the effect of drawing back a curtain that had been pulled across the world, hiding what had once been from the survivors' sight. That invisibility had helped Emily's mind to cope with the loss; out of sight, out of mind, and all that. Now, the ugly, decayed remains of the old world were laid bare, leaving nothing to the imagination, exposing the extent of the utter destruction of their world. She imagined it felt like how she would feel if she had accidentally dug up the moldering remains of an old pet, buried in another life; a better, more innocent life. It left a feeling of profound melancholy in her stomach and heart. *It's all just so unbelievably sad,* she thought.

"Look! Over there," said Petter. He pointed off to his right, through a gap between the shells of two crumbling houses.

Emily shaded her eyes against the glare of the sun and looked where Petter was pointing. She saw a berm of raised earth, maybe two meters tall. But what caught her attention was the wisps of purple energy flowing up the sides of the berm like smoke being pulled by the extractor fan of a kitchen range.

"Let's check it out," Mac said. He added, "Carefully."

They passed between the two homes, weapons raised. "Slowly now," Mac reiterated.

"This doesn't look like dirt," Emily said as she dropped to her knees next to the berm. "It's so smooth." She ran her hand up the curve of the berm. "It's like it's been melted." The mound had an almost glass-like feel to it. Thor nosed around the base of it, his eyes following the wisps of purple energy like they were leaves blown by an autumn breeze.

"It's warm to the touch, too. Not cold like I expected," said Petter, standing beside Emily.

The berm was a little bigger than Emily had guessed it to be, obscuring her view of what lay on the other side. Around it, wisps of purple energy snaked over the ground, played over the berm's surface, rippling and moving into whatever was on the other side. The transference of energy was silent; in fact, Emily noted, the only sound other than the crunch of their boots on the ground was the distant hiss and whoosh of surf, as the ocean broke against the shore a kilometer or so west of where they were.

"Give me a boost," Mac said to Billings. Obediently, Billings positioned his feet shoulder width apart, interlocked the fingers of both hands to form a stirrup, then raised Mac up until his shoulders were over the top of the berm, and he could support himself with his beefy arms.

"Well, shit, love. I think you've found what we're looking for," said Mac, his head moving left and right as he surveyed the ground.

"What do you see?" Emily asked.

"Come on up and have a look for yourself," Mac said, nodding to Billings to lower him down. Mac took Billings' place and lifted Emily up. The berm encompassed the opening to a shaft that was about thirty meters across. She leaned over the edge to get a better look, felt Mac's grip tighten on her ankles, and looked straight down, into nothing but darkness. "Hand me a flashlight," Emily said, holding an outstretched hand behind her. Petter gave her his. She flicked it on and moved the beam into the shaft. The beam pushed back some of the darkness but not much. She played the light across the shaft's walls; they were made of the same smooth material as the berm she leaned against. It was almost as if the tunnel had been melted out of the ground. And there was no sign of a bottom to it. The shaft could drop down for a hundred meters or several kilometers, there was just no way to guess.

"Let me down," she said eventually.

Mac lowered his wife back down to the ground. "This the place, you think?"

Emily nodded. The pinging in her brain had stopped at the same time she had first approached the berm.

"Now what?" Petter asked.

"We need to figure out how we're going to get down there," said Emily.

"We're going to need climbing gear," Mac said.

"We have the equipment back at Point Loma," Billings said.

Mac checked his watch. It was about three in the afternoon. "Better get a move on then."

•••

They spent that night in the same house they had stayed in the night before. There was an odd comfort for Emily coming back to the same familiar spot.

"You have a plan?" Emily asked Mac, her voice hushed, the rest of the team already asleep for the night. They sat next to each other on the same sofa they had spent the previous night.

Mac took a moment to reply. "I don't like the odds of this one, love. We have next to no intelligence on what to expect. We don't know what these Locusts are capable of, other than what Adam has told you, and we have no information on the layout of their lair. I mean, I've walked into some shit-storms before the red rain, but that was against human adversaries; they were predictable. All the cards are off the table for this one and that makes me nervous."

"And you don't like being nervous," Emily said before he could, moving in closer to him.

Mac smiled. "How'd you know? So, is there anything else you can tell me about what Adam expects us to do? Can you contact him?"

"Maybe tonight," Emily said, although she didn't hold out too much hope. This last time Adam had communicated with her, she had sensed how distracted he was, how immersed in his constant absorption of the Caretakers' store of knowledge, to the point that he seemed barely able to maintain his focus on her.

"Okay, I guess that's the best we can hope for then?"

In the remaining time between wakefulness and sleep, they sat silently together, enjoying the closeness of each other, their hands intertwined, watching shadows creep across the window as the last light of day left the sky.

•••

When the team woke the next morning, they grabbed their gear and headed outside, intent on getting an early start back to Point Loma.

"Bugger me," said Mac as he stepped over the threshold into the crisp, damp morning air. Overnight, the ring of energy emanating from the shaft had almost caught up with them. It was now only twenty meters away from where they stood. If they had not woken when they did, the ring would have passed right through the house as they slept.

"It's expanding faster," said Emily. "Look!"

The day before, the ring's progress of consuming the red jungle had been barely perceptible, but now the ring's energetic glow was far more pronounced, its expansion probably twice as fast, Emily estimated.

"Well, that puts a different spin on things completely," said Mac. "There's no more time to waste. We're going to need to hump it back to Point Loma." They had agreed the night before that they would head back to Point Loma as quickly as possible, but in the interest of safety—i.e. "Not getting eaten-a-fucking-live by that big fucker under the bridge," as Mac had colorfully elaborated— they would take a more circuitous route back to the Point, and avoid traveling through SeaWorld.

"We're going to have to take the same route we came in by," Petter said, confirming what Emily was thinking.

Mac added, "Not something I'm happy about, but the risk is one we're going to have to take."

"Well at least we know what to expect," Emily said.

"That makes me feel so much better," Mac said,

mitigating his sarcasm with a sly grin. "Come on then, the universe isn't going to save itself."

•••

Thor smelled the dead titan long before his human companions spotted its rotting corpse wrapped around a pillar of the bridge, not far from where the two creatures had fought their bloody battle. While the humans had seen no other signs of life on land when they passed through the previous day, the water was filled with it, if the hundreds of smaller creatures that now swarmed over the dead monster's carcass were any kind of a gauge.

Rather than take the same northbound span of the bridge they had used previously, they chose the southbound section instead, which meant they would avoid the section the two titans had damaged when they fought their battle. Thankfully, there was no sign of the victorious titan on either of the islands. Still, the team made a concerted effort to move across the bridge as quickly as possible, using the derelict vehicles that littered it as cover.

Moving quickly through the waterpark, they exited through the same gap in the fence they had entered by two days earlier. Emily felt everyone breathe a collective sigh of relief. Now it was just a case of beating feet back to Point Loma as quickly as possible. And they made good time, arriving back just before sundown; exhausted, dirty, and hungry, but thankful that they had made it home without losing anyone else.

STAR CHILD

CHAPTER 14

"Ladies. Gentlemen. First off, I want to thank all of you who are a part of the assault team for volunteering, especially for such an intelligence-poor mission," Mac said, addressing the gathering of soldiers and sailors who had assembled in the camp's cafeteria. All personnel were in the room for the mission briefing, but Mac had decided on a team of twenty volunteers to make the assault on the lair; enough to provide the kind of firepower they might need, but small enough that they could move quickly, and inconspicuously.

Emily leaned against the back wall of the room, watching her husband's briefing.

Mac continued, "Our primary mission is to infiltrate the alien's lair, and identify the enemy's energy reservoir. Secondarily, we will try to locate and extract any potential survivors. Once we've located said energy reservoir, we will proceed to blowing the fuckers back to whatever godforsaken rock they came here from."

Mac's last line raised a few cheers from the group.

"Everyone who's not a part of the assault team will travel with us and provide logistical support topside. Now, if I've made it sound like this mission is going to be a leisurely stroll in the park, I should reiterate that we have next to no intelligence on exactly what we'll be facing once we get inside the lair. Which means we'll be winging it for much of the time. Sounds like fun, eh?"

Now a wave of nervous laughter rippled through the room.

"How are we getting inside?" asked Bishop, a heavyset sailor in his thirties, who seemed to have a permanent scowl on his face.

"Glad you asked," Mac continued. "We've located a shaft that we believe the Locusts use to direct the energy they are harvesting from the surrounding area down into their lair. We'll be using this shaft to pay them a visit."

Bishop looked at Mac expectantly. "And...?"

"Remember when I said all we had was piss-poor intelligence? I wasn't exaggerating. Once we're inside, we'll have to figure out where we go next. We'll be going in completely blind, but there is no other option. If we don't find the Locusts' energy pool so Emily can do what she needs to do, then we're screwed."

The team muttered nervously.

"It sucks, I know," Mac continued. "Now, I don't want to sound too melodramatic, but the fate of the human race rests quite literally on each of our shoulders. Well, everyone but you Simpson..." Mac nodded at a sailor in the front row "...it'd slip right off of yours." The men and women laughed less cautiously now. When the laughter died down Mac continued, his tone turning serious, "I know it all feels and sounds surreal, but it's all true, every word. These Locusts are here for one thing, and one thing only; to steal every resource this planet has. Now, you're all already heroes as far as I'm concerned, but this is some biblical level shit we'll be dealing with. This is the kind of story that, if we manage to pull it off, people will be talking about two or three thousand years from now. This is your chance to be legends."

He let his words sink in for three heartbeats, then stood, checked his watch and said, "Now get your gear together and meet me at the ready-point in thirty minutes. This is *our* world, and it's time to take it back."

•••

"Okay, everyone on board," Mac yelled to the soldiers who had assembled beneath the legs of the *Machine*, their gear in hand. Without further prompting, the group organized themselves into two lines and began to march up the slipway into the *Machine*. Once everyone was on board, Emily, Thor, Mac, and Petter followed, the ramp folding up behind them.

Emily took her seat next to Rhiannon.

The previous evening, Emily and Mac had discussed with Rhiannon her role in the coming operation. As reticent as they both were to involve Rhiannon in the potentially violent events to come, she was the craft's pilot, and the only person who could operate it, and the *Machine* was just too vital an asset to not have it involved. So, they had agreed, somewhat reluctantly, that there was simply no way to keep her out of the coming operation. Initially, they needed Rhiannon to use the *Machine* to transport everyone to a location on the beach about a kilometer away from the shaft. This location would serve as their base camp. There was no way to get the huge craft into the lair, so Rhiannon would stay with it, along with everyone who wasn't a part of the assault team, or the ten-person support group who were going to remain on the surface near the shaft's entrance. Rhiannon and the *Machine*, along with the remainder of the crew would form a rear guard, medical assessment and support section. If Mac's assault crew found any survivors, they would be extracted up the shaft and then directed back to the base camp. Rhiannon's job would be to provide protection for the base camp, survivors, and personnel. Rhiannon had jumped at the responsibility, happy to finally be included in an operation rather than babysitting Thor (even though Emily had already decided that the malamute would remain with Rhiannon for this operation).

Emily looked over to Rhiannon; she was seated in the command chair, her eyes fixed ahead, probably enjoying the super-senses her connection to the *Machine* afforded her.

"Ready?" Rhiannon asked Emily.

Emily did a quick scan of the other passengers, saw they were all settled securely in their seats, and said, "Ready when you are."

"*Machine*, follow the coastline north," Rhiannon ordered.

The seats' protective padding expanded to envelop the passengers, then the *Machine* was off, accelerating rapidly to its breakneck speed. It leaped over the camp's security fence and dropped down onto the beach, its legs kicking up plumes of sand as it powered north, following the beach along the coastline.

The *ping-ping-ping* in Emily's head had returned almost as soon as they had started for home the previous day. Now Emily used it to guide Rhiannon to a spot on the coast parallel to where Emily sensed the shaft was located.

"This is the place," Emily said.

Rhiannon ordered the *Machine* to stop, then lowered its ramp. All in all, it had taken just fifteen minutes to travel as far as Emily, Mac and their team had in two days.

Mac stood. "Everyone off." The group began to disembark, organizing themselves into their assigned groups once they were outside.

Parsons and Rhiannon walked over to where Emily, Mac, and Petter supervised their assault team as they triple checked their gear.

"Good timing," said Mac as the two approached. He reached into a duffel bag and pulled out a handheld radio. "Here you go," he placed the radio in Rhiannon's hands. "You'll be our point of contact here, okay?"

Rhiannon took the radio and nodded.

Mac continued, "The radios aren't going to work once we're in the shaft, all that rock is going to cause havoc."

"Then how will the radio help?" said Rhiannon.

"I am glad you asked," said Mac, sounding like a midnight infomercial. "In this bag," he tapped the duffel bag at his feet with his boot "we have several radio repeaters. I'm going to position them as we go and they'll boost the signal enough that we'll be able to reach you."

"Cool," said Rhiannon, apparently impressed.

"Yes indeed," Mac said, smiling. "It'll be up to you to pass any information back to Parsons, okay?"

"Roger that," said Rhiannon, making all four adults smile.

"Okay then," Mac said, "it's time we were on our way."

Rhiannon silently hugged Emily first, then Mac, and finally, much to his surprise, Petter. The embraces were long, and wordless. When she was done, she turned to Parsons and said, "Can you take me back to the *Machine*?" Parsons nodded solemnly at Mac and Emily then led Rhiannon back toward the craft.

Emily sucked in a long inhalation of air then turned to her husband and Petter, "Ready?"

"You betcha," Mac said, and together they walked over to join the waiting assault team.

•••

The hike to the Locusts' lair was probably going to be the easiest part of this whole operation, Emily decided as they approached the shaft. The constantly expanding circle of energy had devoured everything red for more than five kilometers around the shaft, which left only the remains of homes and stores and other such human debris between the base camp on the beach and the team's target. They reached the opening to the shaft around nine AM.

"Jesus," said Mac, his eyes moving over the raised berm that encircled the shaft's entrance.

The flow of energy that just two days ago had been little more than wisps of purple light was now a torrent. It covered every centimeter of the berm, extending out for thirty meters in every direction, floating several centimeters off the ground like a thin, translucent covering, undulating and shifting in the sunlight. Lightning bolts of energy streaked across the ground from the red jungle in the distance, before merging with the pool of energy collecting around the shaft. It created a disconcerting yet fascinating light show.

"It's obviously picking up its pace," said Mac.

Emily nodded. Adam had given no indication that he had any idea how quickly the Locusts' harvesting of Earth's resources would take, but if the escalation in scale between two days ago and today was anything to go by, they were talking a matter of days.

Jesus, Emily thought, suddenly overwhelmed by a wave of anxiety and dread. *If we fail to complete the mission*...Emily pushed the negative thought from her mind. Failure, as they used to say, was not an option.

CHAPTER 15

Mac had brought along three large, high-powered portable halogen lamps and a portable propane generator that he had planned to use to illuminate the shaft. Except, now, as he and Emily stood on a hastily assembled wooden platform suspended between two stepladders, looking down into the shaft, it turned out they had not needed them. The twisting flow of energy that whirled and swirled within the shaft provided more than enough light to see all the way to the bottom of the pit, and into what looked like a larger, open area.

"That is a *long* way down," said Emily.

"I'd guess somewhere around sixty, maybe seventy meters," Mac estimated. "Not a problem." They climbed back down to the assembled teams. Mac and two of his crew set about fixing rappelling anchors to metal bolts they had already drilled into the side of the raised berm around the lip of the shaft; six anchors and bolts in total, at two-meter intervals. When it was done, the support team quickly threaded rappelling lines and carabiners to the anchors while the assault team readied their weapons, checked that the bags they carried their gear in were securely fastened to their backs, then climbed up onto the berm and positioned themselves near the edge.

On Mac's signal, one after another, the team leaders threw their coiled climbing ropes over the edge of the pit. The lines whirred through the air, uncoiling into the shaft.

Mac breathed in deeply, exhaled, and addressed his people. "Not to sound like a broken record, but remember we have very little idea what we're facing down there, so stay close and stay quiet. I'm going to remind you one last time; our primary mission objective is to get in and locate the energy reservoir for Emily. We do not engage unless I give the order, so keep your fingers off your triggers. If there are any Point Loma survivors, then we'll get them out, but the energy reservoir is our most important task. We want to avoid drawing any attention to our presence, so I'm going to repeat one final time, in case any of you haven't got it through your skulls yet; you engage only if I tell you to. Am I clear?"

"Yes, sir," everyone replied almost in unison.

"Any questions?

"No, sir."

Mac smiled. "Okay, let's rock and roll." And with that, he stepped back into the waiting darkness.

•••

The walls of the shaft looked to be as smooth as porcelain. Emily momentarily stopped her descent, reached out tentatively and laid the flat of her hand against the surface; it was warm to the touch. In fact, the deeper into the shaft the assault team descended, the warmer the air became, to the point that she could feel small beads of sweat running down her forehead.

"All okay?" Mac asked. He had stopped a few meters below Emily.

"The rock's warm," Emily replied. "Shouldn't it be cold?"

Mac touched his own hand to the wall and after a second said, "You're right. Must be related to whatever the Locusts are cooking up down there."

To the left and right of Emily, the rest of the team continued toward the bottom of the pit. Above her, the opening looked small and distant. She could not help but compare herself to the time traveler in H.G. Wells' *The Time Machine* as he descended into the unknown depths of the Morlocks' tunnels in search of the captured Eloi.

Emily felt a hand on her shoulder and turned to see Mac across from her.

"You sure you're okay?" he asked.

She forced a smile to her lips, "Yup! Come on, race you to the bottom."

•••

Emily's feet finally touched the bottom of the shaft. The insides of her thighs were sore; even though she was wearing combat trousers, the rope had still managed to chafe. She resisted the urge to rub the sore spots, knowing that it would only make them itch more.

Mac unhooked her from the rope then spoke into his radio, "All clear down here. Next group, come on down." He turned to Emily. "You okay, love?"

Emily nodded and looked around. They were in a large semi-circular room with walls that curved away from where the shaft ended, about six meters above her head. The room was much wider than it had appeared from the top of the shaft. The temperature had risen to the equivalent of a summer day; a good eighty-plus degrees, Emily thought. Her clothing was starting to feel clammy from perspiration; the rest of the team's tunics also had spreading dark patches between their shoulder-blades. The four other men who had descended with Mac and Emily waited just a few meters away, kneeling with their weapons and flashlights pointing down a tunnel that ran perpendicular to the shaft they had just used to descend from the surface.

The team waited silently as the remaining twelve team members descended the ropes to join them. When everyone was safely down, Mac split them into two groups, ordered one to the left side of the tunnel, the second group to the right. They formed a line one-person deep, separated by gaps of two meters. Mac took point on the left, Petter the right. Emily took her place behind her husband. After a final check of their equipment, Mac signaled to Petter and the two lines of soldiers began to move out along the tunnel, the only sound the quiet scuff of their boots against the tunnel floor.

There was no need for the flashlights each of them carried, the twisting rope of energy flowing down the center of the tunnel gave off more than enough illumination for the humans to see for a fair distance ahead of them. The tunnel was huge, Emily noted, dropping away at a steady 10-degree incline in front of them. The bottom was flat and easy to walk on but on either side the walls curved upward for twenty meters above their heads. Just like the walls of the shaft, this tunnel's walls were smooth as glass, with not even the tiniest of flaws that Emily could see. The river of twisting, undulating strands of energy running down the tunnel's center was probably four meters in diameter, more than twice as tall as the tallest man or woman in the team. Filaments of glowing energy, ranging in size from tiny motes to the occasional strand that was longer than Emily's arm, drifted through the air alongside the main stream of energy, pulled down the tunnel as if by some unfelt draft. The filaments rotated, floating dreamily through the air, some merging with the main stream, the rest drifting ever onward like fireflies.

A couple hundred meters along, the channel diverged, forking into three separate tunnels. The energy stream took a new route along one of the new tunnels that curved to the left. Mac signaled for everyone to stop, and beckoned Petter over to where he and Emily stood. "What do you think?" Mac asked, looking at Emily. "Do we continue on down the same route or follow the energy?"

"It makes sense to me that the energy is flowing either to a storage area or, maybe, even to the Locusts themselves, which means we should follow it," said Emily.

Petter nodded. "Yes, that is logical, but it doesn't necessarily mean that that is where we will find any survivors. We could split into three teams, one for each tunnel."

Mac shook his head. "That would be a mistake, I think. Our handheld radios are limited and the repeaters are only going to add so much range. We should stick together."

"I agree," Emily said. "Our priority is to deliver the cube to the energy source, as Adam instructed. If we don't do that it's not going to matter whether we find any survivors because we'll all end up dead anyway once the Locusts strip the world clean."

Petter and Mac nodded grimly. "So, we're agreed then," Mac said, "we'll continue to follow the energy stream to its destination?"

"Yes," said Emily.

Petter didn't seem convinced of the decision but deferred to Mac. "You are in command," he said then walked back to his team.

The river of energy changed course, now following a smaller tunnel that took a gradual left turn off the main passageway. Mac set off down the new route without a word. Ten minutes of cautious walking later the tunnel made an abrupt 180-degree turn to the right. This section of the tunnel continued for another twenty minutes of walking until the group encountered a second bend that twisted the tunnel back 180-degrees in its original direction, all while dropping ever deeper into the planet's crust. Ahead of the group, a smaller tunnel intersected with the main one, branching off to the right. The energy stream continued to flow past the opening uninterrupted, so there was no need to change course.

Mac was less than a meter away from the intersection when something huge stepped out from the smaller tunnel into theirs.

To Emily, it resembled a giant stick insect. It had a thin body that was about three meters long, its skin color was close to purple with slightly raised bumps of darker purple scattered across its body like the camouflage of a cheetah. Its head, if you could call it a head because the only difference Emily could see from its rear end was that it had a cluster of what might be eyes extending in an arc like a crown across the top of its body. Six legs, two clusters of three on either side of its body, extended from its flanks, close to its rear, which caused the creature to walk with its front end raised well above the ground at a forty-five-degree angle. Two thin arms sprouted from its midsection, each ending in three delicate-looking articulated fingers.

Mac stopped abruptly, fumbling his rifle from his shoulder.

Emily gasped and reached for her pistol. Mac was so close to the alien, if he had wanted to he could have reached out and easily touched the thing. Which meant that when it attacked, as it surely would any second now, Emily reasoned, Mac would be the closest to it and the natural initial target.

Emily's body flooded with adrenalin as she braced for the cavalcade of gunfire she was sure was about to erupt around her. From the corner of her eye she saw Petter and the Jegertroppen directly behind him dropping to a knee as they brought their weapons to bear on the creature. Emily did the same, slowly dropping to one knee.

What Emily did not anticipate was for the creature to do nothing. Instead of attacking, it continued past Mac as though he did not exist, its attention focused squarely on the energy stream. Once it was close enough, a slit opened on the thing's head just below the arc of eyes. A proboscis, tube-like with equally spaced raised corrugated rings along its length extended from the opening and dipped into the glowing flow of energy.

It drank deeply. Emily could see the energy moving up the transparent straw-like proboscis.

Mac raised his right hand slowly into the air, his fist clenched to signal no one should move. If the stick creature showed any sign of aggression, he would unclench his fingers and all hell would be unleashed on it.

For its part, the stick creature appeared to be totally oblivious to the group of humans pressed against the wall of the tunnel, just meters away from it. For several minutes, it continued to drink in great gulps from the uninterrupted flow of energy roiling down the tunnel.

Emily saw beads of perspiration dripping down the side of Mac's face and across the nape of his neck. She could feel dampness on her own forehead but did not dare to wipe it away in case movement, any movement, might alert the creature to their presence.

Finally, after what seemed like an eternity, the proboscis retracted back into the creature's body. Emily's muscles tightened as it stepped away from the stream of energy and turned in the team's direction, its iris-less eyes seemed to look directly at her...then it stepped forward and walked first past Mac, then Emily, close enough to her that one of its legs brushed against her right bicep. It continued past the line of soldiers cowering against the wall behind her, its legs making a *click-clack-click* sound as its feet tapped over the glass-like floor of the tunnel.

When the stick creature was safely out of range, Mac turned to face Emily, his eyes still following the creature as it continued, still apparently oblivious or blind to their presence, down the tunnel in the direction the team had come from. "Was that one of them?" Mac whispered, judging the creature was out of earshot. "A Locust?"

Emily thought for a second, her eyes moving across to Petter and his group who waited nervously, eyes as big as plates, their attention fixed entirely on Emily and Mac. "I don't know," she said, eventually. "Maybe. It just seemed so unaware. It doesn't make sense to me that that could be the mastermind behind everything that's happened to the planet, and yet not be able to sense us when we're so close to it. Right? I think it's more likely something the Locusts have made to assist them, like a helper, or a construct."

"A construct?" Mac's forehead creased as he processed what she had said. He stood up, slowly, and everyone else followed his lead. "Whatever it was, we have to assume it might be back or that there could be more of them. And next time we might not be so lucky. We need to put some distance between us and it as quickly as possible." He motioned over to Petter that they were continuing on their way.

Emily got to her feet, her calves tight from her time frozen in place, her mind still processing the implications of their latest close encounter of the what-the-fuck kind. If that creature really was a Locust, then their job had just become a lot easier, but she had learned long ago that rarely in this world was anything the way it appeared. Subject to change, she thought, *This reality is always subject to change.*

"Keep your heads on a swivel, people. Let's move out," said Mac, and the two lines of humans began to move again, deeper into the Locusts' lair.

•••

Mac raised an open hand—*Stop!*

On either side of the tunnel, both lines of the assault team immediately froze. Fifty meters ahead, the walls of the tunnel abruptly widened, expanding outward into what was clearly an entrance to a larger tunnel or room. From her position behind Mac, Emily was not able to see much of anything because the steady incline of the tunnel coupled with the glow of the energy stream obscured her direct line-of-sight into this new area.

The purple wisps of energy that had escaped the main stream, and, until now, floated freely through the air, became more agitated the closer they were to this new area. Each of the larger strings of purple light that had moved randomly through the air took on the same uniform trajectory and movement as their neighbor, as though they were being sucked into whatever lay ahead.

Emily edged closer to Mac. "What do you see?" she whispered.

"Nothing much from here, I'm going to have to get closer to get a better look."

"Let's go," Emily said, and before Mac could say anything to stop her, she stepped around him and began moving stealthily along the wall toward the end of the tunnel. Behind her, she heard Mac give a quiet sigh, and an order for everyone else to stay where they were.

"Hey, slow down," Mac hissed.

Emily turned and saw him right on her tail.

"We really need to have a discussion about this whole 'You won't even notice I'm here' thing," Mac said, as he stepped past Emily, then, in a low crouch moved slowly down the tunnel toward the opening, his automatic rifle raised and ready.

The energy stream began to narrow as it drew closer to the end of the tunnel, the streams of light within it twisting and turning at a much faster rate than Emily had become used to. The stream pulsed and shifted so rapidly now that

170

Mac and Emily's shadows moved in jittery little circles around their bodies as they edged closer and closer to the end of the tunnel. It was actually a little nausea inducing, Emily thought, feeling her senses swim.

Mac started forward again, Emily an arm's length behind him. They both stopped short of where the tunnel widened into the new area. Mac crept closer until he could get a good look at whatever lay beyond.

"What do you see?" Emily whispered, but when Mac said nothing she shuffled forward and peered over his shoulder.

She gasped in amazement.

The tunnel opened into an almost perfectly spherical cavern that had been carved out of the rock. The floor was flat like that of the tunnel, but the walls of the cavern curved upward for at least fifty or maybe even sixty meters. To Emily it felt as though she had suddenly found herself transported inside a giant snow globe, but that was just about where the similarity stopped. Deep grooves, several centimeters wide formed concentric rings along the walls of the cavern. They spiraled upward around the cavern's circumference, all the way to its domed ceiling. The rings were spaced about a meter apart.

Starting roughly ten meters above the floor, large octagonal fissures pitted the walls. They were easily large enough for an adult man to stand upright in, Emily estimated. Each of the fissures was capped by a dome of translucent material that protruded outward like a blister on a piece of bubble wrap. Within each of the fissures Emily saw a darker shape, shadowy and indistinct, moving almost serenely, slowly rotating, suspended in a cloudy fluid that filled the fissure. There were thousands of fissures, Emily guessed, maybe even tens of thousands. It was impossible to accurately estimate just how many there were because the fissures became a blur in the ceiling's shadows the higher she strained to look.

But what had extracted the gasp of amazement from Emily's throat were the sixty or more constructs that moved between each of the fissures. They looked like exact clones of the construct the team had encountered in the tunnel half an hour earlier. The creatures busily moved from fissure to fissure, their proboscises pushing gently into the membranes covering each cleft in the cavern's wall. The constructs used the deep concentric slits running along the walls to secure themselves, adeptly maneuvering across the cavern's surface.

At ground level, perfectly placed at the center of the cavern was a shallow concavity measuring thirty meters across. The walls of the concavity were made up of angled triangular planes that tapered to a point at the concavity's center. At the center was a three-sided jet-black pyramid-like protuberance, the apex of which rose about three meters above ground level.

The energy stream the team had followed to this point snaked across the floor to the center of the cavern. When it reached the concavity it fractured and broke apart, swirling in a maelstrom of twisting threads that shot upward through the pyramid-shaped object toward the cavern's ceiling in a reverse waterfall of light, before spreading outward in an uncountable array of narrow trails that stretched across the curve of the roof, then split again into smaller ribbons of light. Each ribbon terminated at one of the fissures. The whole cavern glowed and flickered in what would have, under different circumstances, been a visual effect that would have rivaled the aurora borealis.

At exact intervals around the circumference of the central concavity were twenty smaller, shallower indentations that made Emily think of inground spas. These indentations, although smaller than the central concavity, were easily as deep as Mac was tall, and three or four times as wide.

Three tunnels extended off from the cavern, with each new tunnel opening placed at ninety-degree increments to where Emily and Mac now crouched.

Mac turned to Emily, "Does this look like the place Adam said we needed to locate?"

Emily nodded vigorously. "No doubt about it," she said. "The energy stream is being channeled directly from the surface into that cavern and then to whatever is in those fissures. This is the place. It has to be.

CHAPTER 16

Mac nodded his agreement. He did another quick scan of the cavern, then whispered to Emily, "Let's get back to the others," his gaze not straying from the mass of alien constructs scurrying over the walls of the cavern.

While Emily edged back toward the rest of the waiting team, Mac reached into his pack, removed a radio repeater unit, then positioned it just inside the cavern. He turned and followed Emily, signaling the two teams to follow him a short distance away from the opening of the cavern.

"Seems like we've found where we need to be," Mac said, then went on to recount what he and Emily had just discovered in the cavern. "The next thing we have to do is get Emily into that room so she can activate the cube."

"So, are these creatures the Locusts or not?" Petter asked.

Mac looked at Emily, conferring wordlessly. When she shook her head, he nodded, confirming her silent assessment. "We don't think so. They look to be exact duplicates of the creature we crossed paths with earlier. I think they're more like...drones or helpers. They seem to be doing a very specific task of tending to whatever is in the fissures in the wall of that cavern."

Emily nodded her agreement. "I think whatever is in those fissures might be the Locusts." She nodded at the energy stream. "The energy stream is being diverted into each of the fissures through a mechanism in the cavern's floor. Adam told me that the Locusts' only interest in this planet was for its energy, so it makes sense that it would be them that the energy is being fed to."

Mac nodded in agreement. "So, where do you need the cube to go?"

Emily thought back to what Adam had told her. He hadn't actually specified where exactly he wanted Emily to place the cube; just that it needed to be as close to the location where the energy was being collected by the Locusts as possible. For all she knew, she could just toss it into the room and that would be that. But doing that ran the risk of the drones tending the fissures spotting it and destroying it or moving it. No, it needed to be hidden, somewhere that it would not be noticed.

Emily unslung her backpack and reached in, lifting out the cube. It spun gently on its axis, floating above the palm of her hand. "The concavity in the center of the cavern is surrounded by these big indentations," Emily said. "If I place it in one of them it should be out of sight enough until Adam does whatever it is he plans on doing with it."

"Is it a bomb?" Petter asked. He stared (along with everyone else) at the rotating cube. "It seems very small if it is."

Emily shook her head. "I don't think it's a bomb. When I was abducted by the Caretakers, they used the cube to immobilize me. I saw them using it to analyze plants and I'm pretty sure they also used it to transport me to their ship."

"So, it's like some kind of alien Swiss Army knife?"

said Mac.

Emily shrugged. "Maybe. I don't know. What I do know is that Adam wants me to get it into that cavern and that's what I intend to do."

"The question now," said Mac, "is how do we get it into the cavern and get out again without those drones spotting us?"

Petter answered, "The one we encountered earlier seemed oblivious to us as long as we stayed near the energy stream. I think it would be safe for me to crawl in with the cube and place it where it needs to be without being detected."

Before Emily could say anything more, a scream—human and full of terror—echoed down the tunnel from the direction of the cavern. Emily quickly scanned the group, no one was missing, which meant only one thing...

"Survivors," Mac said. He started to jog back toward the cavern, Emily and Petter following right behind him.

Mac stopped at the opening and leaned in. "Shit!" he spat.

"What is it? What's going on?" said Emily.

Mac reached back and slowly moved Emily around until she had a view of what Mac saw; two constructs stood with their backs to the tunnel the humans sheltered in, about ten meters away from Emily, Mac, and Petter. Held between the two constructs, struggling vainly to escape the hold they had on each of his arms was a human, a man. His clothes were streaked with dirt, his arms thin, the hair on his head matted and unkempt. He screeched and wailed and struggled but was unable to shake himself free of the stick creatures' grips.

"What the ever loving—" Mac began to say then stopped as his eyes rose halfway up the opposite wall where a flurry of motion had attracted his attention. "Look at that," he said, pointing.

Two of the constructs converged on a fissure. They

extended their foremost set of legs and made four neat slices through the membrane covering, which fell away, fluttering and spinning to the ground. A small gush of liquid spilled from the inside, then a bulk, rust brown and glistening, slid over the lip of the fissure, only to be deftly caught by the middle set of legs of each of the constructs. Globules of liquid dripped from the motionless bulk as the two constructs heaved it completely from the fissure and began to carry it slowly and carefully toward the ground.

The shape the constructs carried between them was twice as large as the two helpers. Emily could make out a somewhat humanoid body with a pair of powerful, muscular legs. It had two sets of arms. The first—long enough to reach down to its knee joints—culminated in powerful-looking hands that sprouted an opposable thumb-like appendage and three long fingers that each split into two smaller whip-like extensions which writhed and shifted like serpents. A second set of arms—shorter than the first but just as muscular—projected from its midsection, each with a more conventional human-like hand and fingers made for gripping...or crushing. A bulbous, bullet-shaped head sat on a short neck. There were jaws, Emily thought, but she could not be sure. And a single eye that must have been the size of Mac's head sat in a protuberance of flesh that allowed the eye to maneuver in whichever direction it desired. It wore what Emily first took to be a suit of armor that extended outward at each joint but she soon realized this was not armor in the conventional sense and was instead a carapace; a natural (if this thing could ever be described as natural) growth that covered the creature's body in plate armor.

Here, then, the veil of time and distance that had hidden them finally removed, was one of the creatures that had brought so much calamity to the Earth. This thing...this Locust...was responsible for the deaths of God knew how many planets and civilizations, stretching back for thousands or even millions of years. And now it had come here, to

Earth, with the same murderous intent; to strip the planet clean of every resource it could. Emily felt a shudder pass down her spine; part fear, part revulsion, but mostly anger. She unconsciously reached out and laid a hand against her husband's shoulder.

The human prisoner had become still and silent when he had seen the Locust birthed into the arms of its helpers. Now, as the three aliens descended rapidly toward the ground he began to struggle again.

"No! No! Please," he begged.

When the helpers reached the floor and began to carry the limp body of the Locust toward him, the man began to scream again.

Petter let loose a string of expletives in his native tongue. "We must do something to help him," he said. He leveled his automatic rifle at the aliens, took a step toward the struggling man.

Mac spun around and grabbed Petter by his forearm, positioning himself between the rifle's barrel and the Locust and its helpers. "No!" he said from between clenched teeth. "We can't afford to give ourselves away. Not until we've placed the cube."

Emily saw a cloud of anger pass over the Norwegian officer's face, and for a moment she thought Mac was going to be forced to physically restrain him. But Petter's anger quickly vanished, replaced by a new look as his eyes grew wide in horror. Emily's attention flipped back to the captive human...in time to see the Locust—its construct escorts still holding it upright—lift its head and gaze coldly at the wretched man presented to it with that single giant eye. Its smaller set of arms twitched once, twice, as though they had received an order to move but were unable to. The third time, however, they reached slowly, inexorably, for the now gibbering man and clutched him by the shoulders.

The human struggled, his voice already ragged from screaming, now barely audible to the three humans watching in horror as the Locust drew him to its chest like a mother would gather a child to her breast. It was difficult for Emily to perceive what happened next, but the quiet gasp of revulsion she heard from both Mac and Petter told her that what she was witnessing was really happening: the Locust was absorbing the man through its carapace. Even from where they hid, they could hear the fizz and hiss, smell the acrid scent of dissolving flesh as the man's skin and blood and bone and cartilage and clothing began to liquefy, then flow into the Locust. The man, or what was now left of him, jerked and convulsed. The two constructs holding the victim finally released him once he was halfway absorbed, the Locust now able to clutch his rapidly dissolving body to itself.

"Dear God," Mac exclaimed. "Dear God Almighty."

As the Locust continued to feed, its posture began to change. The two constructs that had helped it from its birthing fissure and carried it to the ground released it. It wobbled a little on its two giant legs, then steadied itself as the remains of the unlucky man disappeared into its chest, leaving nothing but a small pool of glistening liquid—Blood? Water? Urine? Emily could not tell—where he had met his demise.

The Locust stumbled, and the two constructs on either side of it grasped at it, steadying the creature as though it were an old decrepit man. Together, the two drones began to carry the Locust toward the concavity at the center of the cavern. They guided it to one of the indentations around the main concavity, helping the Locust into the closest one. The Locust extended itself fully and lay still within the space. The two constructs that had brought the human to the Locust turned as one and vanished into one of the three tunnels, the two others returning to the wall and their duties.

Emily's mind raced at what she had just witnessed and the implications of the entire event bounced around her skull.

"We need to get the cube in there and get the hell out of here right now," said Mac. He was reaching for the cube that had rested forgotten in Emily's hands during the horror show that had just played out before them.

"No!" Emily spat, whisking the cube out of reach of Mac's hands. Then more gently, "Don't you understand what we just saw?"

Mac looked at her blankly, but Petter grasped the true importance. "The survivors," he said. "That man *had* to have been abducted from Point Loma. And if there's one, then there must be more."

"Right!" Emily said, "And if we don't follow the two constructs that dragged that guy here then the chances are we'll never find any of them down here. We need to go now, Mac, or we risk them all being turned into snacks for the Locusts."

"Shit!" Mac sighed. He turned and jogged back to the team of soldiers waiting in the tunnel.

"Here," said Emily, releasing the cube to Petter's outstretched hands. "Give us thirty minutes then get that in the cavern, okay?"

Petter nodded.

Mac was on his way back, Bishop and Cleaver jogging alongside him. "Ready?" Mac asked Emily, knowing he did not have to outline for her what they needed to do next.

"Ready," she told him; then to Petter, "Thirty minutes. Don't fuck it up."

Petter nodded and smiled.

Emily, Mac and their two escorts stepped into the cavern.

180

CHAPTER 17

Emily, Mac, and the two soldiers crept into the cavern. Fifty meters of open ground lay between where they were and the mouth of the tunnel the two constructs had disappeared into. Fifty meters of open ground that would leave them totally exposed to the remaining constructs that continued to blindly work at their task of tending the nascent Locusts. But blindly was the operative word within that observation, Emily thought, because if their experience with the construct in the tunnel was not an exception to the rule, then the humans' presence within this Locust birthing cavern should go undetected.

The constructs, for their part seemed completely oblivious to the humans moving slowly around the cavern's edge far below them. Perhaps, Emily surmised, the idea of there being any kind of intruder within their midst was so unimaginable to them that they did not even bother to look.

Perhaps they did not see as humans did. Maybe they sensed the world in a different manner, on different frequencies, frequencies that would make Emily and the men invisible. Or maybe they were just mindless tools of an arrogant species that had never once faced resistance, created to fulfill one job only; to tend and render help and sustenance to their unearthly masters. It was impossible to be sure, and Emily wasn't interested in finding out if her theory was correct or not. With luck, in a matter of hours, this place would be a smoking ruin and the Locusts and all their helpers nothing but a nightmarish memory.

"Just keep moving, don't stop, don't look around, don't make a damn sound," Mac whispered to Emily and his two men. He was on point, leading the four-person team at a crouch along the curve of the chamber wall toward the second tunnel.

Emily allowed her eyes to move around the huge cathedral-like structure that towered above her. The smoothness of the walls came from a layer of material that was about three centimeters deep. It was translucent, and beneath its glassy surface, she saw the normal rough bedrock the cavern had been excavated from. It was as though the three-centimeter outer layer of rock had been melted by some incredible heat source. Green filaments of dim light danced through the glassy layer, like tiny slow-motion lightning bolts. She had to peer closely to see them they were so dim, but the walls were transferring energy of some kind for some purpose unfathomable to Emily's mind. Above her, the Locusts' helpers continued to move back and forth across the vast expanse of the dome's surface. At any moment, Emily expected to feel the cold touch of their spindly fingers close around her face, to be snatched away, dragged off to be delivered to the wet embrace of a newly birthed Locust. Her imagination was hard at work conjuring up the heat of whatever acid had been used to dissolve that poor bastard against her own skin. "Not going to happen," she whispered under her breath, her eyes dropping to look at her feet. She would put a bullet in her brain before she would let that happen to her.

Emily almost screamed when she felt something brush against her shoulder, but stifled her yell when she realized that she had been so intent on keeping her head down and moving forward, she had almost overshot the mouth of the new tunnel, and it was Mac's hand she felt guiding her to him. He pulled her into the cover of the tunnel's mouth. Emily heaved a sigh of relief and puffed in two deep, stuttering breaths to steady her nerves while Bishop and Cleaver caught up with them.

•••

Emily, Mac, Bishop, and Cleaver jogged down the tunnel, surreptitiously chasing after the two constructs. As they approached a sharp-right corner, Mac slowed to a steady walk, motioning for the others to slow too, then raised a finger to his lips. Quiet!

Emily caught the sound her husband had picked up; it was a faint scuffling noise that came from the tunnel ahead of them, around the corner. She cocked her head to listen. There it was again, a tap-tap-tap sound like something sharp hitting glass. Or alien legs against the smooth surface of the tunnel, she thought. The sound was growing fainter, which meant whatever was making it was moving away from their location.

Mac gave a nod and the four humans jogged quickly to the corner. Slowly, Mac edged around the corner, then beckoned the three others to join him.

Emily took a deep breath and set off down the passage in pursuit.

Ahead of them, the tunnel dropped steeply, so steeply, in fact, that Emily and the rest of the team had to lean against the wall to reduce the chance of a misstep that would send them tumbling. The tunnel went on that way for about two hundred meters, descending ever deeper into the planet's crust, curling downward like a corkscrew. The team descended at a slow but steady rate; Mac at the front trying to keep as close to the constructs as he could without catching up to them or alerting the aliens to their presence.

The incline quite suddenly leveled off as the team rounded a final corner, then angled to the right for a short enough distance that the human pursuers could easily see the two constructs already halfway along it, moving rapidly toward a circular doorway set into a wall at the end of this length of tunnel. The doorway reminded Emily of the blisters covering the fissures in the birthing cavern, but this one was much larger and seemed to be made of multiple fins that overlapped each other like the feathers on a bird's wing, fanning inward from the edge of the door until they met at the center. As the constructs approached, the fins slid apart and the two aliens moved through the opening. Emily caught sight of a weird ethereal glow from beyond the space and what sounded like...people. People yelling, some screaming in fear. Then the fins of the doorway closed again and the sound and the light vanished.

•••

The team jogged to the door, hoping against hope that it might simply open when it sensed their presence.

It did not.

The door was about four meters in diameter, which meant it was twice Emily's height with room to spare. The fins met in the center, interlocking tightly. Emily placed her right hand against the outer edge of the doorway and ran it up and down the surface, looking for any kind of an activator or release mechanism, but there was nothing obvious that she could see or feel. Then she ran her hand over the surface of the actual door. The interlocking fins were made of a weird gelatinous material; it felt almost like warm wax to Emily. She pushed hard against a fin and felt it give a little under the pressure. When she pulled her hand away it left an imprint on the material that lasted for a half second before moving back to its original form.

"Think we can push through it?" said Mac.

Cleaver, who was by far the largest of the group, said "Let me try." He reached up and tried to grip the narrow edge of one the fins. There was just enough of the edge exposed that he could hold it with the tips of his fingers. Reaching up with his left hand, Cleaver grabbed another fin, then pulled himself up. His feet scrambled for purchase, the tips of his boots pressing against the lower fins. Mac stepped up and helped support the soldier, while Bishop covered the rear approach.

Cleaver allowed his legs to take most of the weight of his body, while, through gritted teeth, he let go with his left hand, placed his hand against the middle of the door where the fins met, and pushed. There was no give at all.

Cleaver jumped down. "Sorry, boss," he said.

"No worries," said Mac. "Maybe there's another route or a way to—"

Mac's words were interrupted as the door began to open.

Mac and Cleaver dived to the left, pushing themselves into a corner, Emily and Bishop to the right. Emily pressed herself as tightly into the space where the wall of the tunnel met the doorway as she could. If they had been a second later, the two constructs that walked through the opening would have seen them. They dragged another man between them; he kicked and screamed, trying to break free, his head moving frantically from left to right. His eyes widened when he saw Emily and Bishop crouched in the corner.

"Help! Oh Jesus, please, help me," he pleaded, as the constructs dragged him along the corridor.

The door began to close again.

"Move. Now!" Mac hissed, pushing Cleaver through the rapidly closing portal. Bishop jumped through next, Emily diving through the shrinking space right behind him. She hit the ground hard and rolled away, catching a glimpse of Mac as he dove through head first.

Emily lay flat on her stomach, eyes closed, the wind knocked from her. When she opened her eyes again and looked up, she thought that maybe she had stepped through a gateway straight into hell. She lay on the rough floor of a large cave. The walls of the cave were not smooth as glass like the tunnels and the birthing cavern; these were uneven, hewn inelegantly from the bedrock, cold, wet. Red algae grew in spots across the walls, boulders that littered the area, and the ground. Water dripped from high above, rolling down the ragged walls and collecting in a smattering of small pools. Stalactites and stalagmites of calcium thrust upward from the ground and down from the ceiling. A dim glow illuminated the cavern from several seemingly random veins of incandescent material running through deep crevices, providing enough light to see by, but only just.

And it was cold, *really damn cold.*

Bodies lay everywhere; hundreds of them. Some sat slumped with their backs against the cavern walls, their legs stretched out in front of them, others were huddled together in groups. Some were curled up, fetal-like in small nooks created by outcroppings.

Humans! Point Loma survivors.

Emily didn't think they were dead, at least not all of them, because echoing through the chamber was a background noise of quiet sobbing, muttering, and low-volume conversation. Emily searched for Mac. He was a few feet away, in the process of helping Cleaver to his feet. Bishop was standing with his back to Mac, his weapon raised, covering the entrance they had just jumped through.

Surprisingly, none of the survivors seemed to have

noticed the four strangers who had joined them.

Emily got to her feet and moved to where the three men stood.

"You okay?" Mac asked.

Emily nodded. Apart from a few grazes, she was fine.

"What is this place?" Cleaver asked.

"It's a prison," Mac said. "The constructs are holding the Point Loma survivors here."

"More like a pantry," said Bishop.

The man was right, Emily thought. This was where the constructs stored their human snacks for the newly born Locusts. She shivered with revulsion.

A group of six men, their clothes torn and dirty, their skin muddied, were collected around the body of a man lying face down several meters away. The men were trying to undress the dead man. They had already pulled off his boots and were now going through the pockets of the deceased man's jacket.

Mac strode over to them. They remained oblivious to his presence until he stepped in close and placed the barrel of his rifle against the back of the nearest scavenger's head.

"Afternoon, gents," Mac said.

The men all looked up at once and gasped in surprise. They scurried away, their faces telegraphing their shock at seeing Mac. Their looks of surprise doubled when they also spotted Emily and the two other soldiers. Although she wasn't sure, Emily thought she recognized two of the men, but they were so skinny and dirty it was hard to be certain.

"How? How did you get in here?" one of the men asked. His eyes were huge, his voice rough, croaky, dry.

"Now that would be telling," said Mac. He turned and faced the rest of the cavern. "Hey!" he shouted, his voice echoing off the prison's walls, "get your shit together, we're here to take you home."

Slowly, one after another, heads raised from where they had rested on arms or knees, or from where they lay against the cold ground. One by one, those same heads turned in Mac's direction.

"Over here," Emily called out. She pulled her flashlight from her belt, turned it on and waved it above her head. "Come on, come here to us."

People that had looked dead moments earlier began to stand, then, unsteadily, they walked and stumbled toward Emily and her team, shambling like zombies. Some of them were able to make it on their own, others, too weak to walk by themselves, were helped, until finally a large crowd of stinking, dirty humans stood in an arc around Emily and the team; a sea of pale, disbelieving, gaunt faces. Emily tried not to let her revulsion show at the stench that wafted off the mass of dirty bodies so closely packed around her. Her breath caught in her throat when she first tried to speak. She took a moment, her eyes watering as she stared at her feet, then she breathed in two shallow breaths and lifted her head.

"Is there anyone in charge?" she asked.

A tall man Emily thought she recognized pushed his way from the back of the crowd and limped toward her. His clothes were speckled with blood and dirt, his pants had once been khaki but were now almost black with stains and were torn from the right knee down to the cuff. His face sported an unruly beard and his hair was lank and greasy, reaching to just below his ears. When he spoke, his voice sounded desert dry. "I am, I suppose," the man said. Despite its huskiness, it was his French accent that helped Emily's mind connect the dots of who he was.

"Victor?" Emily said, disbelievingly. "Is that you?"

He nodded, and coughed. "Oui. Yes. I must apologize for my state. I did not expect visitors." He gave a weak chuckle at his joke. Victor Séverin had been the captain of the French submarine, *Le Terrible*, and had gone on to become a member of Point Loma's council. Unlike most of the council, Victor had treated Emily with respect. He looked as though he had lost north of fifty pounds from the time she had last seen him.

Emily looked around at the crowd of people who stood silently watching her, fear bright in their eyes.

"What the hell happened?" Mac demanded, asking the question that had been on the tip of Emily's tongue.

Emily guessed there were probably seven hundred faces staring back at the newcomers, far less than the thousand or so that had disappeared from Point Loma. "Where are the Locusts keeping everyone else?" she asked, before Victor could answer Mac's question.

Victor looked at her quizzically for a second, then understanding flitted across his face as he grasped that she was referring to their alien captors. "All dead...or...worse," he muttered.

Emily's mind faltered. Dead? How could they all be dead?

"How?" Mac demanded, asking the question for her.

"The aliens, they came at night, dragged us out of our beds. Anyone who resisted, they killed on the spot, snapped them like they were twigs. The rest of us, they brought here."

"How long have you been down here?" said Mac.

Victor pursed his lips and shook his head. "I have no real idea. If I had to hazard a guess, weeks." He shrugged. "There's no way to know."

Mac's brow furrowed. "How the hell have you survived for that long? I don't see any supplies."

"There's plenty of water," Victor said, "and we ate the red lichen...and..." his voice trailed off, his gaze dropping to his feet. The man's shoulders heaved as he fought back sudden tears. He steadied himself, raised his head and met Emily's gaze only fleetingly before his head dropped again. It was long enough for her to see the shame and disgust written in them.

Oh, Jesus, Emily thought as she realized the implications of his sudden quietness. Had they turned to cannibalism? Had they eaten their dead?

Emily thought for a second, her eyes moving from gaunt, frightened face to gaunt, frightened face. "You said 'or worse.'"

"What?" Victor seemed confused.

"When Mac asked you what happened to the other survivors, you said 'dead or worse.' What do you mean 'or worse?'"

Victor gave an actual shudder of fear. His knees buckled for a second and Bishop reached out to catch him, but the former submarine captain managed to steady himself. "The aliens, they took many of us. Most never returned, but some did. Those that did, had had things done to them."

"What kind of things?" Emily said.

"The aliens changed them, made them into..." Victor's voice dropped to an almost imperceptible level. "...monsters. They made monsters. The aliens use them to guard us, they take them away sometimes, for what reason I don't know, that's why they aren't here now, but they always come back and when they do..."

Victor began to weep. It was one of the most pitiful things Emily had ever seen; pure fear and disgust and self-loathing. How the man wasn't a raving lunatic, Emily had no idea. She reached out a comforting hand and placed it on Victor's shoulder but he flinched, shifting away from her like a beaten dog.

"No, it's okay," Emily said, "It's okay. We're going to get you out of here." She looked around at the people gathered around them. "We're going to get you all out of here and back to safety, do you hear me?"

"Then we've got to leave now, before she comes back," Victor said, his voice riddled with anxiety.

Mac looked at him, quizzically. "Before who gets back?"

Victor's eyes grew even wider with fear. "Valentine," he whispered. "Before Valentine gets back."

•••

Emily wasn't sure if she had heard Victor correctly. She thought he had said Valentine was coming back. Back from where? The very fact that the woman who had tried to have her murdered was still alive should not have surprised her, but it did. That bitch had the survival abilities of a cockroach, but before she could press Victor further on what he meant, Mac fired off another question.

"Apart from the door, is there any other way out of here?"

Victor turned his face toward the roof. "Just those," he said nodding upward. High above their heads, in the unevenly hewn ceiling of this prison, Emily could just make out several large round openings, about the size of a tall man, cut into the ceiling.

"Well ooo-kay," Mac said, quietly. "They're not going to be much help. Anywhere...a little more accessible?"

"No," said Victor.

Mac glanced toward the doorway. "Then it looks like we'll have to take the same way we came in."

Victor shook his head. "The door won't open. We've tried to break it down more times than you can imagine."

"That's not a problem," said Mac, "I have a key."

Now it was Emily's turn to look confused. "What do you mean you have a key?"

Mac smiled that sly grin he kept for occasions when he knew he was able to get one over on her. He reached up and tapped a bulge in his jacket's breast pocket. "C4," he said. "More than enough to blow our way out of here...probably. But we're going to need a plan for when we blast the door open. If the constructs can hear the explosion or sense it, there's no telling how many of them might come our way."

"Why didn't you mention using the C4 when we were trying to get into this place?" said Emily.

"Well I didn't know who or what was behind door number one, now, did I? And then the two constructs were good enough to save me the trouble. Besides, it would have ruined the surprise." He grinned again.

Emily shook her head, then followed Mac and Victor to the door. Mac ran his hand over the fins, pushing into the yielding, almost flesh-like, surface. "Yeah, I'm pretty sure I can take care of this," he said. "The question is, what do we do once we're out of here? We're going to have to get everyone to the surface and into cover as quickly as possible."

Emily pulled her radio from her pocket. "Bravo team, do you copy?" she said into the radio's microphone.

There was silence for a few moments, then a voice, crackly and indistinct; "This is *brshhhsh* team. *Shhhhsh* have not *shhhhsh* the target. Over."

"There's so much rock between us and Petter, and I didn't have time to set up a relay on the way down here," Mac said, explaining the bad connection. "Just keep trying them."

Emily keyed the radio again. "Tell Major Djupvik we'll be on our way back up and to rendezvous with us at the opening of the tunnel we took. Tell him we're extracting civilians and we'll need his help to get them to the surface." It took three more attempts for Emily to convey the entirety of the message, but finally she was sure Petter's group had at least received the gist of what was going to happen.

Mac turned and addressed the disheveled survivors. "Listen up everyone. I'm going to blow this door, so I want all of you to move back behind cover. When the door comes down, I want you all to follow Emily and my men to the surface, but I want you to do it in an orderly fashion. Am I understood? If there are people who cannot walk, I want those of you who are strong enough to carry them, okay? Do not move off in any direction other than the one we direct you, and obey our commands at all times. Do that and we'll get you all out of here. Do you understand?"

The survivors, fearful and dull-eyed, nodded or mumbled that they did.

Mac continued, "Now everyone needs to move back and find some cover. Put your hands over your ears and open your mouths wide, like you're yawning. That'll help you keep your hearing safe from the shock wave. Got it?"

The survivors stared wordlessly.

"Let's get these people behind cover," Mac ordered his men.

Bishop and Cleaver immediately shifted gears, moving among the survivors, ushering them behind any cover they could find. Slowly, the survivors began to file off into the darkness.

When Mac was sure everyone was safely out of range of any debris, he pulled two blocks of C4 explosives from his jacket pocket, weighed them in his hand for a moment, then slipped one of them back into his jacket. He retrieved a blasting cap and detonator from another pocket, pushed the cap and detonator into the explosives and then molded the C4 onto the doorway.

"Okay, my love," he said, turning to Emily, "you ready for some fireworks?"

Emily nodded.

"Better move our bums then," Mac said, then yelled, "Fire in the hole!" as he activated the detonator and they both ran for cover.

CHAPTER 18

The explosion was not as loud as Emily had expected; it was more of a dry crump than the Hollywood kaboom. It was still powerful enough to send a plume of dust high into the air and a shockwave reverberating around the cave. She was about to get to her feet from behind the outcrop of rock she and Mac had used as cover, when a warning yell of "Watch out!" from Bishop made her look in his direction. The man was scrambling away but his head was tilted up toward the ceiling. Emily followed his panicked gaze and saw several stalactites wobbling crazily, they detached and fell like giant spears toward where she and Mac had taken shelter. They both scrambled away as one of the stalactites smashed into the ground right where they had just been crouched. It broke into a million pieces and showered them with tiny bits of rock that stung any exposed skin they hit.

Mac picked himself up then pulled Emily to her feet. "You okay?" he asked.

"I'll live."

Mac motioned for Bishop and Cleaver to come join them. The two sailors jogged over to their position. "Keep the civilians where they are until I tell you otherwise. No one gets through that exit unless I give the all clear."

The two soldiers nodded that they understood.

A light fog of dust hung in the air, and Emily coughed a couple of times as she and Mac made their way to the doorway. The C4 had blown a hole in the door big enough for two people at a time to squeeze through shoulder-to-shoulder; but it would be tight. Wisps of smoke rose from the edges of the shattered material.

Mac stepped through the newly formed hole to make sure no surprises waited for them. "Coast looks clear," he said after a few seconds and stepped back to Emily, "Let's get everyone over here and we can—"

His words were abruptly cut off by a man's frantic warning cry. The words were quickly drowned out by yells of fear. "They're here," another voice shouted. "Run! Run!"

Several men who stood nearby stared up at the ceiling, eyes wide, mouths agape. One pointed at something Emily could not see from the doorway, her view blocked by an outcropping of rock that jutted from the wall above her and Mac. A small group of survivors, their faces contorted with fear, stumbled toward where Bishop and Cleaver waited, arms spread wide to try and stop the rush of men toward the exit. Bishop managed to grab two, Cleaver another, but the rest slipped by, stumbling past Mac and Emily before either could react, then disappearing through the space in the blown door.

"God damn it," Mac said, as he watched the men stumble their way along the tunnel in the direction of the cavern. Then he yelled, "Everyone stay where you are."

"Please, let me go. Please. Don't let them get me, please," the man Cleaver held begged, struggling to free himself from the soldier's grip. The two men Bishop held were both yelling something similar.

Emily stepped away from the door and swung her flashlight up to the ceiling...and the gears of her mind ground to a shuddering halt. Through the holes Victor had pointed out earlier, three creatures Emily was sure had once been human but who now resembled nothing less than nightmares, climbed out onto the cold rock ceiling to join two already staring down at the humans below. It was difficult for Emily to get a clear view of the five creatures that were now scuttling over the rock toward the side walls because each time she pinned one in her flashlight's beam, it would scurry away into the nearest shadow. But the glimpses she did catch were of humans, people. Pale and naked, the five wretches now had extra limbs attached to their backs; hands that held elongated fingers equipped with claws; heads with multiple sets of eyes; bodies that seemed twisted as though they had been cut in half and replaced facing the opposite direction.

A cacophony of screams, yells, and expletives echoed through the cave as the rest of the human captives now recognized the threat scrambling down the wall toward them. As if they were a single entity, the hundreds of survivors who were still capable of walking rushed toward the door. Some lost their footing, fell and were instantly trampled beneath pounding feet, others ran blindly into outcroppings, crumpling to the ground. But the main throng of panicked humans rushed onward. Cleaver and Bishop stood their ground for a second, then dived out of the way before they could be swept up in the onrushing mob and crushed underfoot.

"Look out!" Mac yelled. He grabbed Emily around the waist and lifted her off her feet as the mob surged toward them. He sprinted, then dived to the floor. Mac let out a grunt of pain as he hit the ground, and a second one as Emily toppled onto him. Together, they scrambled hand over hand away from the periphery of the panicked survivors. The door Mac had blown open was wide enough to allow people to step through two-abreast, but only if they did so in an orderly fashion. Orderly was the last word Emily would have used to describe the frenzied stampede of dirty bodies pushing and jostling and fighting to get through the confined space. Fists were thrown. Bones were broken. Bodies were crushed beneath feet. The sudden bottleneck of humans collected around the exit began to spill in Emily's and Mac's direction, as more and more people reached the exit and tried to force their way through the narrow opening.

Emily got to her feet and pushed a panicked man away as he stumbled over Mac's still-prone form. She reached down, grabbed her husband's arm just above his right elbow and dragged him with all her remaining strength another two meters from the crowd. Panting hard, Emily asked, "Are you okay?" Even though she was only a few centimeters away from Mac's ear, her words had to be yelled to be heard over the screams of pain and terror that echoed throughout the cavern.

"Might have broken a rib or two," Mac ground out through clenched teeth. He groaned as he pushed himself to his knees, then allowed Emily to help him to his feet. He leaned against her for a moment as they limped another couple of meters farther away.

"Do you see Bishop and Cleaver?" Mac asked.

Emily scanned the cave looking for the two soldiers. The pressure of the panicked mob against the exit had broken away pieces of the explosion-weakened door, enough now that four or five people were able to get through at a time. Even so, the press of human bodies seemed to only be growing larger as the slower survivors made up the distance. The crowd acted as a plug in the doorway, blocking any chance that Emily and Mac had of getting out into the tunnel beyond.

"There," she said, spotting Cleaver pushing through the sea of bodies in their direction. Bishop was a few steps behind him. Both men held their weapons above their heads as though they were wading through a river. "Over here,"

Emily yelled at the men, waving her hands.

"You okay, boss?" Cleaver asked when he and Bishop reached Mac.

"I'm fine," Mac lied. "What the hell spooked these people so badly?"

Emily moved her light up the walls trying to locate the transformed humans she had seen come out of the holes in the cavern's ceiling. They were nowhere to be seen on the walls or the ceiling, and for a moment Emily thought that maybe they had turned tail and headed back into those same tunnels they had emerged from. Then her light caught the pale, naked flesh of one of them crouched on a nearby outcropping of rock. It was a man, or, she corrected herself, had once been a man. Now it was a mutated horror.

"That did," said Emily, drawing her three companions' attention to the thing spotlighted on the rock. "There are more of them in here somewhere."

The thing on the rock still retained its original human legs, but the man's arms had been replaced with a second pair of legs; these looked slim enough that they could have belonged to a woman. From the man's side extended two gray tentacles, at the end of each was a curved claw, that reminded Emily of the beak of an octopus. The man's head was bald, the skull dimpled with round pits that made his head resemble the surface of a golf ball. His mouth was a slit, the lips removed to reveal a toothless mouth with black gums. His eyes, still perfectly human, watched the panicked throng of bodies struggling to push through the exit. The abomination's head tilted left and right as it tracked the humans rushing past it, then it let out a curiously high trill, almost like a bird call. The four other creatures Emily had seen climbing from the ceiling ran from the darkness in loping bounds to join the first, gathering around the base of the rock. These mutant-humans all closely resembled the one sitting atop the rock, who, judging by the way it used its whistle to direct the others, Emily assumed was the leader of the group. Two of the mutants had multiple sets of eyes spaced across their skull, which, Emily suspected, would give them almost perfect 360-degree vision.

The pack of mutant-humans regarded the panicked mob but did not move to intercept any of them. Then, from somewhere high above, echoing from the mouth of one of the multiple openings in the roof of the cavern, a shrill screech blasted across the space of the cave. As one, the mutant-humans leaped from their perch and ran headlong at the rear ranks of the escaping humans.

•••

The mutant-humans sprang, claws first, into the throng of survivors; jaws snapping, talons slashing at any human unlucky enough to be within their reach. The screams of the injured could be heard even over the yells and curses of the rest of the mob as they tried to force their way through the opening, unaware that the horrors were now amongst them. A new wave of panic moved through the survivors, as those at the rear tried to fight their way deeper into the mass of heaving bodies to escape the attacking mutant-humans. Others simply ran off blindly into the darkness of the cavern. A man reeled away from the crowd, his hands clasped to his throat trying to stem the gushing blood oozing from between his fingers where a claw had cut deep into his flesh. Another man staggered backward then collapsed into a heap on the ground, the right side of his head staved in. More bodies fell as the mutant-humans cut down human after human.

"We've got to do something," Emily yelled, jumping to her feet. She unslung her shotgun and headed toward the mob. A look back over her shoulder confirmed Mac was following a few paces behind her, his pistol clasped firmly in his right hand, Bishop and Cleaver, right behind him.

Shadowy figures ran or hobbled past Emily, their panic blinding them to anything but their own survival, forcing Emily to sidestep them or risk being knocked to the ground and trampled beneath the stampede of people who were now moving away from the entrance. This at least meant the crowd toward the rear was thinning out sufficiently that Emily could see all five of the creatures as they went about their killing spree.

One of the creatures, the one Emily assumed to be the leader, was clamped onto the back of a screaming woman, its talons sunk deep into her back, causing her to stumble forward as the creature rode her to the ground like a lion on an antelope. It used its claws to cut two long gashes down the woman's back, slicing through her dirty clothing. The woman screeched in agony then fell silent. The mutant-human, knowing it had delivered what was undoubtedly a fatal wound, perched on the woman's back while it searched for its next victim, its head rotating around on the stalk of its neck like an owl.

Emily raised her shotgun and took aim. "Get out of my way," she yelled at the people running blindly in front of her. She couldn't fire without risking hitting some of the survivors, still her finger caressed the trigger in anticipation. "Hey, asshole!" she shouted at the monster. "Come and try me."

The mutant's head rotated in Emily's direction, its eyes locking with hers, then the rest of its body swiveled toward her and the thing began to move across the space separating it from Emily, its two sets of legs working like those of a panther, giving it surprising speed.

"Oh shit!" said Emily, staggering backward, the mutant's agility knocking her off balance. She spat another expletive as the creature leaped at her.

Two loud cracks reverberated nearby. People screamed.

Emily ducked, and the monster sailed past on her left, a spray of blood from the two bullets Mac had put into it splattering across her arms. The mutant hit the ground and lay there, one leg twitching spasmodically.

"Come on," said Mac, taking Emily by the elbow. He guided her toward the next creature which was intent on disemboweling a man it had pinned against the rock wall. The man was dead already, Emily was sure, so she stood about five meters away, took aim with the shotgun and fired. The double-ought buckshot turned the monster's head into pulp. Its headless body and the dead man crumpled together into a tangled heap on the floor.

The concussive boom of Emily's shotgun drew the attention of the remaining three mutant-humans. Simultaneously, they dropped their victims and turned their attention to the humans hunting them. They trilled back and forth in some weird language that a human mouth should never have been able to produce, then sprinted at Emily and Mac, knocking people aside like they were bowling pins.

Bishop killed one before it had taken more than two bounding steps toward them. Cleaver managed to hit another with one shot, wounding it sufficiently that one of its four legs was useless. Still, it did not seem bothered by the wound, as though it felt no pain. It dragged its useless limb behind it while its eyes continued to focus on Mac with murderous intent.

Emily aimed her shotgun at the creature.

A man ran in front of her just as she was about to fire. Then another, and another, blocking her shot, separating her from Mac. She glanced at the doorway. In the confusion of the past few minutes, as more people had run back into the cave those that had stayed at the doorway had made it out into the tunnel beyond the blown door, relieving the press of humans on this side of the opening. Seeing this, the survivors who had run back into the cavern were now making a dash for the exit again, dodging in front of Mac and Emily. One survivor made the mistake of getting too close to the creature Cleaver had wounded and paid with his life; it lashed out with its claws, sending the man reeling away into the rock wall, a trail of blood marking his way.

Bishop approached the mutant-human from the right, leveled his automatic rifle at it and sent it back to hell.

Emily spun around trying to locate the fifth and final mutant, but she had lost track of it in the confusion.

"Anyone see it?" Mac yelled, pushing through the crowd to Emily's side.

Cleaver and Bishop both yelled that they did not.

"No sign of it," Emily yelled. Mac reached her position, placed a reassuring hand on her arm, then turned and faced the opposite direction, so they were standing back to back. Cleaver and Bishop took a similar stance. Slowly, they rotated around, eyes scanning the cavern for the final adversary.

A scream from near the exit caught Emily's attention. "There!" she yelled. The last of the mutant-humans had broken out of the mass of bodies again collecting around the exit, cutting down a fleeing man as it rushed toward Emily and Mac. They both fired simultaneously, killing the creature while it was still three meters from them.

A few human stragglers limped toward the breached exit, moving past broken and bloodied bodies littering the ground. Apart from the moans of the injured and dying, the cavern had become eerily quiet. Then, from far above them, the same sibilant voice that Emily was sure had ordered the mutant-humans to begin their murderous rampage sounded again. This time the voice had taken on a different tone; one of anger, maybe even hatred, Emily thought. She looked up into the blackness of the ceiling, tracking the beam of her flashlight as she ran it over the uneven rock from hole to hole.

"Oh, you have got to be shitting me," Emily gasped, her voice rising several octaves in disbelief.

A swarm of the same ugly-ass mutants they had just dispatched streamed from the holes in the ceiling, leaping across the ceiling to the walls and then down toward her and the team. Emily did a quick count; there were at least thirty of them, and they were moving with speed and obvious intent toward Emily and the men. Leading the attack was a creature that dwarfed the others. It was three or four times bigger than the rest. As Emily's light momentarily illuminated it, the huge creature stopped and turned its head toward her, hatred gleaming in its multiple sets of eyes. It let out a weird alien call from lips that had once been ruby-red but were now black and alien.

And even though the body had been so terrifyingly altered, the monster's features were still unmistakably those of Dr. Sylvia Valentine.

CHAPTER 19

"Is that...?" Mac's words froze in his mouth.

"Yes," Emily whispered, already backing away in the direction of the exit, her eyes never straying from the horror that was Valentine, far above their heads. "We need to get out of here, right now." She felt a rush of fear fill her as she stared back into the inhuman face of the woman who had so desperately wanted her dead. To Emily, Valentine's naked torso looked as though it carried the scars of having been badly burned, but as her flashlight lingered on the monstrous creature, she saw that below Valentine's original arms, two extra pairs of arms had been biologically fused to her body. Around the area where the new arms were attached to her torso, where Emily thought Valentine had been burned, the skin was lumpy and bubbled with scar tissue, like rough welds. The rest of her torso was covered in thin, white, spines, like the quills of a feather, each about thirty centimeters long. The spines vibrated making a sound like a rattlesnake's warning as Valentine glared down at the humans.

The fingers on the blotchy-skinned hands at the end of each arm were elongated, the nails on the fingers black and sharpened to a point. On either side of Valentine's spine, just below her shoulder-blades, two gray tentacles waved, undulating over her shoulders like charmed snakes. At the end of both tentacles were hooks similar to the octopus-like beaks of the mutant-humans that milled around her, except Valentine's were articulated, opening wide enough to fit around a human head, then snapping closed with a cracking sound like a sprung mousetrap. Valentine's head looked almost human, at least if you ignored the row of multiple eyes stretching across her forehead and back around her hairless skull like a crown, giving her, Emily was sure, total 360-degree vision. When she opened her mouth to snarl at the humans below her, Emily saw nothing but black gums within.

Where the woman's hips should have been was only a tightly-wound coil of flesh that connected Valentine's torso to a larger ant-like abdomen with six legs... no, Emily corrected herself as she moved her flashlight over Valentine's transfigured body, they were more arms, muscular arms. The arms were bent backward against their natural articulation. The hands on each looked normal until Emily realized the fingers were twice as long as they should be, with a thick patch of skin between each of them, like webbing, and each finger ended in a slightly curved claw that allowed her to securely grasp the uneven rock of the cave.

She is an abomination, Emily thought. It was almost as though the Locusts had somehow been able to reach inside this woman's soul and use the darkness they found there as a template to create this version of her, giving form to the ugliness within. Emily had no idea whether there was any remnant of the woman she had once been left within this monster, anything that might be appealed to or pleaded with.

But then, she told herself, there had been very little humanity there to begin with.

Emily needed to reload. She had been using double-ought buckshot in her shotgun, which was good enough to take down the mutant-humans, but she wasn't sure it was going to be very effective against the thing Valentine had become. She reached into her pocket and started loading heavy-duty slug rounds. They were basically the equivalent of very large caliber bullets and packed the kind of punch she suspected she was going to need against Valentine.

"Out, *now*," Mac yelled. He tugged Emily toward the exit. They slipped through the hole he had blasted open, closely followed by Cleaver and Bishop, keeping their weapons pointed back through the opening into the cavern as they backtracked down the tunnel. In the tunnel ahead of the team, two men struggled to keep moving forward, each holding the other up as they hobbled slowly along together. They were moving so sluggishly that there was no way they were going to be able to outrun the mutant-humans who were surely just seconds from flooding into the tunnel, Emily judged. The men's emaciated bodies were so weak they were almost dragging each other along the smooth surface of the tunnel. That meant either she and Mac were going to have to abandon them to certain death or help them and risk being caught in the rush of creatures she knew was just moments away.

"Look out!" Cleaver yelled.

Emily turned back toward the cavern in time to see the first of the new wave of mutants drop into the remains of the doorway, eyes flashing its murderous intent, teeth bared. Then it went reeling away as Cleaver shot it between its two sets of eyes. When Emily turned back to the check the two survivors, they had redoubled their efforts, but they still weren't moving anywhere near fast enough to stand a chance of eluding their pursuers.

"Come with me," Mac said to Cleaver and Bishop.

206

Together they sprinted to catch up with the two men, Mac pressing his free hand against his ribcage, wincing in pain from his damaged ribs. As they approached, the two injured survivors turned and stared at the three hulking soldiers with terrified eyes. Emily could see that they weren't sure whether they were going to kill them or leave them for the mutants; either way their terror was heartbreaking.

"One apiece," Mac ordered. Cleaver and Bishop nodded, slung their rifles over their shoulders, then picked the survivors up in a fireman's lift across their backs as though the emaciated men were children.

"Emily and I will cover you. Get them back to the main team," Mac said.

Emily nodded. "Just follow the corridor up, we'll catch up with you in the cavern," she said quickly.

Cleaver and Bishop took off at a jog, the survivors hanging on for dear life, while Emily and Mac turned back toward the doorway to the cave, just in time for the horrifying visage of another mutant-human to appear. It sprang to the ground on the other side of the doorway, landing on its multiple legs, its eyes quickly focusing on Emily and Mac, then it rushed forward at a sprint, spittle flying from its mouth as it roared and bellowed.

Emily raised the shotgun, lined up the sights, and pulled the trigger. The charging mutant was all but split in two as the shotgun slug ripped through its body. The bloody remains rolled off to the side of the tunnel, limbs twitching in its death throes. Another mutant appeared at the entrance, then another next to it. Mac put a round between the eyes of one, dropping it where it stood. Emily pumped and fired, killing the second before it could even take a step into the corridor; it fell next to the one Mac had killed. She pumped another round and shot the next mutant just as it crossed the doorway's threshold. It fell, partially blocking the entrance. Four more mutated heads appeared around the edge of the doorway, then, snarling and spitting, the creatures simultaneously launched themselves toward the humans like a pack of rabid dogs...and jammed in the doorway. Limbs flailed as they tried to force their way through the gap, but they were too large and too eager to get to the humans, their thrashing only succeeding in wedging themselves deeper into the space, effectively blocking it. At least for now, Emily thought. If luck was on their side, it would hold the mutants and the thing that had once been Valentine back long enough for her and Mac to reach the survivors and get them out of this godforsaken place.

Emily felt Mac's hand on her arm. "Time to beat our feet," her husband said.

Emily waited a few more seconds, just to be sure, while she reloaded her shotgun with her dwindling supply of shells, then she turned and sprinted away with Mac.

•••

Perspiration peppered Emily's forehead. Rivulets ran down her face as she and Mac sprinted along tunnel after tunnel back toward the cavern. They rounded a corner and saw Bishop, Cleaver, and the two survivors they had rescued about forty meters ahead of them. Both Cleaver and Bishop had dropped the men. Ahead of Mac's men was the rear line of the survivors they had freed from the cave.

"Boss," said Cleaver, seeing Mac and Emily approach "Major Djupvik is at the front of this lot. He's having a hell of a time keeping everyone in the tunnel."

Emily, breathless and sweat-soaked, ran her eyes over the crowd. Their panic had subsided significantly, now they milled around uneasily, their eyes wide with shock rather than the blind terror she had seen earlier.

"Are...are you going to get us out?" a woman asked.

Emily smiled at her, squeezed the woman's hand. "You bet we are."

"Hand me your radio," said Mac. Cleaver did as he

was ordered.

Mac keyed the microphone. "Petter, do you copy?"

The major's voice crackled a reply. "I'm happy to hear your voice, Mac. We need to get out of here quickly, before this crowd overwhelms my people. Do you have a—" Djupvik's words were cut short as the sound of gunshots exploded through the radio. The ghostly echo of the gunfire rolled down the tunnel to Emily's position a second later.

"Shit," Mac mumbled.

"Mac! Mac!" Petter's voice, loud now as he tried to talk over the sound of gunfire exploding around him. "We're under attack. We have to move, now."

"We're on our way," was Mac's reply. He turned to Cleaver and Bishop. "Stay here and cover the rear," he ordered, then took Emily by the hand and began pushing his way through the crowd toward the cavern.

•••

The sound of gunfire grew louder as Mac elbowed and kicked his way through the crowd, Emily following in his wake. The survivors—*more like refugees now*, Emily thought—had stopped just short of the opening out into the cavern, those at the front trying desperately not to get pushed out into the open space of the cavern.

The sound of gunfire faded away.

"Make a space! Move!" Mac demanded, as he and Emily finally reached the front row of the survivors. "Let us through." Mac came to a standstill, the exit just a couple meters ahead of them. Emily stopped alongside him.

Six of Petter's Jegertroppen troops had formed a cordon across the mouth of the tunnel. The women held their rifles in both hands, using them to push back the crowd, keeping them within the tunnel, but only just. Petter stood near the entrance, covering his comrade's backs from anything that might come their way from the cavern.

"Oh, no," said Emily, looking past Petter into the vast cavern beyond. She estimated there were fifty or so bodies scattered across the glass-smooth floor, bloody and broken and still. The bodies of five constructs lay mixed with the human dead, the smoke still rising from the barrel of Petter's assault rifle proof of who had helped put them down.

"Petter," said Mac. "What the hell happened?"

Petter turned and looked at Mac, his brow was creased with concentration, or worry, Emily couldn't tell. "I did as Emily told me when you did not return in time. I went to place the cube where Emily said I should, in the depression near where the first Locust was. The constructs ignored me as they have always done, but then people began to run from the tunnel. When they saw me, they ran toward me. I think it triggered a reaction in the constructs when they sensed so many people getting near the Locust, because they attacked without warning, dropping from the ceiling and killing everybody. My people were pulling me clear when the rest of the survivors showed up and we've been keeping them here ever since."

"The cube," Emily said, unable to keep the panic from her voice. "Tell me you still have the cube."

"Of course," said Petter. "Here." He pulled the cube from his backpack and handed it to Emily.

Emily sighed with relief, slipping the cube into her backpack.

"We need to get these people up to the surface right now," said Mac.

From somewhere in the cavern, a man had begun screaming. Emily quickly homed in on where he lay, close to the center of the room, near the concavity that contained the recently birthed Locust. The man was dragging himself back toward the tunnel opening where Emily and the rest of the human race now hid within the relative safety of the tunnel. The man's left leg was destroyed, twisted at an unnatural angle just below the knee, and flopping uselessly behind him.

He left a trail of blood behind him as he pulled himself hand-over-hand toward them, his face imploring Emily, anyone, for help.

A shape skittered down the opposite wall, then quickly crossed the floor toward the man.

Emily started to move forward, instinctively wanting to help, then stopped herself because she knew it was already too late for him. The construct grabbed the man with its front legs and snapped him in half as though he were merely a twig. His cry of terror died instantly. The alien dropped the limp body and began to turn away...then stopped, its head tilting left and right as it regarded the large group of humans cowering in the tunnel.

"Ah, shit," said Mac.

The alien gave a high-pitched ululation of its own and bounded across the open space toward the humans.

All hell broke loose.

Mac raised his rifle and poured a stream of bullets into the construct, severing one of its legs. The construct crashed into the floor, spun and skidded to a stop, fluid leaking from multiple bullet wounds along its flank.

Emily and Mac stepped into the cavern, their weapons sweeping the floor and walls looking for any other targets that might be heading their way.

"I've got to get the cube to the concavity," said Emily.

"I'll escort you," said Mac.

"No," Emily countered. "You need to get these people out of here."

Gunfire erupted from the direction of the main tunnel. The rest of the assault team had emerged from the opening, their weapons pointed upward at the aliens that now swarmed toward the ground.

Petter called out to the line of Jegertroppen holding back the survivors. "Malin. Silje." Two of the female soldiers broke away and ran to where Petter stood with Emily and Mac. "I need you to escort Emily to the center of the cavern."

The two Jegertroppen nodded and took up positions on either side of Emily.

Mac looked torn, but before he could say anything, Emily turned and began to sprint for the center of the room, her two escorts running alongside her.

"Everybody, move!" Mac yelled.

Emily glanced momentarily back over her shoulder. She saw her husband ushering the front row of survivors out of the tunnel. "This way. Move! Move!" Mac was directing the survivors along the side of the wall in the direction of the main tunnel that would take them back up to the surface. Pushed forward by the people behind them, the front row began shuffling out of the tunnel, then in the direction Mac indicated, toward the rest of the assault team. "Faster!" Emily heard Mac yell as she turned her eyes front again.

Automatic-weapon fire rattled around the cavern. There were screams, human and alien. Bullets zinged as they ricocheted off the wall. Emily's heart pounded in her chest. She focused squarely on the concavity. When they had first arrived at this cavern, she had witnessed the horror of the newly born Locust feasting on an unfortunate soul. The Locust had been led back to the ring of depressions encircling the central concavity. It had been the only occupant at that point, but now, as she and her two escorts drew closer to the concavity, Emily saw two more Locusts had joined the first.

There was a scream from Emily's left. She turned in time to see one of her Jegertroppen escorts—Malin, she thought the woman's name was—skewered by a construct. Emily stopped and began to raise her shotgun, but the alien bounded away, carrying the unfortunate Norwegian soldier with it.

"Fuck!" Emily spat. She looked to her remaining escort, Silje. The woman's expression was one of pure shock. "Come on," Emily said, as she grabbed the Norwegian soldier by the material of her tunic and pulled her away.

"There's nothing we can do for her."

Emily took off sprinting, trying to cover the remaining twenty meters to the center of the room and the concavity. A construct dropped to the ground ahead of her, but it disappeared in a haze of blood a millisecond later as rounds from Silje's assault rifle shredded it.

Breathless, Emily reached the depressions that surrounded the central concavity like petals around a flower's pistil. She slowed, staring at the huge bulks that occupied three of the depressions. They were far larger than she had thought, their leather-like skin glistening with a sheen of liquid. Each of the Locusts' single eyes were closed. They did not breathe, did not show any signs of being alive as Emily would have defined it, and yet, she felt a dread that was almost paralyzing as she moved among them, inching her way across the half-meter of space separating each of the depressions. She motioned to Silje that she should wait where she was, just on the perimeter of the depressions. The Norwegian fighter took a knee, her eyes moving left and right as she scanned for threats. Emily had to hand it to the Norwegian, her attention barely drifted from her overwatch to the three Locusts lying just a matter of meters away from her.

This close to the concavity and the powerful shaft of energy it directed up to the ceiling of the cavern, Emily felt the heat of the energy stream. Not for the first time she wondered whether there would be any kind of detrimental effect of being so close to such raw power. She pushed the thought from her mind, shrugged off her backpack, loosened the flap, and pulled out the Caretaker cube.

The concavity was deeper than it had seemed from a distance, dropping down around two meters below the level of the surface. If she lost her footing and slipped in there, it would be next to impossible to get out on her own. She got down on her knees, then to her stomach and began inching forward, the cube held out in front of her like some offering to an ancient god. She felt a throbbing pulse run through the ground. It grew stronger the closer she got to the cavern's center. When she reached the lip of the concavity, Emily stole a glance back in the direction of Mac and Petter.

A steady stream of humans ran or jogged or were carried from the tunnel along the wall toward the second team and freedom. Mac was positioned at the midway point between the two tunnel mouths, urging people to move faster. Emily returned her attention back to the concavity, she took a deep breath and allowed the cube to slip from her fingers. It dropped slowly into the concavity, following the curve of the floor, then steadily began to move in a counterclockwise motion like a leaf caught in a storm drain. Gradually, the cube began to descend toward the center of the concavity and the energy beam. She watched, mesmerized, as the cube began picking up speed the closer it got to the beam. Closer. Closer. Then it vanished, sucked into the energy beam.

There was no flash.

There was no explosion.

There was, however, a subtle change in the vibration she felt running through the ground beneath her. A stuttering. It was a change that Emily was sure she felt only because she was lying flat on the ground and felt its passage emanate out from the concavity. The energy beam changed from swirling reds and purples to a deep luminescent green. The color began to spread up the column and out across the ceiling into the fissures containing the growing Locusts. Whatever was happening, it did not appear to have any effect on the energy feeding into the concavity, only the column running to the ceiling.

The ground again trembled beneath her. Emily pushed herself to her feet and began to move back in the direction she had come.

Something was different, she thought, as she made her way back over the narrow bridge of ground that separated two of the three sleeping Locusts. It was only when another, more violent tremor made her pause to keep her balance that she realized the Locusts' eyes were open. And they were staring right at her.

•••

"Run!" Emily yelled at Silje as she sprinted past.

The Jegertroppen must have read the barely restrained panic in Emily's eyes because she did not question the command, easily keeping up with Emily despite being kitted out in full battle-rattle. Every few meters, Emily stole a look back at the recumbent Locusts, expecting to see them rise from their recesses and pursue her, but the aliens had not moved. Perhaps, she reasoned, the eye opening had been a mere reflex, and meant nothing. Better not wait around and find out.

The battle still raged across the cavern. The bodies of fallen constructs littered the ground, no match for the concentrated fire power Mac and his team were able to bring to bear. There were still casualties amongst the humans, though. Across the cavern, a group of five Jegertroppen guided survivors along the wall to the main tunnel. A construct dropped from the ceiling to the floor. It dove at the last soldier who had made the mistake of focusing forward instead of covering her team's six. Emily yelled a warning, but it was of no use, she could barely even hear her own words over the commotion around her. She saw the look of surprise on the Norwegian soldier's face as she was suddenly yanked from her feet, impaled by a construct's front leg, then smashed against the next soldier in line, crushing both to a pulp. The construct released the tangled, bloody bodies and moved toward the line of survivors who cowered and screamed as it approached. The next soldier in line must have sensed something because she turned, then ducked, barely avoiding being stabbed herself. She managed to get two shots into the construct's head, killing it. She took a moment to check her two fallen comrades but must have seen that they were beyond help as she immediately turned back around and ran to catch up with the remaining members of her team.

Emily, breathless and soaked in sweat, came to a stop next to Mac. "It's done," she said.

Mac took his exhausted wife by both shoulders, steadying her. "Here," he said, taking his canteen from his belt and placing it in Emily's hands. "Drink."

Emily drank deeply, then spilled some of the water over her head. "Better," she said.

"How long do we have before Adam does..." Mac let his words drop away because he was well aware that neither he nor Emily had any idea of just what exactly it was they should expect from their son.

"I don't know," said Emily, as she handed Mac his canteen back. "I think we need to just get everyone out of here as fast as we can."

Mac nodded.

"How can I help?" Emily asked.

"If you're up for it, help guide the rest of the survivors to the main tunnel."

"Will do," said Emily, squeezing her husband's hand. She moved off along the wall, her eyes roving constantly over the walls, floor, ceiling, looking for any threat, unable to shake a sense that something momentous had been set in motion, and that time was growing shorter with every passing second.

•••

"Keep moving. That's it." Emily urged the line of frightened humans snaking along the edge of the wall to pick up their pace. She ushered the survivors to where Petter and a handful of his and Mac's soldiers defended the mouth of the main tunnel, the only exit they were aware of back to the surface. Constructs hit the ground all around, then began to squeal and fall as they were cut down. Emily blasted one from the wall just above the fleeing humans, screaming a warning as the body fell to the ground, narrowly missing a man who was just fast enough to dodge away.

The cavern was filled with thunder, adding to the confusion and chaos. Humans screamed in fear and panic, some ran blindly in the opposite direction of where they needed to go, and Emily found herself grabbing the fleeing humans by whatever appendage or piece of clothing she could lay her hand on, shoving them back toward the main stream of survivors and the exit.

The remaining constructs screeched and ululated, calling to each other in that strange trilling language. The constant bam, bam, bam of automatic weapon fire and the thud of Emily's shotgun against her unprotected ears would surely leave those who made it out of this madness alive with permanent hearing damage. But the constructs were dropping like proverbial flies, and that was what mattered. She fired at a construct that was already missing two of its legs, limping across the floor toward the line of escaping humans, dropping it mid-stride as it tried to climb over the body of another of its kin. The ground was littered with alien bodies, and for a moment, Emily thought how terrible what she was doing was: the systematic destruction of these creatures. But then she remembered the survivors huddled in that cave, desperate and deprived. Terrified. How the constructs, cold and emotionless, had ignored their victims' pleas for mercy. And she remembered the world that had existed before this one, a world that despite all its faults had been beautiful. And she mourned for the world that could have been, if the Caretakers' true purpose had been fulfilled, a purpose that would have helped turn the Earth into a paradise, instead of this blood-red planet. A planet corrupted by the Locusts to assuage the constant unquenchable greed of these creatures that took *everything* for themselves and left *nothing*. Emily felt the cold bitterness at the very center of her being. She pulled more shells from her pocket and pushed them into the shotgun, then one after the other she took aim at the constructs and fired until her weapon was empty again. She reached into her pocket and found only four shells remaining, loaded them, then forced herself to mentally step away from the murderous rage that had gripped her. There was still the .45 strapped to her waist, she reminded herself, but that was a far less effective way to dispatch these creatures than the shotgun. She slung the shotgun and pulled out the pistol.

"Move faster," she yelled at the line of humans, urging them onward.

The echo of gunfire gradually began to die away. Minutes later, it ceased entirely.

Emily took a moment to scan the huge dome of the cavern, assessing the situation. There were no more constructs alive up there. All their bodies lay broken and shattered across the expanse of the cavern. If there were other caverns like this and more of the constructs made their way here, it would be impossible to defend against them given the potential numbers, so time, now more than ever, was of the essence. They had to get out. She had done as Adam had instructed her, delivering the cube to the heart of the energy stream, now they needed to get well clear of this place so Adam could do whatever it was he had planned. What that was exactly was still a mystery to her, but Adam had assured her that it would be effective in eradicating this scourge from the universe, once and for all. Whatever it was he had planned, she didn't want to stick around and see it in action. They needed to get as far away as possible in whatever time remained. She saw Mac about twenty meters back from where she stood, guiding the line of people in her direction.

He caught her eye and yelled, "We're getting close to the last of them."

Emily gave Mac a thumbs up and a quick smile, then turned her attention back to the people streaming past her.

"This is all that's left," said Mac a few minutes later, jogging to join Emily. He pointed back over his shoulder as the tail-end of the line of survivors emerged from the tunnel. Bishop and Cleaver stood at the tunnel's exit covering their retreat.

Emily stepped forward and caught an exhausted man as he stumbled over his own feet, his eyes focused on some distant point, moving by instinct rather than purpose. She eased him back into the line and watched him move away, ready to catch him again if he stumbled. There were maybe thirty or so people left between where she stood and where Bishop and Cleaver watched over the last few stragglers.

"Time to leave," Mac said, touching Emily lightly on an elbow.

Emily nodded, and began walking alongside Mac toward the main tunnel. She had taken just a few steps when, from behind her, she heard a yell of warning quickly followed by a scream of pain. She and Mac swung around in time to see Cleaver fly into the air, then drop again head first, his arms windmilling before hitting the ground with a sickening, wet crunch. Cleaver did not move.

Bishop stepped away from the mouth of the tunnel, his rifle raised and aimed back into it. He began firing on full auto, the empty shell cases raining onto the ground around him. Whatever Bishop was aiming at was coming down the tunnel. Emily looked at Mac, and her stomach lurched at the sickening realization at what they both knew was heading their way.

"Get them out of here," Mac yelled at Petter, who was busy trying to herd the last of the survivors toward the tunnel that would take them to the surface. Mac turned back to Bishop and yelled at him to join them.

Bishop ejected the magazine from his weapon and was in the process of reloading it when two shapes bolted from the tunnel's mouth, hitting the man simultaneously, bowling him over and knocking his rifle away. They were on him again in a second. He screamed as the two mutant-humans began tearing and biting at him. Mac raised his rifle and shot one, giving Bishop the chance he needed to pull his sidearm and empty his magazine into the remaining mutant before it could do any more damage to him. Bishop fumbled a fresh magazine from his tunic's pocket, slipped it into his pistol and slammed it home. He turned and began to limp toward the exit where Emily, Mac, and the rest of the team waited, covering his retreat.

Emily gasped.

A shape, huge and terrifying, rose behind Bishop, towering over the man. The soldier barely had time to react before the arms of the Locust enveloped him and pulled him close. Smoke rose from the man's body as he disintegrated before Emily's eyes, dissolving into the Locust's chest, his screams shattering the silence that had fallen over the chamber like a shroud. Then Bishop was gone, nothing but a wisp of acrid smoke and a pool of liquid as evidence he had ever existed at all. The second, then the third Locust pulled themselves erect from around the concavity and joined the first. A deafening howl, deep and throbbing emanated from all three creatures, a thunder that echoed around the cathedral-like cavern.

"Holy shit," Mac hissed. He raised his weapon to shoot, then lowered it again as, from the mouth of the tunnel, a wave of mutant-humans and constructs crashed into the chamber.

•••

Emily and Mac ran for their lives.

A barrage of gunfire buzzed over their heads as they sprinted toward the tunnel and their comrades. Emily dared not look behind her, but the urgency in Petter's voice as he yelled that they should "Run! *Run!*" and the fear on his team's faces told her both she and Mac were only marginally ahead of their pursuers.

Petter's group parted as they approached; Mac and Emily bolted through the gap. Mac immediately turned and began firing. Emily slid to a stop, pulled her pistol, and started shooting too.

The constant *rat-tat-tat* and *boom* of gunfire, mixing with the snarls and screeches of the mutant-humans and the high-pitched trilling shrieks of the constructs, created a symphony that only the Devil himself could have found pleasure in. But above this cacophony of chaos, the deep throbbing ululation of the three awoken Locusts dominated. Whether the Locusts were communicating with each other or commanding the swarm of constructs and former-humans was beyond Emily's understanding, but the overall effect it had on her was not; it was bloodcurdling.

"Fuck! There are hundreds of them," Emily yelled, hearing the panic in her own voice.

Petter shouted back, "We've got to hold them off long enough for the survivors to get to the surface."

Emily grabbed Mac's forearm. "If we pull them into the tunnel we'll at least be able to slow them down," she said. While the tunnel was huge in size, it would funnel the aliens into a more manageable area. Hopefully.

Mac must have thought so too, because he ordered, "Back into the tunnel, everyone," yelling to be heard over the thud of gunfire.

"Getting low on ammo," a Jegertroppen yelled.

"Then pick your targets; single shot where you can. Now, move." Mac grabbed Emily by the shoulder and pulled her away from the mouth of the tunnel. They sprinted about twenty meters farther in. Ahead of them, the tail-end of the rescued Point Loma survivors was disappearing around the first corner. Petter and his group joined Emily and Mac, then as one they turned back in the direction of the cavern and trained their weapons on the tunnel's entrance.

The first construct skidded into view and was

instantly cut down. Another, and another followed behind it, all were quickly dispatched until there was a pile of twitching bodies eight deep lying on the smooth floor of the tunnel, creating a natural barrier that the other aliens had to scramble over.

As if to prove Emily's earlier theory wrong, a group of mutant-humans darted into the tunnel, then leaped onto the walls, the claws that had replaced hands and feet sending chunks of the tunnel's glass coating spraying away as they found imperfect purchase.

"Fuck!" someone yelled as two of the mutants managed to evade the gunfire that cut down the rest of their group. One scuttled along the wall, the other over the ceiling, zig-zagging to avoid the team's bullets.

Emily expected the creatures to launch themselves at the line of defenders as soon as they were in range, instead they kept running, then leaped to the ground several meters behind the group. As one, the entire group turned to track the mutants, opening fire at the two mutants that, rather than attack, seemed more intent on dodging the bullets. One lasted for all of five seconds. The second was more skillful than its deceased brother, leaping left and right in mighty bounds that took it from one side of the tunnel to the other.

"What the fu—" Emily's words froze in her mouth as she realized they had been duped. It had been too easy to think of these creatures as dumb thralls of the constructs or the Locusts. They had forgotten that there was a terrible intelligence behind their actions. She had almost managed to turn back to face in the direction of the cavern when the Jegertroppen beside her was yanked from her feet.

The soldier—her name was Marit according to the badge sewn onto her tunic—began to scream as the Locust that had maneuvered itself into the tunnel pulled her to its chest and began to absorb her.

"Nei!" another Jegertroppen yelled and ran at the alien to help her comrade.

The Locust grabbed the woman around the neck with its second pair of arms with enough force it almost severed her head from her body. It pulled the dead soldier to its chest and began to absorb her body too. It had taken less than seven seconds for all this horror to unfold and in that time, Emily had been rooted to the spot as the Locust loomed over her. Not a shot fired. She leveled her pistol at the Locust's head and pulled the trigger.

Click! Her pistol was empty.

The Locust, finished with the second soldier, returned its attention to the remaining humans. To Emily in particular.

"Mac!" Emily screamed, diving to the floor as the creature's hands clawed through the air she had just occupied.

Mac turned, yelled an expletive and ran the few meters to where Emily lay sprawled on the floor, sliding to his knees, his weapon trained on the underbelly of the Locust that towered over them. The alien was so large it was almost impossible for the thing to do anything other than move backward or forward. That was enough of an advantage for Mac. He put twenty rounds into the alien, gouging pieces of flesh from its body. The Locust staggered backward, orange liquid dripping from the bullet wounds. Emily tried to scramble out of range, but the smooth surface of the floor slowed her, her feet slipping on the blood and liquid that covered the floor. Mac grabbed Emily by the shoulder of her jacket and jumped to his feet. He pulled her with him as he backpedaled to where the rest of the defenders brought their own weapons to bear on the Locust, the mutant-human that had distracted them so easily finally dead.

Shot after shot rang out, riddling the Locust. It screeched and screamed in defiance, its single eye flitting from one human to the next, as if it was memorizing their faces, taking mental notes for revenge it would exact later, or in its next life.

Emily climbed to her feet. She pulled a fresh magazine from her jacket, trying to ignore how empty that pocket now felt, slammed it into her .45 and started firing at the alien's head. The Locust continued to stagger back, then sank to its knees. One of Emily's rounds struck its eye, exploding it and spilling liquid over its chest and the ground. The Locust gave a final screech of pain or defiance, it was impossible to tell, then it collapsed and was still, its crumpled body creating a natural barrier across the tunnel floor.

Emily continued to fire until her pistol again clicked on an empty chamber. She reached into her pockets searching for another magazine but came up empty. "I'm out," she yelled at Mac, swinging the shotgun from her shoulder. She only had the four rounds left in it and for the first time in a very long while, she was truly afraid.

"I'm down to my last magazine," yelled Petter.

"Me too," said Silje, the Jegertroppen who had escorted Emily earlier.

Mac dropped the magazine from his assault-rifle and checked it. "Ten rounds. Shit! We're going to have to make a run for it," he said, firing another round that tore into a mutant-human that had once been a woman as it tried to clamber over the body of the downed Locust.

Emily grabbed Mac's arm. "Do you have any more of that C4?"

Mac's hand went to his breast-pocket and pulled out another slab of the explosive.

"Blow the tunnel," said Emily, an urgency in her voice.

Mac looked torn. "If I set this off down here it might take the whole damn tunnel down all the way to the surface. It could kill everyone."

"If you don't do something, we're all dead anyway," Emily said as two more constructs climbed over the dead Locust's body. She raised her shotgun but both of them disappeared as the two soldiers to her left fired. Another appeared and Mac shot it down.

"God damn it," Mac said through gritted teeth. "Okay,

but you all need to get the hell out of here while I set the explosives. That's the only way I'm going to do this."

Emily looked at him. "I'm not going to—"

"I'm not going to bloody argue with you, Emily. Run now, or we all die here. Your choice."

"I am *not* leaving without you," Emily said, matter-of-factly.

"Look!" said Petter. He pointed past the body of the dead Locust to the mouth of the tunnel where the shape of a second Locust had appeared. Its single eye seemed focused on its fallen comrade. It stepped up to the body and took hold of it with all four hands and began to drag it away.

Emily was sure this second Locust was simply removing the obstruction the dead Locust presented, but instead, it continued to drag the body closer the center of the tunnel. The Locust lifted the bullet-riddled body into the stream of energy and almost instantly the dead alien's wounds began to heal.

It was then that Emily remembered what Adam had told her: that the Locusts were comprised entirely of energy. That they moved from constructed body to constructed body. It made absolute sense now: these things could not die, not in a normal, human way at least. The body would probably have to be completely consumed before whatever connection that existed between it and the—*well*, she thought, *might as well call it by what it was*—the spirit of the Locust, could be considered severed.

"You have got to be shitting me," Mac said as the top set of arms on the 'dead' Locust began to twitch. He leaned in close to Emily and kissed his wife on the lips. "Sorry, love," he said, then turned his attention to the two soldiers standing slack-jawed and exhausted beside him. "West. Mooney. Get Emily to the surface."

West and Mooney looked at Mac for a second, then at Emily.

"Well, snap to it. That's an order," Mac growled.

"Petter, you and your people get out of here, too."

West and Mooney each grabbed Emily by an arm and began to pull her up the tunnel in the direction of the surface.

"No!" Emily screamed, struggling to free herself of the men's grip, but they were too strong for her.

Petter hesitated, then nodded, and he and the two remaining Jegertroppen began to run after Emily and her two kidnappers.

"No!" Emily screamed again. She tried to dig her feet in and slow them down, but the glass-smooth surface was just too slippery.

The last she saw of Mac he was placing the C4 explosive on the wall, then she was dragged around the corner and all sight of her husband was lost.

CHAPTER 20

"Let go of me, or I swear to God..." Emily screamed at the two soldiers for what could have been the hundredth time. Grim-faced, they ignored her threats and continued to drag her along the tunnel, while Emily cursed and elaborated on the pain she was going to inflict on them when she was finally free. She kept trying to look back over her shoulder, but the small glances she managed as the soldiers carried her away showed only an empty tunnel behind them, empty of any sign of Mac.

"He'll be okay," Petter said, jogging alongside. Emily ignored him.

The shock wave reached them thirty seconds later. It rumbled through the tunnel accompanied by a sound like breaking ice. Petter, who had pulled ahead, urged his own people to keep moving toward the shaft. West and Mooney threw concerned glances at each other and slowed almost to a stop. It was enough of a distraction for Emily to first wrestle her left arm free of West, then escape Mooney's hold on her. She took a step away from the men, then two steps in the direction of the explosion, her previous anger overtaken now by an immense sense of dread. West reached for Emily's arm but she sidestepped him and brought her shotgun up to his head. The look of fear on West's face brought a quick stab of pleasure to her, but not enough to even slightly dampen the furious anger that burned within her.

"If you ever touch me again," Emily spat, "I will blow your fucking head off."

West stared down the barrel of the shotgun for a very long second as Emily's finger caressed the trigger. Eventually, his eyes drifted up to Emily's.

"Get out of here. Go!" she yelled. Both men took off at a sprint in the direction of the surface. When they had disappeared around the next corner and Emily was sure they would not return, she turned and faced the direction of the explosion.

Above Emily's head, a crack, about ten centimeters wide had appeared in the ceiling. It ran the length of the tunnel for thirty meters or more, before splitting into many smaller cracks that spread out along the left side of the tunnel wall like lightning bolts. As she neared it, the rock above her groaned, the main crack widening by several centimeters, birthing smaller fractures in the wall.

No. No. No. No, Emily's mind repeated, over and over and over. Her insides felt as though she had swallowed a lead weight. Her emotions—a maelstrom of pain, confusion, and anger—swirled through her body.

She staggered back in the direction of the explosion.

All the pain and confusion froze when, from farther along the tunnel, she heard the unmistakable report of a rifle ring out three times in quick succession. Those same emotions evaporated a second later as Mac sprinted into view.

•••

"Hi, love," Mac managed to say between panting breaths when he reached her seconds later, sweat and dirt covering his beautifully imperfect face.

"You're...alive!" Emily exhaled a sigh of relief.

He planted a kiss on her lips. "The explosion took down a big part of the tunnel, but it's not going to hold those bastards off for long. I heard them clearing the debris away," he said. "Best if...we don't...hang around...okay?" he continued between kisses from his wife.

Emily could not stop smiling...or kissing him.

"Come on, love," he said, pushing her gently away. "Let's get out of here before the whole place comes down around our heads."

The two of them began to run up the incline of the tunnel. A few minutes later they caught up with the tail-end of the exodus. West and Mooney both grinned as Mac and Emily joined them.

"Hello, boss," said West. He looked sideways at Emily but didn't say a word to her.

"I thought I told you to get Emily to the surface?" Mac said.

West blushed, "She convinced us otherwise," he said.

Mac looked at his wife, who was still beaming at him like an idiot, almost all homicidal thoughts toward the two soldiers having vanished. "Yeah, okay, I know what you mean," he said. He glanced back over his shoulder. "How far to the surface do you think we still have to go?"

"I'd estimate maybe another ten minutes," said Mooney.

Mac nodded. "That was my guess. Have you tried contacting the others?"

"I lost my radio somewhere back there. Major Djupvik said he'd try and organize the survivors' extraction, so he's heading to the shaft," said Mooney.

Mac pulled his own radio from his pocket and keyed the microphone. "This is Alpha team leader, does anyone copy?"

Almost immediately a voice crackled back, "Mac? This is Parsons, we were beginning to think you weren't going to make it back in time for dinner."

"No such luck, mate," Mac replied. "We're not too far from the bottom of the shaft. Oh, and I almost forgot, we're bringing some friends."

•••

Ten minutes later, Emily heard Petter's unmistakable voice calling to them from somewhere in the mass of survivors ahead of them. A second later and she saw the Norwegian major's smiling face as he and two of his Jegertroppen pushed their way back through the crowd toward her and Mac.

"Good to see you in one piece," Petter said. He ignored the scowl Emily directed at him. "This is everyone?"

Mac nodded. "Afraid so. Right now, our priority is to get these people up to the surface. I expect some unwelcome visitors before too long."

Petter nodded. "We're not far from the bottom of the shaft. Just a couple more minutes."

"Do you have any spare ammunition?" Emily asked as their group continued on.

Petter nodded. He and his troops pulled out several magazines of ammo and handed them to Mac and his team. Emily reloaded her pistol, but none of the soldiers had any shells for her shotgun.

An excited murmur rippled through the crowd of survivors ahead of them, their pace picked up and they began to move faster along the tunnel. Emily saw why a few seconds later; twenty meters ahead of where she and her people stood was the bottom of the shaft that led back to the surface. She could make out some of the support team that had been stationed on the surface positioned on either side of the tunnel guiding the survivors into the bottom of the shaft then toward a line of ropes that reached down from the surface. It was going to be a slow laborious act to get everyone back up to the surface, but as Emily got closer she could see that more ropes than the original six had been dropped down. They were now pulling up twenty people at a time.

"Someone's getting a workout topside," said Mac as they watched a batch of survivors hoisted upward.

Petter smiled. "Yeah, they've got multiple teams up there pulling these people up. Extra cup of tea for them tonight." He winked at his weak joke but his smile turned into a grin. "Are you heading up?"

Mac shook his head. "We'll cover the rear. You get the civilians topside, quick as you can."

Petter smiled at Emily, clapped Mac on the shoulder and turned his attention back to organizing the survivors' extraction while Mac, Emily, West, and Mooney set up positions at the mouth of the tunnel, using the gradual curve of the wall into the bottom of the shaft as cover.

For the best part of the next hour, the ropes went up with people attached, came down empty, then went up again, while Emily, Mac, and the two other soldiers acted as sentries. Emily found her mind beginning to drift as exhaustion started to take a firm hold on her aching muscles and tired mind. She was jolted back to reality by a hissed warning from Mac.

"Heads up, we've got company," he said, nodding down the tunnel to where the unmistakable outline of a construct had appeared from around the corner.

Emily looked back at the group of survivors still waiting for their lift to freedom. She estimated there were around fifty people left at the bottom of the pit, which meant the ropes would have to come down three more times to get the survivors and the remaining military personnel out. *Not a problem if there's just the one alien,* she thought. *We can deal with—*

Another construct appeared next to the first, then two more filed into view. Several mutant-humans moved slowly between the constructs' legs like attack dogs waiting for an order. The survivors hadn't noticed the new arrivals, not yet anyway, and hopefully it would stay that way, because the last thing Emily and her crew needed right now was for them to panic.

West and Mooney both raised their rifles, but Mac moved his hand to the weapons and gently pushed them back down. "Hold your fire," he whispered.

The constructs' limited perceptions seemed to be holding true, and the humans' presence had gone unnoticed, so far. It would be a mistake to change that with so many civilians still waiting to reach the surface.

"Back up, slowly," Mac whispered. His group edged steadily back into the room below the shaft. At the opposite end of the tunnel, the constructs remained still as if waiting for a command, while the mutant-humans milled around them.

Emily looked back at the rapidly shrinking pool of people still waiting to be lifted out of this hellhole. She quickly counted heads: just ten survivors left. The military personnel who had been tasked with organizing the civilians' extraction slipped a looped end of the rope under the arms of each man or woman, then, once that person was secure, gave a triple tug on the rope to notify the surface team to start pulling them up. As the last survivor rose into the air, the military personnel who had acted as organizers, focusing intently on their job until now, finally saw the threat at the opposite end of the tunnel.

"Shhhhh!" Emily hissed, placing her finger to her lips as the men unslung their weapons, hot panic glowing in their eyes. "No firing. Stay calm and we'll all get out of here," she said, as calmly as possible.

Mac appeared at her side, his voice a whisper. "Everyone get yourselves ready, we're heading up."

Mac insisted on providing cover while one after the other, the remaining military personnel placed the looped rope under their arms and gave the three-pulls signal. Emily looped hers under her arms but held off on signaling she was ready until Mac arranged himself at the rope next to hers.

He gave her a wink then tugged three times on his rope. Emily did the same.

She felt the rope tighten uncomfortably under her armpits, then her feet left the ground and she began to quickly rise upward. Above her, a cluster of barely perceptible heads, silhouetted against a circle of blue sky, had gathered around the lip of the pit, watching as she and the others rose toward the surface.

They were halfway up the shaft when there was a sudden high-pitched twang followed by a short cry of horror as the soldier to Emily's right was suddenly in free fall, his hands windmilling as he fell, the frayed braids of the worn climbing rope he had been attached to trailing behind him like a severed umbilical cord as he plummeted toward the bottom of the shaft. Whether it was shock or simply a last act of patriotism to humanity, Emily did not know, but the soldier did not scream as he fell, even though she could see his eyes were wide with terror, his hands reaching upward toward his comrades.

Emily closed her eyes, unwilling to watch the doomed man's final seconds, but she could not block her ears from the sound of the sickening wet thud when he hit the bottom of the shaft. When Emily opened her eyes again, the man lay motionless below her feet, a pool of blood rapidly expanding around his shattered body. Seconds later, she felt an icy chill roll down her spine as, far beneath her feet, a construct lumbered into view, then a second joined it. Both moved to the dead man's body, their proboscises moving over him, probing, examining. Moments later, Emily's breath lodged in her throat as the unmistakable bulk of a Locust joined them.

From above her, Emily heard someone scream, then several yells of warning. She turned to look at Mac as he tried to signal for them to be silent, waving his hands frantically, but it was too late.

A volley of gunfire echoed through the tunnel, bullets whipping past the humans still suspended from the ropes, cutting down one of the constructs. Less than a second after that, a wave of constructs and mutant-humans rolled into the bottom of the shaft and began to climb toward the surface.

•••

"Take my hand," Mac yelled, reaching for Emily. He heaved her up and over the lip of the pit, pulling her away from its edge. Emily scrambled to her feet, slipped the loop of rope from around her chest and dropped it at her feet. The Point Loma survivors were being herded in the direction of the beach and the base camp by Petter and his crew, while a cadre of sailors stood around the edge of the shaft, firing down at the ascending aliens. Emily pulled out her pistol and joined the other fighters at the shaft's lip.

From the shaft, constructs screeched as they were hit and fell from the wall, spiraling to the ground far below, trailing streamers of blood behind them. Some hit others on the way down, dislodging them, and they went spinning off to their destruction. The mutant-humans were harder to hit; smaller and faster, they dodged and darted as they scrambled ahead of their masters. One appeared just below Emily's feet. She fired her pistol pointblank into its head, splattering gore across her pants. The body fell silently away into the depths, plummeting down to where she now saw the second and third Locust had joined the first. The alien masters seemed content to allow their minions to fight on their behalf, staying out of range of the human's weapons, for now at least.

"There's too many of them," Mac called out to Emily, then yelled to his men, "Prepare to fall back to cover." He waited a few seconds until they had cleared the nearest threat from the shaft then yelled, "Fall back! Fall back now!"

The guns fell momentarily silent as Emily and the soldiers slid down the side of the berm encircling the shaft and sprinted in the direction of the desiccated remains of a house twenty meters from the opening. The only sound Emily could hear over their feet pounding across the ground and the panting of their breath was the *click, clack, click, clack* of the constructs as they moved up the face of the shaft.

To the right of the ruined house, an arroyo formed a natural trench. Scattered along its edge were several large boulders that could provide minimal cover but would be better than being caught out in the open. Mac pointed at the nearest boulder and altered course toward it. Emily followed closely behind him. She ducked behind the boulder and slid down beside Mac and a couple other men. The rest of the team took cover behind their own boulders, dived into the trench, or ran into the ruined house.

"You okay?" Mac asked, trying to look confident.

Emily nodded, catching her breath.

"Listen," Mac continued, "if things get hairy, I want you to run, okay? You've got to get out of here...for the kids, understand?"

"When the time comes, we'll *both* get out of here," Emily replied. "Do you understand?"

Mac closed his eyes for a second. When he opened them again, he nodded his agreement to Emily. He edged around the side of the boulder and looked back toward the entrance to the shaft. A few seconds passed in silence then he shouted, "Here they come."

Emily stood, positioning herself on the opposite side of the boulder as her husband. All along the arroyo, men and women got to their feet and prepared for battle.

A tidal wave of constructs and mutants flooded from the pit, spreading out as they bounded toward the waiting humans.

"Pick your targets," Mac yelled as the creatures continued to advance across the fifty meters of open ground between them. Then, "Open fire!"

Constructs and mutants fell one after the other as a barrage of automatic weapons opened fire, but not enough to truly stem the advancing wave of walking, scuttling death. Emily estimated there were easily a hundred or more of just the constructs, not even counting the mutant-humans, leaping and running ahead of them. The single advantage the humans *did* have was that the constructs seemed ill-equipped to handle the rough terrain they now found themselves in, slowed by the weathered ground's furrows, ruts, and ditches, and the litter of humanity's lost civilization strewn all across the landscape.

"Watch out!" someone yelled from Emily's left, then the voice turned into a scream as a mutant-human leaped over the boulder the soldier sheltered behind, grabbed him by the throat with its multiple sets of hands, and squeezed. By the time his comrade put a bullet in the creature's head, the soldier lay writhing on the ground, his throat crushed, blood and spittle bubbling from his lips, already as good as dead.

More and more constructs spewed from the mouth of the shaft, a seemingly never-ending stream of alien killers replenishing the ones the humans had already cut down. One broke through the human's defensive line, grabbing a soldier. Emily shot the creature three times and it fell to the ground in a heap. The soldier rolled away, gasping for breath but alive. He pulled himself to his feet, grabbed his rifle and started firing again.

"I'm almost out of ammo," Emily yelled at Mac. She was again down to her last pistol magazine. She looked around the edge of the boulder and screamed for Mac, whose attention was focused on a group of three mutant-humans who had flanked the combatants sheltered in the wrecked home. He turned and looked in the direction his wife was pointing.

From the mouth of the shaft, the three Locusts they had seen earlier now pulled themselves up to the surface, their heads turning left and right as each of their single eyes surveyed this alien world that had fallen to them without a single shot having been fired. More constructs climbed from the pit, leaping past their masters and racing toward the humans.

A deep, bellowing howl sounded across the area, as if the Locusts were announcing their ownership of this new world, and they began to advance. Quicker even than their constructs, the Locusts strode across the ground like ancient giants reborn. The two men who had taken shelter in the derelict house leaped from the ruins and started to run for the trench. The largest of the Locusts spotted them and angled to intercept the fleeing men, quickly bounding over the space between them. It plucked the men from the ground, one with each of its upper arms, then with a finesse that belied the horror that unfolded, pushed them together like a child who insisted her dolls kiss. Bolts of lightning rose from the blanket of energy that still covered the ground around them, playing over the Locust. The two men did not cry out, but that, Emily thought, was only because they could not scream. Face to face, they began to melt into each other, their skin sizzling where it met, as their bodies melded into a single lump of flesh. Their limbs began to twist and rotate, and Emily realized that what she was witnessing was the very same process that had created the mutant-humans who were so hell-bent on destroying every last one of them. In a matter of fifteen seconds, the two men became a new entity, something that could never, should never, have existed on this world. When it was done, the Locust had created a work of macabre art, a horror that belonged in the halls of hell. The Locust lowered the aberration to the ground as gently as a human might lay down a baby.

What had just seconds ago been two individuals with minds, with hopes and fears and aspirations of their own, had now become a multi-limbed thing that followed only the will of its master. And its master willed it to destroy.

The second its feet touched the ground, the aberration took off at breakneck speed toward the trench—slather flying from its mouth, a mouth that was now full of fangs sharp as knives. Leaping over any obstruction, it dove into the arroyo where the soldiers had taken refuge, its head low to the ground as if it was tracking a scent. Quickly, it followed the trench, leaping on any human it found. Two men fell in bloody succession to it before it was finally taken down with a burst of automatic fire from a blonde-haired Jegertroppen.

Mac turned to his wife. "You need to go now, Emily," he insisted, worry lines making his face look twenty years older than he really was.

"No," Emily said, "not yet. I can still help."

Mac grabbed her by her arm. "We've lost, Emily. It's a matter of minutes at best before we're overrun. You need to leave now, while you can still—"

A shadow, vast and fast moving, passed over the battlefield, blotting out the sun, turning day to evening. In its shade, it seemed to Emily as if everything and everyone was suddenly frozen in place; even the once-human mutants and their alien masters appeared to have been shocked into immobility.

"Ho-lee shit," Mac exclaimed, his eyes fixed on the sky.

Emily looked up, too.

High above their heads, the outline of a Caretaker ship, huge beyond comparison to anything humanity had ever created or envisioned, moved silently and serenely over their positions from the east, led by its shadow as it swept across the dead ground surrounding the entrance to the Locusts' lair.

"Adam!" Emily whispered, from between lips devoid

of any moisture. When she and Rhiannon had first encountered this Caretaker vessel at the end of their search for Adam, she had thought the ship was made from the same material as a black hole, sucking in all light to create a perfect blackness. Now, watching the ship—it was the same ship, she was certain—as it blotted out the sky above her, that same thought held true. But back then, only the dome-like upper section of the ship had been visible, the rest of the spacecraft buried deep within the Earth's crust. Now the full size of the ship was revealed...and it was mighty.

Beneath the convex dome of utter blackness, jagged mountain-sized protrusions, like gigantic shards of broken glass projected toward the ground. Each multi-faceted surface shimmered and scintillated, giving off color of every hue and shade; as though the light that could not escape the perfect blackness of its upper portion was somehow broken down into all of its possible component frequencies. It was, Emily thought, the most beautiful and terrifying thing she had ever seen.

The ship came to a dead stop, positioned perfectly over the opening of the shaft. For several moments, it hung silently in the sky, then, in Emily's mind, she heard her son's voice, *"Prepare yourselves."* Before Emily could ask what she should prepare for, the shards beneath the ship turned as obsidian as the top of the craft, creating a hole in the sky so devoid of anything other than its perfect black nothingness that Emily was forced to avert her eyes, for fear she would find herself falling into that never-ending void. When she looked again, glancing through half-shut eyelids, the flow of energy into the open mouth of the shaft had changed; now it flowed upward from the ground into the abyssal nothingness of the ship.

A violent, deafening roar shook the ground beneath Emily's feet, as a vortex of energy spewed up from the shaft, surging into the blackness that was Adam's ship. The ground heaved and buckled beneath Emily's feet, sending plumes of gray dust spiraling into the air where it hung like fog, then slowly began to drift to the ground. Through the gray haze, Emily saw the Locust that had created the mutant begin to twitch and convulse, its arms spasming. The single eye rolled back into its socket. Emily searched through the pall of falling gray dust until she found the two other Locusts. They were experiencing the same effects as the first. Simultaneously, the three Locusts became rigid, as though a high voltage electrical charge was passing through their bodies. Streamers of yellow light drifted from their skin like finely spun yarn. The streamers flowed upward, toward the black ship, growing thicker and brighter with each passing second. The light was so intense it hurt Emily just to look, but she forced herself to squint through half-closed eyelids. There was a sudden flash of brilliant orange and yellow, like the flare of a struck match, as each Locust was simultaneously engulfed in a shimmering yellow bloom of energy that streamed from their bodies, joining with the pillar of energy flowing into Adam's ship. The light grew brighter and more intense by the second. The air seemed to be alive, crackling and sizzling with static. Emily thought she smelled burning but could not be sure, her mind overwhelmed by the multiples of sensory input flooding her body. The bloom of light surrounding the Locusts was ripped violently away from the aliens' bodies, flowing back to the main column, where it mingled and became one with the rush of energy as it roared into the ship high above. The three Locusts collapsed into a pile of twisted twitching limbs, fine wisps of yellow light still drifting from each body over the next few seconds until finally, that too stopped and the Locusts moved no more.

The roar of energy pouring from the shaft's mouth was deafening, its brilliance blinding, flooding Emily's senses almost into nonexistence. The roar grew louder. The light brighter. The ground beneath her feet shifted and undulated like water...

There was an abrupt change, a sound like something

unimaginably huge tearing far, far above her head was followed by an earsplitting boom that echoed across the land...

Then there was only silence.

Emily forced her eyes open, the afterglow of the visual assault still a lingering ghost, haunting her optic nerves.

Slowly, Emily's vision returned and she surveyed the devastated battlefield.

Nothing moved other than the gray dust that swirled and rushed around her.

The three Locusts did not stir, but the constructs and the mutant-humans were still very much alive, unaffected by whatever force Adam had unleashed on the Locusts. They seemed as stunned by what had just happened as the surviving humans who were slowly pulling themselves to their feet around her were. The constructs and mutants were beginning to regain their senses too, but she noted, as her eyes drifted to the opening, no more of the fiends came from the shaft. Now there was only the column of escaping energy flowing into...an empty blue sky.

The ship, Adam's ship, had vanished, gone, leaving behind nothing but a faint smoky outline in the sky. Globes of white light, like falling stars, spiraled to the ground, impacting the dead ground surrounding the shaft.

"No," Emily whispered, then louder "No!"

Mac staggered to his feet a few meters away from Emily. He lurched his way to her.

"Are you okay?" Mac asked. His face was dirty and dust-striped.

"No. Yes," Emily said. "But the ship...Adam...He's gone."

Mac looked confused. "What?"

Emily was unable to speak. A terrible emptiness filled her chest as she watched what she believed could only be the burning debris of her son's ship fall from the sky. Her son.

The ship. It was all gone. He had kept true to his promise, the Locusts were gone, dead—but at a terrible price. Adam, she was sure, was dead.

Without warning, the ground heaved beneath Emily's feet. She staggered, almost fell, but felt Mac's hand grab her own and pull her to him. They were barely able to remain on their feet as the ground continued to roll and dip, like waves on the surface of a storm-blown lake.

Emily frantically looked around her; some men and women had been knocked to the ground and were in the process of trying to get to their feet, others were leaning against rocks like she was, holding on for dear life, others were simply sitting on their butts trying to ride out whatever the hell was happening now. A loud crash marked the collapse of the ruined house as it crumbled into a pile of dust and rubble; if anyone was inside it they were surely crushed.

"What is it? What's happening?" Emily cried, steadying herself against the boulder.

Mac wobbled like a drunk as the shock waves continued to turn the ground beneath their feet to liquid. "Earthquake," he declared. "I think it's an earthquake."

Emily pulled herself hand over hand out of the trench. She gasped. "Mac! Mac! Look!" She pointed with her right hand and instantly regretted it as she lost her balance again and fell to the ground. She quickly scrambled to her feet and stood next to her husband, staring back toward the shaft's entrance. Blue, red, and green ribbons of energy shot from the shaft's mouth, rushing upward for kilometers into the California blue sky. From the ground, bolts of the same multi-colored light jumped and sparked...and killed.

Emily saw a bolt of energy hit a construct, it crumpled immediately to the ground, its legs curling into its abdomen like a dead ant. Another fell and another. The aliens were as unable to maneuver across the undulating ground as the humans and, exposed in the open, they were quickly falling prey to the energy pouring out of the shaft. The bucking grew more violent. A creaking, cracking, snapping sound unlike anything Emily had ever heard before pulled her attention away from the carnage being inflicted on the aliens to the ground just behind where she and the remainder of the assault team stood. A rupture, already a meter wide and growing wider by the second, opened in the earth five paces away from where Emily and Mac tried to keep their feet, tiny streamers of the same multi-colored energy leaked into the air from it. The rupture spread across the terrain at a steady pace, the ground snapping asunder with a terrifying crack.

"What the hell is—" Mac's words were replaced by a sudden expletive as the ground under their feet dropped violently, canting downward toward the rupture. Loose rocks and spent cartridge cases began to gradually roll toward the freshly opened fissure. Emily still had a firm grip of the boulder she had used for cover, others had no such anchor. She saw bodies tumble to the ground and begin to slide down the now-slanted shelf of ground they stood on toward the gaping mouth of the rupture. Mac started toward the nearest man but the ground beneath him abruptly dropped again and he stumbled, his hands flailing as he pitched forward, his legs trying to find some purchase to slow his steady fall in the direction of the ever-widening fissure.

"Mac!" Emily screamed, as her husband plummeted toward the edge of the rupture...and stopped, his boots finally catching on a thin crack of uneven rock, perilously close to the edge of the fissure. Mac's feet kicked gravel into the opening as they slipped then found their grip again. He had slowed his movement but not stopped it entirely; now he was edging toward the fissure by a couple of centimeters each time his feet lost their purchase.

Emily let go of the boulder she clung to, dropped to her butt, and began to scoot toward Mac.

"Help them," Emily yelled at the men to her left and right who had not yet noticed the growing fissure behind them, their minds transfixed by the tower of light thundering into the atmosphere or holding on for dear life to their own boulders and outcroppings.

Mac looked up at the sound of his wife's voice, his face set in a determined grimace as he fought to maintain his precarious foothold.

"Stay where you are. Don't risk it," Mac yelled at her.

Emily said nothing, but continued to edge closer to him, all the time praying that the ground would not suddenly drop again, while trying to ensure that she did not lose her own tentative balance. When she was a half-meter away from Mac, she planted her left foot into a small indentation in the ground, barely big enough to slip the edge of the heel of her right boot in. It was not much for her to trust both her own and Mac's weight to, but it was all she had. She unslung her shotgun, quickly loosened the leather sling, took the weapon by its barrel and leaned forward so it passed between her knees, the leather strap dropping to where Mac struggled to hold on for his life.

"Take it," she hissed.

Mac reached for the strap, his fingers almost touching it. Emily leaned in farther, trying to stretch every last centimeter out of her tight muscles, but Mac's fingers could not quite reach.

The ground kicked again, launching Emily and Mac into the air. Emily dropped back down hard onto her butt, landing almost exactly in the same spot, her foot quickly scrambling to find the same small indentation and steady herself. Mac landed face first, his nose erupting in a gout of blood. He shifted closer to the edge of the widening fissure by a few centimeters. A yell for help to Emily's right momentarily drew her attention away. She saw a man who had been clinging to a rock and the soldier who had gone to rescue him tumbling down the incline. Both men slipped over the edge of the fissure and disappeared, their screams trailing behind them. Emily returned her focus to Mac. He lay completely still on the rock, a thin rivulet of blood flowing from his shattered nose. "Mac! Mac!" Emily cried.

He remained motionless for a few moments, then groaned, his hands clenching and unclenching. His head moved across the dirty ground as he lifted it toward the sound of Emily's voice.

"Grab the sling! Grab it!" Emily hissed, nodding at the leather sling of the shotgun that now lay within easy reach of his right hand.

Mac looked confused for a moment, then his hand began moving toward the end of the sling. He finally found it and pulled it closer to himself, wrapping it around his fingers. He closed his hand in a tight fist. Then his head sank to the ground again. Emily leaned back, planted her feet as firmly as she could and pulled with all her might. Mac moved a few centimeters closer to her with a sound like dry sandpaper on wood as his body moved across the rock. Emily scooted her butt back up the sloping ground, repositioned her feet and pulled again.

"When...we...get...out...of...this..." she hissed through clenched teeth, drawing in a deep breath between each word, "you're...going...on...a...diet."

A high-pitched screech from behind Emily made her jump in surprise. She swiveled her head as far back over her left shoulder as she could...and felt the breath leave her body. Two constructs stood on the boulder she and Mac had sheltered behind. Somehow, they had managed to evade the energy that killed their comrades and now these two creatures stood surveying the helpless humans below them. One after another, the constructs leaped from the boulder to the ground and began making their way nimbly across the slab of rock toward Emily and Mac, their spiked legs giving them the purchase they needed to move quickly and confidently.

Emily froze. Her shotgun was Mac's only lifeline, his hands were entwined in its leather strap, so there was no way she could untangle it in time to turn it on the constructs. And if she reached for her pistol, one hand would have to let go of her end of the shotgun, and it was taking all her strength and grip just to hold on to Mac as it was.

Emily screeched and flinched as two bullets zipped past her head, followed the briefest of moments later by their reports. She looked in the direction of the gunshots and saw Petter kneeling on the other side of the widening fissure, a bolt-action rifle in his hands, smoke drifting upward from its muzzle. Emily screeched again as the body of one of the constructs tumbled past her and disappeared into the rupture. Two more shots rang out in quick succession and the second construct was down, whatever it was that passed for blood oozing from two large caliber bullet wounds that had ripped through its body.

Her hands shaking from fear and exhaustion, Emily turned back to Mac. His eyes met hers. He was conscious, at least. She pulled again, grunting with the exertion. Mac planted the flat of his free hand on the rock and used it to leverage himself upward, easing the burden somewhat on his wife. Emily scooted her butt back and pulled, repeating the process over and over until finally Mac could pull himself the remaining distance to her. When they reached the safety of the boulder, Mac's eyes were clear again, but his nose was obviously broken and the blood was refusing to stop. He spat a glob of blood from his mouth, then flopped down next to her, panting.

Emily pulled the radio from Mac's jacket and keyed the microphone, "Back to the beach, now. Everyone. Get out of here!" Most of the remaining team had already managed to make it over the rupture and were stumbling toward where Major Petter and a collection of two Jegertroppen and four sailors waited, the sniper rifle he'd used to dispatch the constructs cradled in his arms like a baby, his eyes fixed firmly on Emily and Mac. The growing fissure separating Petter from them had expanded even farther, the ground opening up in a gradual curve that expanded to Emily's left and right.

"Can you stand?" she asked Mac.

Mac nodded. Unsteadily, he got halfway to his feet, leaning hard against the boulder.

Emily scanned the incline leading down to the fissure, searching for anything that would help her and Mac. She identified several large rocks and indentations between where she and Mac sat and the lip of the fissure. As she was formulating her route, the ground shook again, sending gray dust into the air, and pebbles and dirt skittering away into oblivion. "We've got to move now!" Emily told Mac. She stood, offered both hands to her husband, and pulled him unsteadily to his feet while she tried to retain her own balance.

Mac swayed for a second.

Emily looked back toward the shaft opening; the ground was littered with the smoldering bodies of the Locusts, their constructs, and mutant-humans. Nothing moved in that desolation now besides the twirling pillar of energy stretching skyward. In the distance, her eyes followed the still-expanding line of the rupture, its route betrayed by a sudden puff of dirt and the glitter of energy where the ground continued to split apart. She moved her eyes to the right and found the opposite end of the rupture. The two ends were less than a hundred meters short of meeting and becoming one massive, continuous chasm that would encircle the entrance to the Locusts' lair, she realized.

"Oh, shit!" Emily whispered, as she finally understood what was going to happen when those two ends met.

"What?" Mac asked, his right hand positioned under his nose to try and slow the bleeding.

"No time to explain." Emily took Mac's left hand in her own, then together they began to move gingerly from foothold to foothold down the escarpment toward the glowing fracture. On the opposite side of the fracture, Petter waited a few safe meters back from the gradually crumbling edge. He shadowed their every move, repositioning himself as Emily and Mac made their zig-zagging way down to the edge of the crack. Emily spotted a large rock close to the edge; she angled toward it. She and Mac both let out a sigh of exhaustion when they reached it, using it as a foothold to momentarily catch their breath. The fissure was over a meter and a half wide now, and still growing, loose pieces of dirt and rock crumbling away from the edges even as they momentarily rested.

They needed to move. Now!

"Ready?" Emily said.

"As I'll ever be, love," Mac replied, his broken nose giving his words a nasal tone.

Emily kissed him gently on the tip of his shattered nose, then stood and signaled to Petter that they were going to try and make the leap across the chasm. She repositioned herself slowly around the edge of the rock until the only thing that was between her and certain death if she slipped was about twelve centimeters of slowly crumbling ground. Mac edged around beside her.

Emily turned to her husband. "I want you to go—"

Mac grabbed her under her arms and in one swift motion lifted her off her feet and threw her with all his remaining strength.

Emily spun through the air, her arms flapping uselessly, her mind unable to register the shock or even have a chance to scream, as she sailed through the air. She did however have just enough time to glance down into the crevice and the maelstrom of energy swirling within it. Then she felt another pair of arms grab her. She looked up into the handsome face of Major Djupvik.

"Welcome, little sparrow," he said, smiling, then set her down beside him.

Emily watched wordlessly as Mac braced his feet

against the rock, swayed his body back and forth as if he was winding up in preparation for what was to come, and used the momentum to propel himself into the air, a trail of blood flying from his nose as he soared across the chasm. He landed close enough to the edge that his heels hung over the precipice, then he fell forward and rolled, only to spring up in front of his wife.

"I'd punch you in your goddamn nose if it wasn't already broken," Emily said flatly. Then grabbed her husband and kissed him hard.

Mac grimaced in pain as Emily's cheek pressed against his busted nose and her arms squeezed his broken ribs.

"Come on you two. There'll be time for all that later," Petter said.

They took off at a jog in the direction of the beach. As they ran, Emily re-threaded the sling into her shotgun, and slipped it over her shoulder. They had gone no more than thirty meters when a sound like rolling thunder filled the air, growing in volume with every second. Again, the ground shook and rumbled beneath the retreating humans' feet. Emily slowed to a stop and turned to face the direction they had just come from. The pillar of energy had vanished, replaced by a cloud of gray dust that billowed outward from where the edge of the fissure had been. Beyond that, a huge expanse of land where the entrance to the Locusts' base had been centered had vanished, collapsed in on itself, leaving behind a massive gaping hole in the earth that stretched for half a kilometer from one side to the other. A caldera Emily thought it was called, like when a volcano collapses in on itself.

"Wow!" said Mac, apparently impressed by the level of destruction. "I did not see that coming."

Through the pall of dust rising into the air, Emily thought she saw movement near the lip of the newly formed caldera. "May I?" she asked, motioning to Petter's binoculars. He passed them to Emily and she raised them to her eyes, adjusting the focus until she could see clearly. An indistinct silhouette moved within the dust near the caldera's edge. Someone was alive back there.

"Mac, I think there's still—" Emily stopped short. Through the binoculars' lens the indistinct shape finally resolved itself. Emily hissed a warning as the huge bulk of what had once been Dr. Sylvia Valentine emerged from the swirling dust, striding into view. Twenty mutant-humans clung to her body. They spilled onto the ground around Valentine, like baby wolf spiders from their mother. Valentine's head moved left and right, surveying the ruined landscape. Her multiple sets of eyes fixed on the group of humans standing as still as petrified trees. Even at this distance, Emily sensed the monster's gaze seeking her out, and when, finally, Valentine found her, the creature let loose a terrifying screech of hatred. Then, as one, the horde rushed toward the waiting humans.

•••

Mac was the first to open fire, blowing away one of the smaller but much faster mutant-humans as it sprinted ahead of Valentine. The rest of the team opened fire a second later, knocking down five of the mutants in quick succession. Emily stole a glance back toward the ocean; the tail-end of the survivors and their military escort were about two hundred meters away. There was no chance her people would be getting any backup from that direction before Valentine and her minions reached them. Besides, if they could not stop Valentine right here and now, the bitch would be on the retreating survivors in a matter of seconds after dealing with Emily and her party.

Emily drew her pistol and fired shot after shot at the line of mutants rushing toward her. More fell, but it wasn't enough. The mutants were on them a moment later, while

Valentine waited in the distance, watching as the once-human minions did her bidding.

"Mac," Emily yelled, "We need to—"

Mac turned and pointed his pistol at Emily.

"Mac? No! Wait—"

Mac fired two shots in quick succession.

Emily felt the wake of disturbed air as the bullets ripped past her, then spun around to see the mutant that had been just a few steps away from her crumple to the ground, its still-human face frozen in a grimace of pain.

Petter was yelling orders in Norwegian. While neither Emily nor Mac nor the other Brits could understand the words, the intention was clear. They ran to join the major, forming a semi-circle of two rows, facing their attackers. The rear rank stood while the front rank knelt, each weapon covering part of the ark of fire. Emily caught a blur of motion from her right. A man screamed. She turned in time to see two bodies rolling away, the mutant-human tearing at the soldier's chest with its claws, spraying blood everywhere as the man tried to fight back against the stronger adversary. Petter shot the creature in the head. It collapsed onto the now-still form of the soldier.

A Jegertroppen let out a scream of pain, that turned into a roar of defiance as she shot the thing that had sunk its claws and teeth into her unprotected arm. She ripped her bloody arm from the mutant's jaws, cursing wildly in Norwegian as she kicked the dead body away from her, clutching her hand to the wound. Blood quickly seeped from between her fingers.

The last two mutants died in quick succession.

Breathing heavily from the battle, his bloody nose finally stemmed, Mac reloaded his rifle. Emily stepped up beside him and eyeballed Valentine. During the short fight, Valentine had remained close to the edge of the caldera, moving back and forth crab-like while her foot soldiers did their work. She had stopped pacing, and was now watching the humans as intently as they watched her, her head dipped low, contemplating her next move.

"We need to catch up with the rest of our people, right now!" Petter hissed, coming up behind Emily and Mac.

"Roger that idea," said Mac. He and his remaining men pushed the dead mutant off their fallen comrade, then Mac knelt and checked the soldier's vital signs. Mac cursed and stood back up. "Let's move."

Emily, Mac, and the others took off at a jog toward Point Loma. Mac grunted quietly in pain with each alternate step he took, and a thin dribble of blood began to flow from his nose again. Periodically he would flip around and check on Valentine's location. Emily focused on the distant outline of the sand dunes that delineated where the beach began and their people should now safely have assembled. She knew that if Valentine moved, Mac would let her know.

The third time Mac turned to check, he let out a sharp curse, followed by a screamed warning to "Watch out!"

Emily half-turned, reaching for her shotgun. She saw a blur of black heading toward the group. Heard the first report of Petter's weapon firing even as she saw one of Valentine's tentacle-like arms snap whip-like through the air and hit him, sending his weapon flying away. Petter's body spun twice through the air, and stopped directly facing Emily, a narrow slice cut through his tunic from his abdomen up his chest to his right cheek where the tip of Valentine's tentacle had caught him. Blood was already welling up through the wound. Petter staggered, tried to keep himself upright, but collapsed to the ground and lay still, blood pouring from his wound. Whether the Norwegian was unconscious or dead, Emily had no way to tell. She turned in time to see Valentine's huge bulk barreling directly toward Mac, her intention obviously to crush him where he stood. Mac dived to his right, but he wasn't quite fast enough. Valentine caught him with the edge of her shoulder, knocking him six feet through the air before he landed hard on his back, his arms raised skyward from the elbow up, hands clenched into fists in the tell-tale autonomic response of someone who had been knocked senseless.

The remaining soldiers fired their weapons in unison as Emily fumbled for her shotgun. Valentine screamed in pain as bullets ripped into her, gouging out large pieces of flesh, but her reactions were faster than the soldiers. She dipped to avoid the continuing spray of bullets, then swung a tentacle out in a vicious arc that knocked two men to the ground, leaving one man's arm almost severed at the elbow. The remaining Jegertroppen, already injured from her run in with the mutant-human, fired shot after shot, then screamed in pain as one of Valentines tentacles smacked with a sickening thud against her head. She collapsed to the ground.

Emily finally managed to wrestle her shotgun off her shoulder, aimed it at Valentine's head and fired. Valentine must have sensed the shot because she dipped away just as Emily pulled the trigger, then screamed in blistering anger as the slug tore across her back, gouging a thick furrow through her tissue. Emily managed to rack another shell into the chamber before Valentine turned on her. She did not see which tentacle hit her. All she felt was a burning sensation in her hands and then the shotgun was no longer in her hands. Emily stared at her right hand and saw nothing but a bloody stump where her pinky finger had been. She let out a gasp of pain and surprise as Valentine grabbed her, wrapping her tentacles tightly around her chest and squeezed. It felt like she was being crushed by two anacondas, the grip so tight she could not breathe, let alone scream.

Three shots ripped through the air. Valentine bellowed in pain.

Mac!

Through vision that was quickly growing dark, Emily saw her husband lying on his back, his head moving as though his neck was barely able to hold it up. His finger continued to pull the trigger of his pistol, but nothing was happening, his magazine empty. Mac ejected the spent magazine from his pistol and fumbled for another one in his belt, but by the time he managed to slam it into the pistol, Valentine was gone, running toward the beach, Emily clasped firmly in her grasp.

CHAPTER 21

Emily's world turned monochrome. The edges of her vision became tinged with a black mist as she fought to draw in air, Valentine's grip on her cutting off all but the tiniest of breaths as the once-human abomination raced away. Valentine had her clasped like a baby to her ice-cold naked chest, so tightly it allowed Emily to catch only fleeting glimpses of the terrain, barely enough information for her oxygen-deprived pain-sliced brain to attempt to make sense out of.

Hills? No, they were...sand dunes, rising on either side of her. Valentine was taking her to the beach, putting as much distance between her and Mac and Petter as possible.

Why?

Emily shuddered. Because Valentine wanted to take her time with her, that was why. They had some catching up to do, after all. Valentine had singled her out, had been so fixed on pulling her from the group alive when she could have undoubtedly killed her right then and there, instead of bringing her here, to the dunes. That meant only one thing; that even after all the mutations and changes that had been inflicted on the woman to turn her into this...this *thing*, there was still sufficient humanity left within her, still enough of Valentine's twisted excuse for a soul, that she recognized Emily and wanted her revenge. And Emily was sure it would be a terrible revenge.

She sensed they were slowing. The continual bumping up and down as they climbed and descended the dunes now reduced to little more than a vibration as the dunes gave way to beach. She felt the pressure around her chest ease then disappear altogether as Valentine released her. She fell. Hit something soft that gave beneath her weight. She barely noticed any of this because when she hit the ground, pain raked her chest, and the blackness that had almost completely receded closed in on her vision again. She managed to turn her head and vomited onto her shoulder. Then sucked in a puke-flavored gasp of air.

Oh, dear God, I hurt.

But there's air!

Emily sucked in huge rasping lungfuls of it, her hands clasping at something fine and coarse that ran through her fingers. *Sand*, she realized as her fingers shifted within its warmth. Her chest hurt every time she breathed in.

Broken ribs.

And her hearing was filled with a pounding-hissing sound that Emily wasn't sure was her heart or the crashing of the waves onto the beach. She tried to lift herself up to a sitting position, and moaned in agony as lightning shot through her right side. She fell back into the sand.

Definitely broken ribs; just hope they haven't punctured a lung.

Then the breath was crushed from her again as Valentine snatched Emily from the ground and raised her high into the air until the two were face to face. Valentine held her there for a few seconds, her multiple eyes studying her prisoner. Then, without any warning, she dashed Emily to the ground. Emily's left leg smashed against the sea-worn remains of what had once been a Titan tree limb. She felt her left leg snap with a sickening crunch.

Emily screamed silently, the excruciating agony freezing her mouth wide open, imprisoning the scream in her throat. Pain rolled in and out like the ocean waves for what seemed like an eternity. Finally, she managed to exhale a pitiful mewl of agony that faded slowly to a panting sob of despair and misery. Even through the pain-induced haze that had turned her vision a raw red, she saw Valentine's mouth twist into a sadistic smile of pleasure. Her smile grew wider at Emily's scream as she reached out a tentacle and pressed hard against her shattered leg. Valentine timed the torture perfectly; as Emily fell helplessly toward a welcome unconsciousness, her captor released her hold on the injured leg, and Emily began to slowly rise toward full consciousness again.

Tears flooded down Emily's face; part pain, part anger, part frustration at the realization that it was going to end like this, and that she would not be able to do a goddamn thing to save herself from this mutant bitch. Her weapons were all lost. All she had now were her hands. She beat her clenched fists weakly against Valentine's chest, a slow pathetic *thump, thump, thump.*

It was useless. She knew it. Valentine knew it. But damn this monster to the hell she deserved if she thought she, Emily Baxter, was going to go down without a fight. *She would never give up. Not this woman. Not now. Not ever.*

Her hands sank to the sand. Strangely, the sound her fists had made against Valentine continued. Well, not exactly the same, her befuddled brain thought, this was more of a...

Emily tilted her head slowly to the right, trying to focus her eyes through the pain and the afternoon sun which had become intolerably bright. Behind Valentine, in the direction of Point Loma, standing atop a dune that seemed to Emily's pain-slit eyes to stretch way up into the sky, an indistinct black blob of shadow appeared. Valentine, still fascinated by Emily's suffering had not noticed it yet. The blob of darkness moved quickly down the eastern face of the huge dune, resolving into a four-legged silhouette. As the shape drew closer, she realized the sound she heard was the low, snarling bark of...

"Thor!" Emily hissed, as the indistinct shape resolved into the unmistakable form of her Alaskan Malamute. The dog ran full tilt toward Emily, his barking turning to growls of fury as he darted around Valentine, sinking his teeth into the meat of one of her rear legs.

That got Valentine's attention. She howled in anger and spun around, her feet coming down close to Emily's head, sending sand flying into her eyes and mouth as she yelled out to her dog. Spluttering, Emily tried again to shout; *Thor, run! Run!* That was what she wanted to say, but the words would not leave her lips, the sand choking her.

Thor continued to bark and growl, relentlessly hounding Valentine, diving in and out of her legs, nipping at her muscles, while Valentine howled more in frustration and anger than pain as she tried to grab him with her tentacles or stomp him with her powerful legs. If Valentine got hold of Thor, Emily had no doubt that she would tear him to pieces in a heartbeat. Still the dog continued to harass the monster, as if he knew that this was the same woman who had so callously rejected his affection when first she had arrived at Point Loma.

Emily spat the sand from her mouth, and forced herself to a sitting position, "Thor—" she managed to say, before a thought appeared unannounced in her head. *How did he get here?* The last she remembered she had left Thor with—

A shadow passed over Emily, easing the burn of the

too-bright sun.

Emily raised her eyes in time to see the giant form of the *Machine* rising over the top of the sand dune Thor had appeared from. A second later, Rhiannon clambered over the top of the dune too, and stood there, jaw set in concentration, her hands outstretched as she guided the *Machine* nimbly down the side of the dune toward the three figures on the beach.

Valentine must not have sensed its approach, her attention still focused on the distraction that was Thor. The first she knew that she had lost was when the *Machine*'s front tentacles lassoed her around the waist, then yanked her from her feet, high into the air as if she were nothing. Valentine let out an indignant screech that turned quickly to a squeal of mortal fear as she stared into the sightless face of the massive engine of destruction that now held *her* struggling within its grasp.

The *Machine*'s head turned to look directly at Emily, and Emily understood that through its sensors Rhiannon was looking at her, waiting for an answer to her silent unasked question.

Emily nodded. "Do it," she managed to mumble from between her bloody lips.

The *Machine* tore Valentine in half, sending her head and torso spinning far off out to sea, where it landed with a splash and vanished beneath the waves. The rest of her body went spiraling away from the beach, entrails and bodily fluids flying behind her to land with a wet *thunk* somewhere in the dunes.

Emily's head sank back into the warm sand. She closed her eyes and allowed the heat of the California sun to wash over her, turning her world from red to blue. The last thing Emily Baxter sensed before she passed into unconsciousness was Thor's warm tongue against her face.

CHAPTER 22

Emily sat alone by the bank of a stream. The water gurgled and babbled, bouncing over rocks and pebbles, creating a symphony that was at once gently chaotic, but irresistibly beautiful. *If I close my eyes*, Emily thought, *I'll fall instantly asleep.* At least, she would have if it had not been for the obvious clues that she was already asleep.

The grass she lay on, and that stretched out in all directions around her was a luscious green. The trees, maples and huge green birch, were in full leafy splendor, vibrant and glistening with life. The air, warm and clean, was redolent with the smell of chlorophyll and apple blossom. A few white clouds drifted serenely across the azure sky, serenaded on their journey by the song of birds, who in turn were accompanied by the lively chatter and laughter of children.

Emily sat up and allowed her eyes to search for the source of the laughter.

A little farther along the bank of the stream, a group of maybe fifteen children were gathered around a tall man.

The man, dressed in white linen trousers and a shirt of the same material, stood in the stream, the water up to his knees. The children splashed and laughed in the stream around him. The man smiled at them as they excitedly danced around him, each one clamoring for his attention, each receiving it in turn. The stranger was tall, had a full but tightly cropped beard the same color as his blond shoulder-length hair, and, as he waded through the stream toward Emily, eyes of the deepest blue. His face, peaceful and kind, seemed...familiar to her. It was as though she recognized him from her past, but could not quite grasp the memory of who he was.

"Hello," Emily said, smiling first at the children who followed behind the man, then at the stranger as they drew closer. "Am I in a dream?"

The tall stranger dropped to his knees beside Emily and looked deep into her eyes, his smile widening. He reached out and took Emily's hand in his—it was warm and comforting, and she felt a gentle wave of electricity run over her skin where his hand touched her own.

"Yes, a dream," said the stranger, "of sorts." His voice was calm, gentle, soothing.

"You look...familiar. Do I know you?" Emily asked, canting her head to one side, the sleepy, dreamlike quality of her existence slowing her thought process. She felt so very, very relaxed. At peace.

The stranger-who-was-not-a-stranger leaned in close to Emily, placing his lips close to her ear. He whispered, "Hello, Mommy," then drew back, his smile widening.

The realization that this was Adam, her son, did not come as a shock to Emily, not here, not in this place, wherever this strange dream world was, if it was at all. Instead, it felt the same as when she knew the answer to a question, or a problem, but her brain was unable to release it; the solution waited on the tip of her tongue, and, when that answer finally revealed itself, it completed rather than surprised. *This* was *that*.

Emily smiled, "Hello, baby." She wrapped her child in her arms, pulled him to her, felt the warmth of his skin pressed against hers as his arms enveloped her. She breathed in deeply, inhaling the scent of her boy.

"Is it over?" she whispered into her son's ear.

"Yes. It is done."`

Adam squeezed his mother tightly, then slowly released her. The children—other children, Emily thought, because to her Adam was and always would be a child—milled around Adam's legs, smiling and quietly chattering to each other, their eyes moving from Adam to Emily and then back to Adam again.

They are beautiful. Beautiful, Emily thought.

"Who are they?" she asked, unable to contain the joy she felt at the sight of the children as they frolicked and played in the grass at her son's feet.

Adam smiled again. "My sisters and my brothers."

Confused, Emily started to say that he had no brothers or sisters but stopped before the words left her lips. She knew that that was not correct. It was this place, she realized, this other world. In this dream-place, no untruth could be spoken or thought. How that was, she did not know, did not care. She was just content that it was.

Adam continued. "They are future echoes. Probabilities waiting to be realized. Children of the new world. The new Earth." He reached a hand down to stroke the hair of a little girl, no more than four or five, who clung to his leg, her arms wrapped around his calf, her cheek resting against Adam's thigh just above his knee. She had blonde hair, glittering eyes, and a radiant smile. Her eyes focused on Emily, never leaving her.

Emily's smile grew wider. "You're beautiful," she said.

The little girl giggled, then dipped her head behind Adam's leg.

"Is this the past or the future?" Emily asked.

Adam smiled, "This is both past and future. It is what once was and what will be again should you choose the right path."

"The right path?" Emily asked.

"You are on the path. You have always known that it was the right one. Simply continue. Do not falter," he said.

"What about you, son? What path have you chosen?"

Adam's smile faded, "I must leave."

"No!" said Emily, reaching to take her son's hand in her own. "I can't lose you again. Not now. Please."

Adam squeezed his mother's hand. "I am already gone. There is so much left for me to understand. The destruction of the Caretakers has left a vacuum in the universe. I must find those who created them and tell them what has happened. I must understand them."

"But what if you can't find them? What if they are all dust, as dead as the Caretakers?"

"Then I will take their place."

"But why? Why does it have to be you?"

"Because the universe has always needed a steward. Left on its own, it teeters toward chaos. If there is to be order, life, then someone must help to direct it."

Adam dropped to a sitting position in the grass, squeezed his mother's hand and released it. He ran his hand over the head of the blonde-haired girl who now sat in his lap, quietly working at something unseen in her hands. The little girl had made a daisy chain from the wild flowers that grew all around. She stood, walked to Emily and placed the daisy chain solemnly over Emily's head.

"Thank you." Emily smiled at the little girl as she returned to Adam's lap.

The little girl smiled shyly, leaning against Adam's chest as he spoke.

"You have given this planet and countless other worlds and civilizations a second chance, and in return, I have given you and those who stood at your side a gift. Do not allow it to be squandered."

"A gift?" Emily asked, although she felt as though she already knew the answer to her question. Felt it within her.

Adam smiled. His head tilted skyward.

Where had the clouds come from, Emily wondered. She had not seen their approach but now they covered nearly the whole of the sky. Emily sensed that with their approach, her time in this place had drawn almost to a conclusion.

"Will I ever see you again?" Emily asked. She looked up at her child, squinting because the sun was directly behind his head, creating a fierce halo of light.

"One day," Adam said. He lifted the little girl from his lap, placed her between his mother and him, then pushed himself to his feet. Adam took a step back toward the stream.

"No, please. Don't go. *Please...*"

Adam took another step backward, still smiling.

"Please," Emily begged, "stay."

"I love you," said Adam.

"I love you, too," Emily whispered.

Then Adam was gone and the clouds filled the sky.

But the beautiful blonde-haired child remained.

•••

Emily opened her eyes to a world that was darker than the one she had just left. As her mind gradually returned to the reality of this world, memories slowly began to return to her. She had been in a fight...? Yes, that felt right, but in that moment, she could not recall the exact details of it all, they eluded the grasp of her mind. It took several seconds for her senses to fully return to her, but when they finally did, she saw that she lay in bed in a room with dull white walls. There were several machines and monitors next to her bed, quietly doing whatever they were designed to do. An intravenous tube fed a clear liquid from a bag hanging from a stand into her right arm. Obviously, she was in a hospital, but

Emily didn't think it was Point Loma's infirmary.

Mac sat in a chair near her bed. His head cradled by a hand whose elbow rested on the armrest of the chair. He was breathing rhythmically. Asleep. Snoring quite loudly, a large y-shaped adhesive bandage strapped to his broken nose.

Mac! The memory of her husband, lying unconscious on the ground returned with a blinding flash of panic that quickly began to subside, because there he was in the chair, alive and well. Another image flashed into her mind, this one of Petter; unconscious, and covered in blood. And then all her memories just seemed to pop back into existence at once: the assault on the Locusts' lair; the survivors they had found deep within; their flight from the lair and the ensuing battle and final destruction of the Locusts, along with the abominations they had created; the terrible, terrible losses that had once again been inflicted on her fragile species. Valentine, and her ultimate death at the hands of Rhiannon.

And finally, there was Adam.

Oddly, she felt no sense of loss for her son; probably, she reasoned, because the profound emotional heat of her 'dream' still burned within her; a dream she suspected was actually a farewell from her son, her very much alive son, who was now out there, somewhere in the heavens, traveling on a mission to find the creators of the Caretakers. Where there should have been soul-breaking pain at his absence, there was only a profound sense of love, a love that burned at the center of her mind and in her heart; a parting gift from her beautiful, irreplaceable star child.

Emily's eyes drifted down her body to her left leg...it was in a cast from the knee down, two large pillows beneath it for support. Her right hand was also encased in a bandage, wrapped around all her fingers down to her wrist. Wrapped around her remaining fingers, she corrected herself, because there was a space where her pinky finger should have been; a permanent reminder of her battle with Valentine. She felt absolutely no pain. Zero. Nada. *That*, she quickly deduced, was because she was dosed up-to-the-gills with painkillers; the unmistakable soothing fuzziness of opioid-induced peace and wellbeing flowed warmly through her veins.

And with that realization came a sudden sense of panic.

Emily tried to call Mac's name, but her lips refused to move, fused together by a lack of moisture. Her tongue felt like a strip of the Mojave Desert in the middle of summer. She looked to her right then left, stretched past one of the monitors for a red plastic cup on the bedside table. It had some water left in it and she emptied the cup in one gulp, swishing the water around her mouth and over her lips before swallowing. Her throat felt like it had constricted to one-third its normal size. She tried to speak again, this time more successfully.

"Mac!" she croaked. He did not react. "Mac!" she repeated, this time a little louder.

Her husband's eyes flickered open. He blinked twice, then his eyes grew wide, and in a second he was out of the chair and at her side.

"Emily! Oh, thank Christ. I thought you..." His voice trailed off as tears began to flow, emotion holding his throat in a stranglehold of love and relief.

Emily pulled Mac's hand to her cracked lips and kissed the back of it.

Her husband gulped down his emotion, closed his eyes for a second, exhaled a breath that Emily had the distinct impression he had been holding for a very, very long time, and smiled. He leaned in and kissed her on the forehead. "I...We...I..." he stuttered, unable to form a coherent sentence. "God damn it!"

They both laughed gently at his verbal stumbling.

"It's okay," Emily croaked. "*I'm* okay."

Mac took the empty plastic cup from her and refilled it from a pitcher on a table in the corner of the room. He returned the cup to his wife and she drank it slowly, savoring the coolness of the water against her mouth and throat.

When Mac spoke again his powers of communication had miraculously returned. "We weren't sure if you'd come out of it, the coma...*You* were in a *fucking* coma..."

"Petter?" Emily asked.

Before Mac even spoke, she knew from the cloud that seemed to move across his face that the news would not be good. "He didn't make it. I tried to help him, but his blood loss was just too much. We returned his body, along with the bodies of his people that we could find to Svalbard for burial."

"How?" said Emily, confused at how they could have done that so quickly.

"Rhiannon's been bringing people back and forth between Point Loma and Svalbard. Did I mention that's where you are? Svalbard Island. She ferried you to the hospital here. Doctor Johansen and Doctor Candillier have been looking after you since we brought you here. Captain Constantine's in the room next to this one." Mac smiled brightly, as if that little nugget pleased him greatly. Then, anticipating her next question, he added, "Eight days. You were in a coma for eight days."

Emily allowed that piece of information to sink in for a second, then discarded it, because it was not important. What *was* important was that she convey her message to her husband quickly, because she could feel exhaustion beginning to creep into her mind again.

"Anesthetic," she said. "Pain killers."

Mac stood up quickly. "Christ! Yes, of course, sorry. Let me go and get Doctor—" he started to turn away, his fingers releasing Emily's hand as he started toward the door.

Emily grabbed his hand, refusing to allow it to slip from her own. "No. No more painkillers. No more anesthetic. None, understand?" The clouds of exhaustion were approaching faster now. There wasn't much more time.

Mac stepped in closer. "What? I don't understand.

Why don't you want painkillers?"

Emily pulled him in as close to her mouth as possible, and as reality slipped away she managed to speak. "Pregnant," she said. "I'm pregnant."

EPILOGUE

Time passed quickly, as it inevitably does when you are focused on a goal. And when that goal is the survival of humanity, time, at least for Emily, had seemed to fly by faster than she could ever remember it doing. Today was no exception; although time had gotten away from her for all the right reasons, which made a pleasant change.

She rose quietly from the bed, took her dressing gown from the back of the bedroom door and walked out onto the balcony, looking briefly back at the bed, where Mac lay naked beneath the sheets breathing gently, a sheen of sweat from their afternoon lovemaking glinting on his shoulders. Thor, who had been lying on the floorboards, leaped up onto the bed, settling into the space she had just vacated, his tail shushing gently across the sheets, as if giving his approval to the love that Emily felt so strongly within this room. She pulled her robe around her, more to cover her nakedness than for warmth, the California air as perfect as it had always been. As she tied the robe, her eye unconsciously moved to the space where her right pinky finger should have been, then to her left ankle where the bone had not quite set properly, pushing out against the skin. She still walked with a limp, even after all these years, and would, she knew, for the rest of her life; a parting gift to remember Valentine by. She could live with that trade-off, she told herself, as she did every day when these thoughts inevitably invaded her mind, especially when she counted everything she had gained since those terrible, distant days.

Emily leaned against the balcony's wrought-iron railing, her eyes moving across the square below her window to the twenty-or-so other two-story family homes clustered around it, the late-afternoon sun pushing their shadows out over the space. Eight trees—poplars, if Emily recalled correctly—offered shade to anyone who chose to spend a few moments resting on the large plots of succulent green grass that grew beneath their leafy branches. The houses surrounding the square were white-walled, blue-roofed, in a classic Greek style, thanks to a native of the Greek island of Kos, an architect and former resident of Svalbard who had brought his skills to bear on the new communes. Emily's commune was just one of fifty or so similar projects that followed the line of the coast north of the survivors' original Point Loma home in kibbutz-style communities.

She looked over the roofs of the homes. In the distance, the edge of the red jungle was unmissable, but between the jungle and the collection of houses, and also to the west, and the south of the commune...was color. Acre-upon-acre of green and yellow fields. Here and there, scattered amongst the crop fields like diamonds, the sun glinted off large glass hot-houses, that held the fruits and vegetables for the community.

It was humanity's best hope for a future and it was beautiful.

Her mind drifted back through time. When, after many months of recuperation and therapy, and even as her belly swelled with the new life growing within it, Doctor Johansen had finally judged Emily fit enough to be discharged from the hospital, the first thing she had done was to keep her promise to Magda Solheim, the Governor of Longyearbyen. She offered any of the island's residents the chance to return with her and Mac to California. Almost everyone on Svalbard had taken the chance at a new life, a fresh start, with only a handful of longtime residents choosing to remain behind, the lure of sunshine and warm seas no match for the ice-cold beauty of their island home. Emily couldn't blame them, not really; the island was the last vestige of normalcy in their lives, and leaving it, seeing what the planet had become, would have forced them to accept the horrors that had been perpetrated on the world. There was solace in not knowing, in ignoring the reality that lay beyond their sight, she understood that. No, she couldn't blame the holdouts one bit for wanting to stay right where they were.

Rhiannon had spent many months ferrying Svalbard residents and supplies from the Norwegian archipelago to California, rendezvousing with boats from the island in warmer areas to ensure the *Machine* did not die. The replacement *Machine* had eventually died, of course, as all things must; but that was okay, because Rhiannon had discovered that she, too, could speak with the red creatures of the world and ask for their assistance in making new machines. It had, as Rhiannon told it, come as a complete surprise to her that she was able to summon their help; a profound experience that had changed her, subtly. *Rhiannon had become...centered,* Emily thought was the best description of the calmness that had settled over her surrogate daughter. Emily was sure that Rhiannon, would, one day, help to guide the survivors down the path that they had started along together, toward a better, brighter future.

The first time Emily set foot back on American soil after her long recuperation, she had been greeted as a hero by the survivors she had helped to rescue, all unrecognizably healthy after months of freedom and food shipped via the *Machine* from Svalbard had put some meat back on their bones. Still, both physical and mental scars persisted; the latter a burden every one of them carried, able-bodied or otherwise. But, if the universe was kind, theirs would be the last planet, the last civilization, the last generation to ever worry about the terror that had been the Locusts. And it was on Emily's return that those who had been present at the battle, fighter and rescued alike, had begun to discover the meaning of what Adam had described to Emily as 'a gift' for his mother and those who stood at her side. It manifested as skills that the recipient had never trained in; abilities they had never mastered; insight into the world around them that had not yet been uncovered; and knowledge, new and undreamed of, that granted the survivors an understanding beyond that which the old world had possessed.

Each year, as the commune continued to grow and expand, new knowledge filtered into the collective consciousness, arriving as a memory or an inspiration or a sudden awareness, seemingly from nowhere. But Emily understood where it originated; her son. Her star child.

The drip-by-drip feed of empowering information and understanding and knowledge of the world and the great universe it floated within, was Adam's parting gift to the people. It was a gift meant to feed and nurture them, guiding them toward a greater understanding of the stewardship required for the planet and the vast complexity of life that lived upon it. *Earth*—humanity's home; unique and precious and irreplaceable. A blue, red, and growing-green ball of potential.

The caldera where that final apocalyptic battle had taken place was now nothing more than a natural tombstone marking the remains of the Locusts' time on this planet. It had been silent for many years, but as the survivors told it, for seven long weeks after the Locusts' defeat, energy had continued to pour out of the ruins into the sky, before finally, ceasing forever.

Upon her return, with the help of the Longyearbyen council and Victor Séverin, Emily and Mac had formed an interim council to oversee the original Point Loma survivors and the camp's new Svalbard residents. One of the first agenda items the new council pondered was what to name their new society. They finally settled on Arcadia, named after the ancient Utopian ideal. A year later, the first full and free elections were held, and Emily was unanimously picked as the official President of this fledgling nation, a title and position that she accepted willingly but not without much embarrassment. In her acceptance speech, she jokingly pointed out that it had only taken the end of the world for what had once been the United States to finally elect a female president.

The first order of business for their new community had been to focus on creating a sustainable food source from the seeds stored at the Svalbard Seed Bank. With the collected knowledge of the horticulturists, botanists, and other scientist transplants from Longyearbyen, the fertile soil, and the perfect California weather, the first year saw successful crops of wheat, corn, lettuce, carrots, Chinese loquats, South American cherimoya, and other assorted vegetables and fruits. The second year saw tea and coffee, cotton, and flax. Part of the phenomenal success was due to a rich new fertilizer derived from the root of Titan trees that increased growth and yield in the crops by almost two hundred percent. That knowledge had been another gift from Adam, conveyed through, of all people, Mac, who now found himself one of the community's leading horticulturists. With zero previous knowledge, interest, or experience in the field, the man of war, Emily's husband and love, found himself at the forefront of ensuring that human life continued onward, a role that he accepted wholeheartedly.

And, of course, there was new life. The community now had many children, with more on the way each year. It would not be long, Emily knew, before all those children would be old enough to play in the square below. She looked forward to that day, it would be good to hear their laughter.

Emily smiled to herself. These days, she found herself waxing more poetical than ever before in her life. *Happiness*, she thought, *has a habit of doing that to you*. Her thoughts returned to the present moment as her eyes drifted past the grass and the poplar trees to the center of the square; a fountain pumped water high into the air, a symbolic representation of the day Emily, Mac, and the other survivors had helped Adam free the planet and the universe of the scourge of the Locusts. The fountain had been the last project Parsons completed before the cancer he had kept secret from all but Emily and Mac finally claimed him, almost a year and a half prior to this day. Despite the melancholy she felt at the passing of the Welshman, Emily's smile was because this day was a very special day, and one that she knew Parsons would have given anything to be a part of.

From the nursery, Nicholas began to yell for his mommy. Mac stirred, sat up, well trained now in the habit of responding to their youngest at just three-and-a-half years of age. "I got this, love," he said, quickly pulling on a pair of pajama bottoms and heading out the bedroom door to the nursery.

"Mommy."

Emily turned to see Eloise standing in the doorway Mac had just exited through. The little girl dangled a teddy bear by its arm. "Hello, baby girl. Come and get a hug." Emily crouched down and held out her arms. The little blonde girl, her eldest now at almost six years of age ran across the space and into her mother's waiting arms. Emily pushed a stray lock of hair from over the child's eye and

274

kissed her forehead. "Are you ready for this afternoon?" she asked.

Eloise nodded and snuggled into her mother's neck. Emily closed her eyes and stood with her child for a few moments, savoring the feeling of completeness, before reluctantly lowering her to the floor. "Let's go get ready, shall we?" They walked out of the bedroom toward Eloise's room. "Come on, Thor," she said as she passed by the bed.

Thor stretched and climbed down off the bed. These days, the malamute was a little grayer around his muzzle and a little stiffer in his joints, but age had not curbed his love of life. In the corridor outside the bedroom, Samantha, the White German Shepherd Emily had first met at her owner's home in Longyearbyen, lay sleeping on the cool tile of the corridor. She opened her eyes and wagged her tail when she saw Emily and the little one leave the bedroom. Samantha got to her feet and followed alongside Thor, who nuzzled and licked at his mate's face.

Edith Vikra had given Samantha to Emily when she moved to Point Loma in the first wave of relocated islanders. "They just seem to belong together," Edith had told Emily, "So who am I to deny true love?" In return, Edith had received her pick of the first litter of six puppies born to the two canine lovebirds. There had been three more litters since then.

"How's he doing?" Emily whispered, pausing at the doorway to the nursery. Mac held Nicholas to his chest, bouncing lightly on the balls of his feet, trying to coax the child back to sleep.

"We're good," Mac said, winking at his two girls.

"I'm going to get this little devil ready, then we can head out," Emily whispered.

Mac smiled and nodded.

Ten minutes later, Emily met Mac back in their bedroom with a freshly washed Eloise.

Mac had showered and slipped into a pair of homespun linen pants and a matching shirt.

"You look very handsome," Emily said, straightening the collar of his shirt. She handed Eloise to her husband and headed to the shower herself. A little later, clean and refreshed, she changed into a comfortable summer dress and rejoined her husband. Mac successfully collected Nicholas from his bed without waking him.

"Are we going to see Aunty Rhia?" Eloise asked, holding her mom's hand as the family headed downstairs.

"You bet we are," Mac replied, smiling broadly.

By the time they closed the front door and walked to the square, six rows of chairs had been placed in two neat sections on the western side, with space left between them to form an aisle. Up front of the chairs, near the fountain, was a small dais, a lectern placed on top of it.

Guests were already beginning to take their seats. Emily greeted everyone by name; smiling and shaking hands, hugging friends, kissing their kids, as she and Mac slowly made their way down the aisle to the front row of chairs. Emily sat with Eloise and Nicholas, while Mac took a few moments to talk with a young Belgian man named Pascal, who was sitting in the first seat across the aisle with his parents. Pascal made eye contact with Emily, smiling nervously. Emily winked and smiled back. By the time Mac rejoined Emily, a four-piece band—named, appropriately enough, *The First and Last Band*—had set up just to the left of the dais, and most of the seats were now full.

Captain Constantine took the seat next to Mac. The woman he had been dating, a statuesque Danish climate researcher, sat next to him, and the foursome chatted quietly while the last of the remaining guests arrived.

"You ready? " Mac asked Emily after ten minutes had passed, checking his watch.

"Is it weird that I feel so nervous?" Emily answered him.

Mac laughed. "Course not. It's a big day; no need for

you to be nervous. And there's a first time for everything, right?"

Emily took a deep breath then she and Mac handed the kids off to Captain Constantine and his lady. Emily stepped up to the lectern, while Mac headed in the opposite direction back down the aisle. Pascal and his father rose and joined Emily at the foot of the dais. The young man's father placed a reassuring hand on his son's shoulder. When *The First and Last Band* struck up the opening notes of Mendelssohn's *Wedding March* Emily removed her handwritten script from her pocket and placed it on the lectern in front of her, spreading the creased pages out.

Dressed in simple white and wearing red flowers in her hair, her smile larger and brighter than the afternoon sun, Rhiannon walked gracefully down the aisle, her arm linked with Mac's as he guided her toward Emily. Rhiannon had long ago abandoned wearing the sunglasses Mac had given to her, the strangeness of her crimson eyes paling by comparison to her intelligence and kindness, while only adding to her ethereal beauty. Thor and Samantha trotted alongside them, tails swishing happily back and forth.

For his part, Pascal outwardly looked calm enough, but as Rhiannon and Mac reached the front of the aisle, he flushed bright red, a slight tremor noticeable in his hand as he adjusted his shirt. And well he should quiver, Emily thought, because there were no words to describe how radiant Rhiannon looked.

The two had first met when Rhiannon ferried Pascal and his parents from Svalbard, where his mother had worked as an engineer, his father a botanist. The two youngsters had quickly struck up a friendship that had endured and eventually grown into love. Three months, when Rhiannon celebrated her twenty-first birthday in this very same square, Pascal had asked her to marry him. Now he stared deeply into Rhiannon's red eyes, his own eyes wide and glistening with moisture.

Emily cleared her throat. "Well," she said, addressing the seated guests, "these are words I never dreamed I would speak." She took a deep breath and from behind a wide smile, began the ceremony, "Dearly beloved, we are gathered here today to witness the union of Rhiannon and Pascal in matrimony..."

The ceremony lasted twenty minutes. Rhiannon read her vows from memory, Pascal from a slip of paper that shook slightly either from the cool breeze that blew across the square or nerves. The couple exchanged rings carved by the groom's father from wood he salvaged from the leg of a scrapped oak table. With the rings exchanged, Emily concluded the ceremony, "And, by the power vested in me as President of Arcadia, I do hereby pronounce you husband and wife. You may kiss the—"

To cheers and laughter, Rhiannon pulled Pascal to her and kissed him passionately.

The band began to play an up-tempo tune, and the crowd cheered again as Rhiannon and her new husband made their way hand-in-hand down the aisle for their first dance, both smiling so widely that Emily just knew their cheeks would ache tomorrow.

As the night moved in to surround the celebration, torches were lit around the square, bathing the area in their subtle glow. The wedding guests danced and ate and drank and laughed and talked and loved and did all of the things that make being alive, being human, such a wondrous, fleeting, amazingly fragile experience. Finally, as the evening turned to night and the music grew slower, Emily excused herself and wandered away from the celebrations, toward one of the poplar trees. She sat, her back against the young tree's trunk, watching from the sidelines for a change. Mac and the children sat at a table off to her right; the kids enjoying the constant attention they received, Mac, smiling and talking freely, as relaxed as she had ever seen him. Every now and then, his head would turn her way, and he would smile. She would smile back. Pascal guided Rhiannon from table to table, talking to the guests and smiling at the compliments that fell from everyone's lips.

Everything was right with the world. *Finally.*

Emily allowed herself to relax, her mind to drift. Between the kids and work, it was rare that she found even a moment to herself these days, but when she did, she liked to take advantage of it, to just *think.*

Inevitably, her mind would always drift to Adam.

Knowledge. That had been the gift that her son had given to his people; what they chose to do with it, well, that was up to them. Everyone who had been present at the last battle—soldiers and survivors alike—had received that wondrous gift of insight.

Emily's gift, though, was different.

It was a special gift from Adam to her, and for her alone.

Emily closed her eyes. She felt a momentary disorientation when, instead of the black screen of the inside of her eyelids, she found herself hurtling through space; ahead of her, a star, bright orange and shot through with strands of purple and red growing larger by the second, coming at her so fast her hands dug into the grass beneath her fingers. She breathed in slowly, allowing herself to relax, reminding herself that she was only a passenger in Adam's mind, observing these events through the augmented eyes of her son. Adam was millions of light-years from where his mother rested beneath the tree, traveling the lanes between worlds and star systems and galaxies. Following a route invisible to her, tracking back along the path of the Caretakers. Moving from star system to star system, inexorably searching for the last alien civilization the Caretakers had helped before their encounter with the Locusts' had irreversibly changed the destiny of both the Caretakers and Earth.

Over the last six years, each time she linked with her

son's mind, Emily had witnessed for herself the destruction the Locusts had wrought; dead, barren planets followed one after the other. All evidence of the life she knew had surely once existed on them swept clean. The planets' histories, every accomplishment, experience, or discovery...wiped away forever.

In her mind's eye, a speck, no bigger than a pinpoint, appeared. The speck quickly grew into a planet as Adam altered course and sped toward it; a black disk silhouetted against the brilliance of the alien star. Emily felt her stomach lurch as Adam began a graceful spiraling arc to intercept the planet. Closer and closer, until the new planet began to fill her vision. They passed between two moons revolving aimlessly around their larger brother, both as barren and gray as earth's own satellite.

Adam guided his craft toward the planet's twilight zone where night turned into day, crossing the terminator line as though he were the bringer of dawn. Below her, Emily saw a huge continent resolve out of the darkness; half of the land obscured by cloud, gray and white and voluminous. Lightning flashed here and there across the great storm, but beyond the storm's edge Emily saw mountain ranges capped with snow rising high into the air, giant fingers of rock stretching across the continent; vast tracts of forests and grasslands spread swirling, bountiful greens and vibrant yellows, like a Van Gogh watercolor; rivers cut through the swaths of color snaking down to an iridescent aqua-green sea, where islands and archipelagos peppered the ocean.

Life! There was life on this planet.

It was, without question, the single most breathtaking moment Emily had ever experienced.

Fire appeared around the periphery of Emily's vision as the ship penetrated the planet's atmosphere, drawing ever closer to the surface. Clusters of light appeared across the land, reflections of the rising sun bouncing off the faceted sides of towering glass-spire cities that thrust into the air like spears of white crystal. She counted eight similar collections of these magnificent structures caught in the dawn's early light, each at least a hundred kilometers in diameter.

It was a magnificent, awe inspiring sight.

Far below, from a city of mirrored spires on an island off the western coast of the continent, a subtle motion caught Emily's eye; three craft—large spheres of shimmering pearlescence—left the ground and ascended quickly skyward, rising to meet the child-traveler who had journeyed so very far to find them.

Emily Baxter...smiled.

~ THE END ~

ACKNOWLEDGMENTS

Well, it's taken us a few years to reach it, but here we are, at the end of Emily's adventures. As with every book before this one, it's been a joint effort to bring her story to print, so I'd like to take a few more seconds of your time and acknowledge the people who helped make this happen.

First and foremost, I have to thank my wife for her guidance with some of the toughest parts of this book, and for helping me shape the story. Next is my editor Karen Boehle-Johnson who, once again, brought her keen eye for spelling and grammatical mistakes to bear on the manuscript, along with her uncanny ability to spot plot holes and inconsistencies.

Now it's my beta-readers turn for some recognition: April Taylor; Kelly Graffis; Rosemary Gaskell; Mathew Carter, and Britanny Grossman. My thanks to all of you.

And then there's *you*.

Thank *you* for spending your time in Emily's world, I truly hope that you have enjoyed the adventure. This series wouldn't have happened without your affection for the characters.

Oh yeah, and make sure you stick around; I have a new series coming out that I'm sure you'll enjoy, with lots of new characters, and one or two that you might have met before.

Don't be a stranger...

Paul Antony Jones
July 2017

ABOUT THE AUTHOR

A native of Cardiff, Wales, Paul Antony Jones now resides near Las Vegas, Nevada, with his wife. He has worked as a newspaper reporter and commercial copywriter, but his passion is penning fiction. A self-described science geek, he's a voracious reader of scientific periodicals, as well as a fan of things mysterious, unknown, and on the fringe. Paul is the author of six books, including the best-selling Extinction Point series and Toward Yesterday.

You can learn more about Paul and his upcoming releases via his blog at www.DisturbedUniverse.com
or his Facebook page
www.facebook.com/AuthorPaulAntonyJones/

23513824R00166

Printed in Poland
by Amazon Fulfillment
Poland Sp. z o.o., Wrocław